HAUNTING TALES OF
Old *New Orleans*

VOLUME ONE:
HISTORY, LEGENDS AND LORE

ALYNE
PUSTANIO

Cover Design and Interior format by The Killion Group
http://thekilliongroupinc.com

"Bouqui the Clown": Rabbit, Photograph Detail, Anonymous. Retrieved from Wikipedia Public Domain Image Resources, www.wikipedia.com.

"The Bloody Lady": "Silence" by Odilon Redon c. 1885. Retrieved from Public Domain Images, www.public-domain-images.com.

"Mariquita": Photograph Detail, Anonymous. Image is in the Public Domain.

"The Swamp Golem": Original Artwork Contributed by Andrew Goldfarb © 2013, San Francisco, CA.

"Bras Coupe, The Zombi King": Original Artwork Contributed by Andrew Goldfarb © 2012, San Francisco, CA.

FOREWORD

Welcome to the new Queen of Classic Horror, Alyne Pustanio.

In *Haunting Tales of Old New Orleans: History, Legends and Lore*, Alyne Pustanio gives full rein to her remarkable abilities with elegant and rich language tuned perfectly to stifled screams of terror and cries of fear. Be prepared all ye who open the pages of this book, Alyne Pustanio is a sorcerer of the English language. She doesn't simply tell a story, she spins a vortex of mystery that pulls the reader into the actual tale itself. Readers will be transported back in time into the very fabric of Old New Orleans, and they will find themselves becoming witnesses, rather than mere readers, of the tableaus being enacted before them.

Whether she is showing us the combination of dread and revulsion when witnessing a somehow mobile rotting corpse or pitting us against vampires lusting for our blood, we know that we have in some magical manner crossed the borderline between fiction and ghostly reality.

I was somewhat prepared for Alyne's particular style of literary Voodoo because she has been a contributor to a number of my books, such as *Real Zombis, The Living Dead, and Creatures of the Apocalypse* and *Real Vampires, Night Stalkers, and Creatures from the Dark side*. I discovered with her first contributions that she could transform the written page into a living panorama of sights, sounds, and smells. Truly, when she writes about the Louisiana swamps, you will begin to sweat with heat and humidity, inhale the myriad odors of vegetation and animal life, and you will also feel your gut gripping with the horror that you know must lurk around the next clump of trees.

Lest I paint Alyne as a total creature of the shadows, I have co-hosted her on The Jeff Rense program and found her to be an extremely articulate spokesperson for our field of the paranormal, the strange, and the unknown. Her wit and her obvious knowledge of the history of both the genre of her craft and the region about which she writes prompted Rense to proclaim that she was really intelligent and well-informed.

There is no better way to discover just how well-informed Alyne Pustanio is about Old New Orleans and its seen and unseen inhabitants of Witches, Voodoo Queens, Vampires, Zombis, Werewolves, and Restless Spirits than to immerse yourself in *Haunting Tales of Old New Orleans: History, Legends and Lore.* I highly recommend that you now put aside this Foreword and begin turning the pages at once.

~ Brad Steiger, March 2013

For Amanda, and for my Family who believed

A NOTE ABOUT DIALECT AND VERNACULAR USED IN THIS BOOK

It may be noted by some that the stories in this book contain comments, words, and discourse that today would generally be considered "politically incorrect" in the mind of the average informed reader.

The inclusion of these examples of antique vernacular and colloquialisms is a conscious effort on the part of the author to reproduce, to the greatest extent possible, the atmosphere and mindset of the time in which the tales originated. This is not meant to offend or provoke, but rather to preserve the daily realities and cultural nuances of an era in New Orleans and Louisiana – the "Creole Epoch" – that, though familiar to older generations, is fast fading from the memory of the city.

It is hoped that the reader will enjoy these tales in the context and spirit in which they are intended.

INTRODUCTION

To those who know her New Orleans is a sentient, living being – unique, charming, gracious, full of history and tradition and pulsating with a fascinating charm that is always felt but which can rarely be put into words. She is in almost every sense a mother to those born to her, and every native is weaned on her vitality; like mother and child, the one is part of the other and know each other intimately, in a way no "adopted" child – no matter how beloved - ever could.

The children of New Orleans are familiar from the cradle with her ever-changing moods and complexions, and the continuing expressions in our culture of her long, noble lineage. Her beautiful face smiles at us from lush, sheltered courtyards and bloom-laden balconies; she walks with us under the wide promenades of spreading oaks and sits dreaming in the cool seclusion of magnolia-laden bowers. In the antique desuetude of her turrets and gables we see her body, changing in vibrant contrasts as it turns with the sun through the days and seasons; and we sense her long memory when she is melancholy and pulls on her grey shawl of rain and fog. We learn her traditions at her riverbank knees or running our fingers through her moss-hung hair, and we thrive on her charm as she sings to us in a voice full of laughter and music. Only when we have grown do we become aware of the wistfulness in that voice, how it grows gentler and sadder with the passing years. When we are parted from her, her perfume lingers in our memory, redolent of night jasmine and honeysuckle and the heady scent of old roses glowing in her tropic sun. When we are parted from her, we children of New

Orleans long for her, our tender and faithful mother in whom love and memory are eternally bound, and who throws her arms wide to welcome us at each return.

In likewise manner, New Orleans welcomes her visitors, openly, alternately alluring and inspiring them, and finally bringing them, whether they will or not, under her spell of mystery and nameless charm. Visitors cannot resist lingering here beneath her wide, sunny skies, the long fingers of her tropical palms beckoning them with every breeze. They must wander her ancient streets, gaze into her courtyards, and peer in at the threshold of history that is her old Creole cottages, her weatherworn buildings, her markets and her squares. New Orleans welcomes newcomers with the constancy of tradition and the promise of new, yet undiscovered days; she puts them at ease, until at last, unable to resist any longer, the visitor comes to stay.

But it is she who always has the final word in these relationships; and New Orleans, this "fair child of two continents, imperial daughter of France and Spain," will very often reject the visitor's suit, indeed, even drive the stranger from her door. Those whom she turns away will forever try to reclaim her, to be held again in the magic of her gaze, like desperate lovers who are foresworn and find themselves defeated anew at every turn: once bestowed, her rejection is absolute.

New Orleans carries an old soul, a spirit born of her historic descent and proud heritage, and she preserves her traditions in a heart filled with poetry, romance, and a joie de vivre that have fed the world for generations. Not only France and Spain, but many other places have poured their culture into the vessel of her being, and her history is told in a multitude of voices.

As with any woman, the spirit of New Orleans dwells within the chambers of her heart – this is where she has stored the memories of her long lifetime. In her heart, light and dark dwell side by side, playing like children against the tapestry of her laudable history or in the fading autumn glow of her quaint traditions. But sometimes they run in fear from the night of dark memories they find locked inside with them; and some of these memories can be very dark, indeed. It is from her heart's shadow play that this book of New Orleans has been crafted.

The reader seeking a strict history lesson can look elsewhere – her story has been set down in a thousand volumes, told and retold over generations. Here we are not concerned with dry statistics or the posturing of governments and armies that have tried to tame this edge-of-the-otherworldly outpost over the long years of her life: such is the province of other works. Beyond the scholarship of history necessary to cast the shadows more starkly, or to better illustrate the terrifying tale in the mind's eye, the reader will not find much here. What is set down in these pages, however, is a hint of the dazzling splendor of a New Orleans that is now barely a memory; a time, an age swiftly disappearing into the gloaming of a dreamy twilight, here set against the shadows of her secret memories.

The stately dignity of those old days, with customs and mores that have passed forever, lives in New Orleans like a vision on the edge of sight. Into that vision we will peer, and listen while this grand old dame tells us tales in old world pictures, until at last, with long, lingering "adieus" she snuffs the light completely and leaves us, reluctantly, in the care of those old, familiar nurses—Darkness, Dread, and Fear.

PART ONE: HISTORY

Whenever one thinks to describe the heart of New Orleans it is the Vieux Carré, the Old Quarter that most immediately comes to mind.

In the Old Quarter – most often called the "French Quarter" and sometimes colloquially "the old Carré" – there is still much to be found of the fabled poetry and romance, the drama and legend that have made New Orleans famous wherever its name is known. Tradition, history, and folklore all combine to cast this oldest section of the city in an air of dreamy timelessness, and each turn past a different corner only deepens the allure of the spell. Every picturesque street and building seems to have its own story to tell, echoing with the sacrifices of the city's founding, the challenges and romance of the French and Spanish dominions, and the gay light-heartedness of the Creole epoch, the "golden age" that flourished between the Purchase and the Civil War.

But it must be said that the New Orleans of today is not the New Orleans of yesterday, and the Quarter as it stands today – building upon building peering down upon crowded urban streets and narrow alleys, more bricks and mortar and iron than it seems any one place could hold – looks nothing like it did in the days when the tales with which this book is concerned occurred. In order to bring about the proper perspective, the reader must cast the mind back to earlier times – let it absorb the quaint customs, the continental atmosphere, and the ethereal beauty of this old city; indeed, must truly immerse every sense in the life of days gone by.

✦✦✦✦

On his approach to what would be the spot chosen for the founding of New Orleans, Bienville and his comrades explored the marshlands along what is today called Lake Pontchartrain, pushing inward through the thickly-wooded swamps. Once the perfect spot was chosen, on the highest rise overlooking the Mississippi River, Bienville's engineers immediately began oversight for the protection of the new city.

A series of forts – five in all – were constructed inside a wall of timber beyond which, on the north, west, and south, was a water-filled rampart seven feet deep and forty feet wide. At the southeast end of the city overlooking the river, where the Rue de la Levee met the Chenin des Tchoupitoulas (the long, southward road where the Tchoupitoulas Indians sold their mystical herbs), was a military gate; another gate stood at the northeast corner near a barracks that housed 150 men. Gates at what is now the intersection of Canal and Royal Streets, and where present-day Dauphine Street meets the Esplanade, provided the main access and egress for the population; in the early days, these were also strictly guarded and locked at nightfall.

Within its fortifications Bienville's city grew: twelve squares (or city blocks) wide along the river and six squares deep, from the Rue du Quay to the Rue des Ramparts. Street names recalled the noble heritage of the French homeland: Chartres, Condé, Royale, Bourbon, Dauphine, and Burgundy ran parallel to the river; and crossing from east to west were Bienville, Conti, St. Louis, Toulouse, St. Pierre, d'Orleans, St. Anne, Dumaine and St. Phillip. When the Ursuline nuns established their convent on the edge of the city in 1727, the street on the south side of their property received the name Rue l'Ursulines. The next street northward became the site of the city's first military hospital and eventually received the name "d'Hospital"; the barracks lay one square beyond on the Rue d'Arsenal, later renamed simply "Barracks Street." The open thoroughfare on the northern edge of the city, from the river to Fort St. Ferdinand, quickly became a popular area among the citizenry for taking the air and was called the "Esplanade."

Here, also, the wealthy men of the city housed their mistresses
– the beautiful quadroons, or "yellow women" – in small,
colorful cottages, close to the des Ramparts. Nearly all the
street names of the Old Quarter are still unchanged; they have
endured through the years, reminders of a storied, romantic,
and sometimes troubled past.

The citizens of New Orleans have continuously worshipped
in churches on the site of what is now St. Louis Cathedral since
1727 when the first church, dedicated to St. Louis IX of
France, was founded. Capuchin fathers arrived with the French
explorers, and long shepherded the faithful under the vaults of
St. Louis and through its many challenges, including damages
from a hurricane in 1779, and its near-complete destruction in
the infamous Good Friday Fire of 1788; another fire, in 1794,
was almost as devastating, but afterward rendered the building
in the form now recognized so far and wide.

The Capuchins did not labor alone, however. French
Ursuline nuns were also present since the founding, and
worked shoulder-to-shoulder with the Capuchins among the
sick and needy of New Orleans. The Ursulines built a beautiful
convent – today it is the oldest surviving building in the city –
and established a plantation on a large tract of land located on
the city's northern edge. Late in 1727, the Capuchins and
Ursulines were joined by another religious order when the
Jesuit brotherhood arrived, founding a monastery and a
working plantation south of the city, just above the Chenin des
Tchoupitoulas.

Through the doors of the church of St. Louis, so awash in
history and tragedy, many of the noted of New Orleans passed
to be baptized, married, and mourned. When death finally
claimed these citizens and the burial rites had been rendered,
many went to their final rest in the little cemetery of St. Peter
nearby. This burying ground, the first established within the
limits of the city, was located at the southwest corner of the
Rue St. Pierre and the Rue Burgundy. Burials in St. Peter's
were below ground with space reserved for local clergy, and
the wealthy and distinguished of early New Orleans society. St.
Peter's received burials from 1721 until approximately 1790 by
which time the larger St. Louis Cemetery No. 1 had been

established beyond the Rue des Ramparts. The original site of St. Peter's Cemetery has long been built over, though occasional street repairs and renovations nearby have turned up bones and other artifacts, and the location is believed to be haunted.

Regular arrivals of new settlers soon began to grow Bienville's city. Many were aristocrats and officials of the French government. But the majority were simple French low-brows who had taken the option of deportation over the ignominy of debtor's prison or the workhouse. There were some widows and otherwise ruined women to whom the Louisiana colony might mean a new marriage or a new start; and there were also masses of deportees that France had long sought to offload in one way or another. Refugees of the Natchez Indian Massacre of 1729 also significantly swelled the new city's population; supported by slaves and supplemented by newcomers from the American territories and the peaceful Indian populations of the local Chitimacha and Acolapissa tribes, a burgeoning microcosm of European society soon firmly took root.

Under its French founders in the 1700's, New Orleans society busily sowed the seeds of genteelism and romance that would come into full bloom a century later when Creole society reached its height. When many titled noblemen and officers of France brought their families here to join them, an aristocratic coterie was established that soon came to rival the European world of wealth and privilege that had been left behind. Balls, soirees, state dinners, the theatre, masquerades – society life in New Orleans was so filled with excitement that the city quickly (and rightfully) earned the nickname "Le Petit Paris."

But when France ceded the Louisiana colony to Spain in 1757, a move unanticipated by its colonists, a pall was cast over the glamorous lifestyle of the "Little Paris." Many influential citizens banded together to protest the cession; under the leadership of the Sieur de Lafreniere, a successful planter and businessman, they declared Louisiana an independent colony and called for rebellion against what they saw as the impending "Spanish occupation." But this first act

of revolution on American soil was not to be long-lived. The
Spanish arrived well-prepared and firmly resolved to put down
any hint of rebellion in the colony. With a military fleet
anchored up and down the Mississippi River, and officers of
the Spanish government already in place, the Spaniards easily
rooted out the conspirators. Lafreniere and his compatriots
were swiftly tried and sentenced to death. He and his highest-
ranking conspirators were taken to the Place d'Armes - New
Orleans' equivalent of the town square - where they were tied
to stakes and shot; the remainder of Lafreniere's men were
sentenced to life in prison and shipped off to Havana. Protests
and French discomfiture aside, New Orleans passed into the
Spanish dependency.

Under the Spaniards, the city took on much of the character
and charm we see in modern times. Indeed, the so-called
"French Quarter" can more accurately be described as the
"Spanish Quarter" since nearly all the oldest buildings in it
were erected under Spanish rule and in the Spanish style.
Despite the deepest fears of Lafreniere and his revolutionaries,
Spanish governance actually helped the city to thrive. Business
opportunities multiplied in trade with the wealthy Spanish
homeland and all its New World holdings; as commerce with
the New England territories also increased, the groundwork for
the later entrance of the city into a young America was soundly
laid. At the end of the century other refugees fleeing the bloody
slave rebellions of the island of Sainte-Domingue – they
numbered at least 10,000 – doubled the city's population and
paradoxically transformed it, at least culturally, into a French
city once again. These whites and free people of color also
brought slaves and by 1810 those in bondage comprised
roughly a third of the city's population.

The Spanish also significantly improved the general welfare
of their people by establishing the first Charity Hospital to
replace the poorly-run New Orleans Hospital founded in 1726
under French rule. Located on the Rue des Ramparts between
present-day St. Louis and Toulouse Streets, the St. Charles
Charity Hospital provided much-needed medical care to a
population that easily – and often – fell prey to unpredictable
outbreaks of yellow fever, malaria, and cholera. Destroyed by

three successive hurricanes in 1779, 1780, and 1781, help from local benefactors enabled a new, larger Charity to open in 1784 below Canal Street in an area that would later be known as the "American side" of the City.

The new hospital was generously supported by ranking Spanish philanthropists, encouraging an influx of excellent physicians from Spain and her colonial territories throughout the New World. These doctors, combined with the near-constant flow of practitioners from France and other parts of Europe, made a higher standard of care available to more people. Though the specter of virulent epidemics remained ever-present well into the nineteenth century, overall the Charity Hospital at New Orleans represented one of the best state-of-the-art medical facilities in the colonies - much to the benefit of local citizenry.

Not only did the Spanish do much to increase the size and health of the city, to grow its economy, and deepen its pockets, they also made a special effort to adapt to its society. After a period of acclimation, the Spanish and French proved more than amenable to intermarriage and from this happy alchemy came the blood of our first true Creoles.

"Creole" is a term widely misused and broadly bastardized. Many wonder, What is a Creole? Encyclopedias and dictionaries present varying definitions, and unfortunately even in New Orleans one will probably not get the absolutely correct answer, that is to say the definition set forth by founding members of the original Creole Society of New Orleans, to wit: a true Creole is a white person descended from the French or Spanish, or French *and* Spanish, settlers of Louisiana and the Gulf States, who preserve their characteristic speech and culture, and in whom the line of descent has not been diluted by intermarriage with other ethnicities. By this definition, descendants of other ethnic groups such as the products of mixed marriages between the French or Spanish and their African-American slaves, the Native Americans, Italians, Germans, or Irish, among others, are not Creole.

Some of the resulting ethnic confusion can be laid on the original Creoles themselves who, perhaps in an effort to identify everything they found, owned, or created in their new society as their own, used a broad brush in applying the "Creole" label. Thus to a true New Orleans Creole his cottage became a "Creole" cottage; his cow a "Creole" cow, and as well its milk and cheese; his mule a "Creole" mule; the vegetables from his garden "Creole"; and – most significantly – even his slaves were labeled "Creole." But in modern times the lines of such strict ethnicity have truly blurred, and the scope of who can rightly be called "a Creole" has been expanded to encompass much of the progeny of those long-excluded groups by virtue of the simple fact that they were children of the New World born into the rich, diverse culture, the "gumbo" of New Orleans.

After the same manner the Creoles also gave their name to an entire way of life in New Orleans. Historian Henry Rightor, writing about the Creoles at their apex in the golden, prosperous days before the Civil War says they "at once kept an eye to the material wants of life, and cultivated the most princely and refined society of the day, educating their sons in Paris, their daughters in the refining and spiritualizing atmosphere of Catholic convents, and so producing a race of fiery, spirited, chivalrous, cultured men and delicately beautiful, modest and charmingly feminine women." Suffice to say, a true Creole is a rare thing to find today!

When the Americans did finally arrive in New Orleans, they discovered their greatest challenge in adapting to life here was not the inhospitable climate or the untamed environment, nor even the frequent outbreaks of yellow fever and the danger of the local hoodoo. The biggest challenge facing the Americans was to be accepted by the Creoles who held sway over the Old Carré and thus the keys to doing business successfully anywhere in Louisiana.

The Louisiana Purchase did much to alleviate tensions over what Creole society viewed as encroachment on the part of the Americans prior to 1803. But even after the Purchase and despite the fact that the two societies had put aside their differences long enough to fight the Battle of New Orleans, Creole society held to its old boundaries, with the Vieux Carré as its heart. Americans, with their industry and fine houses, decamped to the areas south of Canal Street, or the "American side." But always, business and social intercourse in New Orleans was governed by the old rules and mores of the Creoles. And although everyone thrived, it would not be until the end of the nineteenth century, when confronted with the nation's brutal Civil War, that New Orleans would finally amalgamate into a single community of multiple and equal ethnicities and traditions to face that bitter threat and finally take its place among the other shining cities of the United States.

At the time of the Purchase, one standing on the riverfront in the Rue du Quay, at approximately the center of the Place d'Armes, and gazing out at the city of New Orleans would see the spires of the St. Louis Cathedral soaring to the sky as they do today. Beside it to the left, separated by Cathedral Alley, at the corner of Rue Condé and Rue St. Pierre (Peter), is the famous "Cabildo" where the old Municipal Council of Spanish times met and where each transfer of government – from French to Spanish, back to French, and finally to American – peacefully took place.

Beyond it, just visible against the skyline, is the Calaboose, the old Spanish jail. The deep cells of this old jail will continue to receive prisoners until 1834 when the new Parish Prison beyond the Rue des Ramparts opens its doors. Runaway slaves and black offenders, however, will continue to languish inside the moldy old edifice until mid-century when the jails behind the Cathedral will be torn down. Vaults discovered underneath, littered with skulls and bones, do much to confirm the long-held suspicion that the Inquisition had successfully been established in New Orleans. New Orleanians will later rename adjacent Cathedral Alley, dubbing it "Pirate's Alley" for no apparent historical reason; subsequently a "fakelore" concerning pirates, smugglers and their ghosts will grow up around this old alleyway. An exact replica of the Cabildo flanks the Cathedral on the opposite side, between St. Anthony's Alley and the Rue St. Ann and is the location of the Civil Courts. This building occupies the former site of the Capuchin monastery that was destroyed in the great fire of 1788.

Market stalls and the wagons of produce vendors and the *rabais marchand* or "little needs" men ring the square of the Place d'Armes all about. Here and there are seen the Native Indians, sitting on blankets spread on the grass, selling their strange herbs and wares. Devoted "mammies" watch with a sharp eye from the shade of cypress and wild magnolia trees as their charges – white and black – play together nearby. The scene is rather surreal when set against the well-used wooden gallows that are ever-present in the foreground, perhaps the last thing one would expect to see where children are at play.

Looking left toward the Rue de la Levee one sees the wide expanse of the dockyards and workers swarming like bees over tall-masted schooners, steamers, and deep-hulled seagoing ships, loading and offloading their exotic cargoes. Northward are reams of cotton rolling like great wheels under the sharp hooks of the dock men; southward are large staffs of sugar cane and barrels lined up in chutes waiting to shuttle forward into the deep, dark hulls of the merchant ships; here and there are tall piles of banana stalks brought up through St. John's Bayou, and great mounds of the prized, emerald-green Spanish limes brought from Cuba. In the river beyond the docks, floating along the swift current, deftly navigating through the press of larger vessels, the narrow little boats of the Filipino luggermen ride low in the water; heavy with their cargoes of oysters, their spindly masts bob up and down against the sunlit waters of the great Mississippi.

The city is populated from the Rue du Quay back to the Rue Dauphine, with the wealthy massed near the Rue Condé and the Rue Royale; the Rue Chartres is the main business artery of the city. The lower caste cluster around the Rue d'Orleans; beyond the Rue Dauphine the population is sparse and live mostly in shacks scattered here and there inside the old ramparts. There are very few inhabitants on the western side of the Rue des Ramparts where the basin opens that joins the Carrollton locks. Here and there more shacks and some small patch farms break the monotony of the continuous woods. The Bayou Road pierces the trees on this side of the city, plunging bravely through the verdure to connect with the Gentilly Road, the Grand Route, and the Spanish docks on the banks of St. John's Bayou.

The Governor's House stands at the corner of the Rue Toulouse and the Rue du Quay. Along the river the city expands from the Rue St. Louis to about the Rue St. Phillip. Beyond St. Phillip the old Spanish barracks occupy the whole square between the Rue Hospital and the Rue d'Arsenal, facing the river. One square over, where the Rue Chartres meets the Esplanade are the common kitchens and the docks where slaves are offered for sale in a busy riverside market.

Downriver the Rue de la Levee joins the old King's Walk and the Chenin des Tchoupitoulas and is a popular place among the citizens for promenades in good weather and in the evenings. Braces of young willow trees and benches line the riverfront from St. Louis to St. Phillip to encourage such recreation. Nearby Canal Street lacks a navigable waterway and is a swath of grassy land that separates the Creole city from the American side, terminating at the old military gate of the Chenin des Tchoupitoulas.

Throughout the city its streets are in poor condition—dusty and dry-rutted in the sun, boggy and near-impassable in the rain. The first paving projects will begin in earnest in 1821 when ships bringing in stone as ballast receive credits from the city that can be exchanged for cash. The walkways alongside the streets, what the locals call "banquettes," are made of wood and edged with an unwholesome wooden drainage ditch. These ditches are regularly cleaned by teams of heavily-chained slaves, all of whom have previously run away, in a job specifically designed to discourage any future attempts at escape.

Drinking and potable water is drawn from the Mississippi river at a place above the Rue St. Louis where the current runs deep. It is filtered through a stone filtering process and distributed to watermen who go through the streets carrying kegs and large pails from which the residents purchase refills for consumption and home use. By the middle of the nineteenth century enclosed water cisterns will be introduced to supplement the river collection method. Dairymen distribute milk from metal cans loaded onto large wagons; the familiar rattling of the cans are usually the first sounds to come with the early hours of the day. Produce vendors make daily rounds, passing through the narrow streets hawking their wares as they make for the market stalls of the Place d'Armes. The *rabais marchand* men, offering all manner of small household items, from sewing needles to storage jars, rattle along through the neighborhood as the morning grows. Bakers, candy makers, and vendors in everything from flowers to coffee pass through the streets; their familiar cries are the music of everyday life in the Old Carré.

Throughout the day the city is guarded by a police force culled from the old French gendarmerie and Spanish military guards. At nightfall the city gates at Rue Royale and Canal Street and at Rue Dauphine and the Esplanade are locked; admittance to the city after dark requires a pass signed by the governor or other high official. In the early part of the century a curfew is enforced by small cannon fire – nine o'clock in the summer months and eight o'clock in the winter; a curfew bell would later supplant the cannon. Throughout the night, military watchmen assume patrol of the streets and cry out the time and weather conditions on every hour.

The city is lit by large oil lamps suspended on posts at major intersections and along the riverfront. These lamps will be modernized beginning around 1825 when larger lamps equipped with metal reflectors will replace the old ones. The new lamps will be suspended from long hangers fixed in the sides of buildings at corners and in the middle of most blocks; the larger lamps shed more light and are more numerous. Even following these improvements, citizens will still find it necessary to use lanterns to guide their way after nightfall. A typical family, out for a night at the theatre, for example, would require a lantern-carrying servant to walk ahead of them and occasionally one following behind. The streets being what they are, it is sometimes necessary for the well-to-do to dress at their destination; sometimes a slave carrying a trunk filled with the family's evening dress will be seen plodding behind the rear lantern-bearer. Inside their homes, the wealthy employ elaborate oil lamps and the finest beeswax candles to drive off the shadows of the night. The poor commonly use messy, fast-burning candles made from green myrtle wax that smoke awfully and are quickly used up.

Transportation is invariably by foot. Carriages are used by the wealthy and only in the driest weather, except where the streets have been much improved; diligences operate regularly between stops in the city and more distant locations such as Milneburg and St. John's Bayou docks. Heading out for entertainment after dark the Creoles and other ranking members of society sometimes patronize the Theatre d'Orleans, located in the middle of the block in the Rue d'Orleans between the Rue Royale and the Rue Bourbon. Gentlemen and rogues alike often linger until the wee hours at Le Coquet, the largest gambling house in the city, one of many operating round-the-clock and located in the area where the Rue Orleans meets the Rue Bourbon. Beyond the Rue Dauphine are a number of commoner's taverns, frequented by the working class; here, too, many of the poor residents are known to keep their own brewing stills.

Gambling and drink can also be had, albeit with very real risk, in the Rue Gallatin, a short, foul square facing the river not far from the barracks and the Esplanade slave markets. This is the tenderloin district of New Orleans and every kind of debauchery can be had here for a price. Most taverns here never close and the brothels are constantly crowded with soldiers, dock workers, sailors, and flatboatmen from the river trade including, very often, bootleggers and pirates. Gallatin is flush with pawn shops and storefronts where stolen goods can be "fenced." Prostitutes display their wares openly from low windows facing the street, and there is always a game of dice or cards going on in the alleyways nearby.

On this side of the Old Carré the Rue du Quay joins the Old Coast Road that leads down past the cotton mills and slaughterhouses to connect with the Shell Beach Road winding eastward through St. Bernard's Parish. This area will become significant during the War of 1812 when the Battle of New Orleans will be fought here, feeding history with tales of courage and folklore with ghosts. The Shell Beach Road rolls past many gracious plantations with their neatly-ploughed fields and manicured parks before cutting into the wild again on its way through the expanse of the Marais Tremblement. In those swampy wastes, where the high grasses whistle in the lonely marsh winds, the Filipinos have their little village of St. Malo and keep their secrets close. The Shell Beach Road winds finally through the little settlement of Ste. Croix and comes to an end at Lake Pontchartrain, near the location of the Last Oak, at the very edge of the old colonial boundary.

But back on the riverfront in the heart of New Orleans, where we stand taking in the panorama of this beloved old city, we will cross the Rue du Quay and leave behind the high grasses of the Place d'Armes and the ancient corridor of Cathedral Alley, emerging at last in the Rue Royale where it meets the Rue d'Orleans. Here we are suddenly aware of a new sound - a strange rhythm, a distant drumming that calls to us, compelling our feet to follow its irresistible beats. We are drawn ever on, passing square upon square of the Rue d'Orleans until at last we step out upon the wide expanse of the Rue des Ramparts.

Before us is another square laid with ancient Spanish tiles, broken and pressed into the earth, and bounded by iron stanchions from which the chains have long gone missing. This is the old Circus Square. Once home to the Congo Circus, a thriving, continental-style circus of slave performers under the guidance of an Italian maestro, it is now an impromptu gathering-place where people of all sorts come for recreation; children, their faces plastered with the sugary remains of swiftly-devoured candies, squeal in delight and chase each other in the wide acres, with mothers and mammies all in pursuit. Recalling to mind the history of the place, acrobats and clowns in parti-colored costumes still perform; a magician in a tall top hat does sleight-of-hand from a little tabletop; Italian organ grinders stroll here and there, serenading the small crowds; the praline ladies call out the quality of their wares; and flower girls sell "tussie-mussies" from clapboard boxes for handsome young gentlemen to give as gifts to their lovely Creole belles. But the drumbeats are yet distant, and so we walk on in search of them.

Beyond the Circus Square, wide grasslands open: here are the Congo Fields, stretching over the ramparts on the edge of the old city, flowing westward to meet the swamps and the banks of St. John's Bayou. These fields are the province of slaves and free people of color who have come here for decades to greet each other and to enjoy recreation in song and dance. This is where the music of the drums has drawn us – to one of the great weekend "bamboulas" of the slaves where they dance in wild abandon to the mystical rhythms of their dark homeland. In the midst of a great circle of people, ringed by smoking torches, men and women move together in exotic, near orgiastic gyrations, caught up in the irresistible power of the African drums. Wrinkled old crones sit looking on, selling talismans and strange little sachets called "gree gree" from the tops of upturned barrels; and hovering in the shadows, wavering in the darkness like black flames, we see the tall figures of the root doctors mixing with the much-feared "bokor men" – sorcerers who will do any sort of magic for you, as long as the price is right.

And so it is here in this fantastic atmosphere, amid the leaping glow of pagan torches, the gyrations of a mysterious race and the rumbling of their dark drums, with the sun a bright copper disk sinking in a mango sky, here in the wild Congo Fields that our haunting tales truly begin . . .

PART TWO: LEGENDS

The Ghost

It is doubtless that isolation and loneliness exaggerated the fears of the earliest settlers who came to New Orleans. In the city growing up beside the river, the worst superstitions and fears of its European cultures became starkly real to early residents, encamped as they were, together yet completely alone in the vastness of a dark, undiscovered country. Against the very real physical dangers lurking in that darkness, these citizens quickly threw up fortifications and guards; against the deeper and ever-present fear wrought by the fantastic new environment, only faith provided refuge.

Ghosts were well known in the folklore of these European settlers. Spirits could take myriad forms, coming and going with ease, defying the ordinary boundaries of the natural world. Some revealed themselves as they had appeared in life; others manifested in the varied stages of death, reminders of the mortality awaiting us all.

The purposes of ghosts were inscrutable. Some lingered only long enough to bid goodbye to a loved one or to complete some business; some were held in thrall by the unyielding grief of those left behind; and some resisted moving on, lingering in fear of the unknown or of a hell filled with perpetual punishment. Other specters, perhaps the victims of grievous wrongs in life, were driven by hatred to haunt the world of humankind until their quest for vengeance was satisfied. Denied the peace of death, a malevolent spirit such as this cannot rest until the authors of its suffering have been given their just reward: a lonely plot of barren earth far from the sight of God where they, too, will bloat and grow foul, and waste away to nothing . . . but not until the avenging spirit has taken its due.

Bouqui the Clown

"I cannot describe the monstrous, the horrible sight. Hours ago – and yet it plagues me every time I close my eyes!

He was haggard and glassy-eyed as they dragged him away from the Congo Fields, and away from any scrutiny on the Rue des Ramparts. They beat him and pushed him inexorably forward, while Alphonse and I, and a few other right-minded men, stayed directly on their heels. When he fell, and we made a move to lay hold of him, they beat us as well and one man, a tall, brutish German, yelled, 'Juden! Juden! Get away Jews, or we will hang you with the nigger!'

When the constables arrived upon the scene I thought, 'Surely, most assuredly, they will put a stop to this!' But to our amazement - and their everlasting shame! – the cowards stood by silently and did nothing!

Alphonse roared at them all, 'Beasts! You are not fit to be called men!' and all the while the poor, sad eyes of the Negro searched us wildly, for we were his only hope – and we were failing him.

A few men, maybe four or five - the ringleaders I suppose - pushed the poor man to his knees and formed a circle about him. When we tried to break through, others crowded round – ignorant laborers, unschooled docksmen – tightening the ranks. They struck out at us randomly with fists and sticks, none finding their mark; a few brandished firearms and at this we drew back.

Then, a strange new horror – the men brought out a white rabbit, the clown's little pet that he was wont to use to entertain children, and tied a cord about its neck. The absolute horror! The tall brute, so prominent in the other lurid acts, flung the poor creature into the air and swept it about, like a falcon's lure – then, finding the act had not killed it, he threw the rabbit into the air one last time and caught the rope up short as it came down. The little neck snapped. The animal writhed a little and was dead.

Then, and for the first time, the poor, beaten Negro reacted. He cried out in pain, as if the snapping of the rabbit's neck had struck like a poniard through his own heart; he wept for the death of the innocent creature and now begged for his own.

Alphonse and I protested anew, and fought our way through the circle until at last he had hold of the poor, broken man. But we were thrown off and chased, and again the cries of 'Jew!' and 'You are next, Jew bastards!' For our safety, indeed for our very lives, we had no choice but to withdraw at some distance, from which we observed as a long rope was threaded round a stout oak tree branch and a makeshift noose was tightened around the poor man's neck.

'God!' Alphonse growled. 'My God! They do *mean to hang him!'*

*No sooner had he said those words then the shouts of
'Heave!' went up, like those one might hear from sailors
squaring yards on a ship at sea. The thin, ragged, and bloodied
Negro was lifted from the ground and there hung, kicking,
weeping as all the while the men around him laughed and
struck out at him as he slowly died.*

*Neither Alphonse nor I wished to leave, but we knew we
could now do nothing for the man and, the danger to us being
quite real, we departed those fields for the safety of my home,
where now I write these lines.*

*But we are the worse for it and find no comfort: –My
brother Edward has brought me news of what happened after
we departed: that when the mob took down the body of Bouqui
the Clown, they subjected it to the grossest indignities, finally
cutting it in half at the waist with a Kaintuck's logging saw!
They threw the remains into a ragged wooden coffin that
someone dragged to the spot from the St. Louis cemetery: –The
dismembered pieces of the beloved pet were thrown in with
him. No one knows where they have buried him, or if they have
buried him at all. As to why this awful act was committed, my
brother has it, on some authority, that the mob believed Bouqui
to have been responsible for the several disappearances and
murders of children of the poorer caste that have occurred
over the last few weeks.*

*But in my mind this is all impossible, and Alphonse is of the
same opinion. So kind, so carefree and gentle was the Clown to
all the children who visited him in the Circus Square that to
accuse him of such acts and, with no proof but hatred, to make
him the victim of such a horrible demise is an affront both to
reason and justice! Alphonse is correct: The beasts responsible
cannot rightly call themselves men! The man they murdered,
the man we knew as Bouqui the Clown, could not have harmed
any living thing!*

Jos. V. Gottschalk, Notes."

"Joooo-sieeee!" Paddy called out his sister's name in a
playful sing-song. "Josie!" he repeated, now in earnest. "Ye
know we're not supposed to play in dere! Ma's goin' t'tan yer
hide if she catches ye!"

Josie, who had until now successfully ignored her brother's teasing, turned on her heel and stuck her tongue out at him, then went back to pitching acorns at a nearby headstone.

The brother – about eleven years old, thin, wiry, with a mass of ginger hair and all the energy of a tightly-wound spring – and sister – some two years his junior, with the flaming red hair, flashing green eyes, and natural defiance of her Irish mother – were occupied near a singularly eerie playground: the overgrown, disheveled burying fields that lay between the city and the edge of the La Chaise estate, and that had for decades received criminals, suicides, unwanted infants, and other unsanctified dead of New Orleans.

"Alright! Alright!" said Paddy. He buried his hands deep in his pants pockets and kicked about distractedly in the dirt near the cemetery gate. "It's yer own hide!"

"Aye," Josie replied smugly. "It is!"

It was a golden afternoon in late October with a cloudless sky bending over a copper sun, deepening the shadows across the rooftops and in the narrow streets of the Old Carré. The branches of the Esplanade oaks shook in the cool river breezes and scattered their little brown acorns all about their gnarled roots where earlier Josie had knelt, gathering them and stashing them in her apron pockets one by one, with all the care of a miner sieving for gold.

A steady line of vendors and *rabais marchand* men wound its way from the Rue du Quay, passing through the mottled shadows along the Esplanade as they made their daily retreat from the riverside markets. Beyond the city limits they would disperse to points hither and yon and then, with the first light of day, they would retrace their steps into the city, crying out and hawking their wares on the way back to their stalls.

"Ho! Paddy!" called a familiar Italian man with a long, curly moustache and bright smile. He held out three bright oranges and Paddy accepted them thankfully. "Be sure your mama gets one!"

"I will! Thank ye, Nunzio!" Paddy called back and began to juggle the bright fruit in the air. He stopped short and let out an exasperated sigh at the sight of his sister standing where he had left her among the graves. With all the determination he could muster, Paddy marched past the rickety iron cemetery gate to where Josie stood, quite still.

"Josie!" he barked, but his sister hissed and put a finger to her lips. She nodded, and Paddy followed her gaze to where, among the ferns and weeds choking the boggy ground near the roots of a cypress tree, a large, white rabbit sat. But for its snuffling pink nose, Paddy could have mistaken it for a statue, it sat so still. Then slowly and, it seemed to the boy, quite deliberately, it turned its head and regarded them with its thoughtful, rosy eyes. Josie marveled and moved toward it with her hand held out, entreating. But Paddy was seized with an unexpected and inexplicable fear.

"No!" he cried and grabbed his sister's arm; the rabbit immediately bolted, disappearing into a hole underneath a crooked headstone.

"Paddy! You frightened it!" Josie exclaimed in a girlish whine, pounded out with her every step as she stomped off through the cemetery gate. "Why did you do that?"

Paddy stood for a moment in thoughtful silence, gazing at the hole into which the rabbit had fled – littered with Josie's acorns, it yawned at him like a small, round mouth protesting from the deep shadows of the trees. A sudden gust of chill wind swept up and blew over him; the trees shook their dead leaves down and they rattled in a tiny whirlwind about his feet. The rusty cemetery gate swung shut with a loud "clang" just as Paddy ran clear of it; he sprinted for the safety of home, and did not once look back.

Home for Paddy and Josie was a simple, three-room cypress shack propped up on flagstone piers, which their father had built by hand. Located outside the city in a kind of "no-man's land" that paralleled the Old Carré and skirted the Bayou Road, the house stood among other rustic dwellings built to accommodate a local population of mostly German and Irish dock laborers and their families. At three rooms, the children's house was one of the largest, its only fault being that it stood closest to the dilapidated cemetery. From their tiny bedroom window, Paddy and Josie had an unobstructed view of the melancholy old burying ground with its primitive stone crosses and wooden markers rotting under old, gnarled trees. Josie was not much bothered by their proximity to the place, but Paddy – more superstitious and impressionable – disliked this fact intently. Unlike his sister, who could lose hours among the graves picking flowers and daydreaming, Paddy rarely played there.

Josie ran crying through the kitchen with Paddy right behind her. "Oranges!" he cried, and shoved them into the pockets of his mother's apron.

"What on earth is wrong with tha' child?" she wondered aloud, gazing after Josie.

Paddy shrugged. "Don't know," he fibbed as he spooned out a mouthful of rich stew from his mother's pot.

"Here! Put tha' spoon down or I'll beat ye wit' it! T'ere won't be enough for your Da!" she admonished, narrowly missing him with her own heavy spoon.

Paddy ran away laughing into the bedroom where he found Josie on her bed playing with a poppet and sulking.

"Ah, yer not poutin' over dat rabbit, now?" he said. Josie was silent. "Sure, it'll be back t'morrow if it came t'day!" He tried to sound reassuring as he gazed out the window toward the burying ground, fading swiftly from sight in the cool, shadowy gloaming.

"Ye might have caught it fer me!" Josie sniffed.

"What?" Paddy replied, incredulous. "Yer off yer noggin! Even if I could," he added quickly as his sister folded her arms and rolled away in a huff to face the wall, "And even if I *could* catch it," he repeated, "sure Da won't let ye keep it anyway!"

Josie was silent. Paddy sat on his own bed. "Ye know he'd only kill it and eat it," he said thoughtfully, "and make us eat it! No," he almost whispered then, gazing vacantly at his feet, "I would'na bring dat poor t'ing into this house fer nothin' – not t'him . . . not even fer ye!" A brooding silence settled over the little room. Josie turned and gave her brother a puzzled look.

"Padraic! Josephine!" their mother called from the kitchen. "Cam' 'ere and get washed fer supper! Yer Da'll be here soon, I'm sure of it!"

Their father's late arrival always presented a quandary for their mother and an ominous circumstance for Paddy and Josie.

While their mother made her best guess, the children often sat, faces and hands washed, hair neatly combed, napkins in their collars, stomachs growling as the evening meal sizzled or bubbled on the hearth nearby, and yet could not eat. Too many times, when at last their father did arrive, their mother had been admonished and abused for feeding her children before her husband; too many times they had watched as their supper was thrown away uneaten and later, when her husband had passed out from drink, their mother would come to them, face swollen and red with crying, and bring them bowls of brown bread in milk. This night, however, for better or worse, the children did not have long to wait.

Their father, a great, blonde hulk of a German man, burst into the kitchen smelling of pitch, tobacco and whiskey. He said nothing, but stood still for a moment, surveying the scene; at last he swaggered over to a chair and sat down. As his wife spooned out his meal, he turned a slanted eye on Paddy and held out his hand. Paddy reached deep into his pants pocket and produced a nickel and three picayunes; he placed them in the center of his father's massive palm.

"Is this all?" the man grunted through a mouthful of stew and bread, the sauce trickling down his stubbly chin.

Paddy nodded and hung his head over his own bowl. The coins were his earnings from the work he did delivering for some of the French Market vendors, among them the Italian man who had earlier given him oranges. But no matter how much or how little he earned, he had to turn it over to his father at the end of each day. It never seemed to be enough and it didn't comfort Paddy much to know that every cent went into the bars and brothels of Gallatin Street.

"Pah!" his father grumbled as he pocketed the coins. "A pittance! You had better get fleeter on those clumsy feet of yours!" He meant that Paddy should make his deliveries quicker and earn more money; he drove his point home with a kick under the table at Paddy's shin.

"What about you?" their father said thickly, turning his attention to Josie. Unlike Paddy, she looked up, straight into her father's watery, bloodshot blue eyes, and chewed in defiant silence. Then she reached into her apron pocket and pulled out a handful of acorns. She set these on the table in front of her.

He gazed at them. "Why you insolent little –!" her father growled and lifted a hand to strike her.

"The Daliets paid!" her mother cried, jumping up and producing a half-dollar from her own apron. "But we've not been paid by the Letelliers yet," she added nervously, checking the tone of her voice. She quickly swiped Josie's acorns from the table. "Dey pay reg'lar on Fridays, ye know. Dey'll have sometin' fer Josie then."

Josie earned a small amount for the household by helping her mother do laundry. It was hard, back-breaking work that kept her mother near exhaustion; Josie did what she could, helping to starch collars and cuffs, and to press the tiny pleats on infants' clothes which she smoothed with her thin little fingers.

Her father grunted and looked at her; even though she had just heard her mother tell a bald-faced lie (the Letelliers had, in fact, paid) she never flinched or turned her eyes away. Her father, unable for some reason to withstand his child's gaze for very long, mumbled something inaudible and went back to eating. The meal went on in silence.

Later, after the children had helped with the washing up and readied for bed, and long after their father had passed out bent over the kitchen table, their mother came quietly into their room to say goodnight. She went first to Paddy, who was already dozing; she bent down and kissed his cheek and brushed his tufted hair aside – something he'd never allow without protest were he awake. Then she rose and moved toward Josie's bed.

"Oh!" she gasped as a litter of acorns cracked under her feet, casting her off balance before skittering away into the darkness under the bed. "Honestly, child!" she sighed and settled onto the bed next to Josie. "Sure I'll fall and knock me head one of these nights! Why do ye clutter yer room with these t'ings," she wondered, kicking the acorns away. "Yer to sweep 'em up first t'ing, alright?"

Josie nodded, but said nothing. Her mother petted her softly and smiled. "There's my sleeping beauty," she laughed softly as she ran her hand over Josie's blankets, tucking them neatly down. Suddenly she stopped. She could feel her daughter tense, and when she drew the sheets away she found Josie's hands folded tightly over her chest like little red balls, desperately clutching something in each.

"Wha's the matter 'ere?" Josie's mother said now. "Wha' do ye have 'ere, child?" She pulled at Josie's hand, but the child's grip was like iron. "Now, enough of this! Show me wha' ye have!"

Josie slowly peeled open her hands and displayed their contents. In the midst of her palms, now white from the tightness of her grip, were two small caches of acorns.

"More?" her mother gasped. She held out her hand. "Tsk! Give them to me," she said sternly. "Come on! Right now!" Reluctantly, Josie did as she was told.

"Sure it's a mystery to me what ye want wit' these t'ings," her mother said, shaking her head. "Go to sleep," she whispered as she bent to kiss Josie's forehead. "We'll let it alone fer now!"

Josie's mother turned around and blew a kiss to her daughter as she left the room. Josie waited, listening to her mother's soft footsteps padding away to her own room. After a few moments of silence, broken only by the loud rattling of her father's snoring, when she was certain her mother would not return, Josie reached under her pillow and drew out another little handful of acorns. She hung over the side of her bed and quietly scattered them onto the floor. Satisfied that there were still enough surrounding her bed, she turned over and passed into an unquiet sleep.

The beautiful townhome in the Rue St. Louis still had a new smell about it – fresh paint and plaster, new jute under the fine, imported rugs, pungent pecan oil on the floors and woodwork. It stood as the perfect example of an increased social status, and this was just what the new owners intended to convey: the father, a French immigrant who had worked his way up through years of laborious tasks on the river docks into a position of means; his wife, the light of the home, about to bear a third child; and two beautiful twin daughters in whose daydreams the exquisite new dwellings were a fairytale castle in a sunny land of constant play. But when evening came and the shadows of night finally drove out the last golden beams of day, the newness of the home – especially its unfamiliar feeling and its vastness in comparison to the humble intimacy of the cottage the family had lately vacated – made of the girls' dreamy "castle" a nightmare landscape full of undiscovered fears.

One accoutrement that inspired particular nighttime anxiety in the girls was a simple, nondescript model of convenience found in only the very finest new homes: a mechanical dumbwaiter. During the day it provided no end of amusement as a conveyor of dolls and toys of all kinds; though the girls' play interfered with the daily work, the newly-acquired household staff took it in stride. At night, however, while the servants completed the evening tasks, the familiar rattling of the dumbwaiter's chains and pulleys took on an ominous sound as they echoed deep inside the walls; and when the blustery autumn wind that tampered with the doors and windows found its way into the dumbwaiter's shaft, it whistled and cried, and caused the chain to emote with a noisy clanking.

It was just such a night, and little Minette awoke in a state of fear. From the hallway, she could hear the rattling of chains and the bumping of the dumbwaiter in its hollow shaft. It was too late for the servants to be about, so Minette knew the dumbwaiter should not be in use. She lay there, shivering and listening anxiously to its every rattle and bump, magnified in the overwhelming silence of the house, wondering how her parents could not have heard the sounds; at last, when she could stand no more, she whispered for her sister.

"Mignon!" she said. "Mignon!" she called a little louder. Minette heard her sister rustling in her bed nearby. At last her dark, curly head popped out from under the covers.

"What is it?" she whispered sleepily.

"Listen!" Minette replied.

Mignon listened; instantly she recognized the sounds. "Oh, no!" she said wide-eyed, and pulled the blankets up around her face.

They lay still and the minutes ticked by interminably slowly. The rattling and clanking went on, and the bumping of the dumbwaiter against the side of its shaft was like a malingering heartbeat. Minette put her hands to her ears and shut her eyes. But Mignon was suddenly struck with a strange courage: fierce and impatient of fear, she threw off her bedcovers and jumped up.

"I'm going to see!" she said, shuffling into slippers and pulling on her robe.

"Mignon, no!" Minette cried. "Don't go out there!"

Mignon gave her sister a narrow look. "Don't be silly, Minette! It's nothing but the wind! Let's have a look together!" She held out her hand to Minette, still cowering in her bed. The bumping and rattling continued; Mignon was already at their bedroom door.

"Oh, very well!" Minette sighed and got into her own robe and slippers. "Wait for me!" she cried, and rushed up close to Mignon as she slowly opened the door. They peeked out.

From their doorway the girls had a good view of the gallery and the top of the winding stairs. Across a wide landing and a few steps down was the door to their parents' room. Soaring windows lined the staircase and this night let in only the barest light of the waning moon so that the complicated pattern of the drapery sheers looked more like a blurred stencil across the floor. The girls' doorway did not allow a view of the dumbwaiter in its recessed alcove; to see it at all, they had to venture out into the passage. So, hugging each other, the sisters moved with careful, quiet steps, from the relative safety of their room and out into the darkened gallery. Immediately, Mignon gasped, and Minette put a hand to her own mouth to stifle her shock: there, in the middle of the passage, sitting in a thin patch of moonlight, was a large, white rabbit.

At first it ignored them completely, snuffling and rubbing its pink nose with its paws. It sat up, then back down again. Then it rolled slightly and lazily scratched an ear. When it righted itself, the rabbit turned its head and looked at them with large, thoughtful eyes.

"Oh!" Minette whispered with delight. "Look at how lovely he is! How did he get in?"

"He must have come up the dumbwaiter!" said Mignon, smiling and holding out her hand. "That's a good boy," she purred, making soothing whispers, "that's right, we won't harm you."

Transfixed by this unexpected delight the girls inched forward, not mindful that despite the presence of the rabbit in the hall strange noises continued to sound from inside the dumbwaiter shaft.

"Come here," Minette coaxed.

"That's right," Mignon whispered.

The rabbit sat still, its pink nose still snuffling. It did not attempt to run, and even as the sisters slowly closed in upon it, there was no hint of fear.

The girls were smiling now, bending low over the rabbit and about to reach out for it when, suddenly, and to their horror, the doors of the dumbwaiter flew wide open with an echoing BANG! The girls jumped back in fear and instinctively Mignon moved to draw the rabbit to her for its safety, but when she reached out to grab it, her hands closed on empty air! Her startled gasp was enough to momentarily draw Minette's attention away from the yawning blackness of the dumbwaiter shaft; she looked just in time to see Mignon's arms go right through the spectral hare. At this the sisters ought to have cried out in fear and run away, but before either could think a full thought, they were transfixed by a horrible new sound.

Strange, hollow, yet it had a sort of rhythm – first a thud then a drag, then a *thud-thud* and another drag, *thud-drag, thud-thud drag* . . . the noises coming from the shaft were growing louder with each excruciating minute. The girls backed away slowly, clutching each other, eyes fixed upon the square of impenetrable darkness facing them. Then a wave of horror and fear broke over them as they watched two gray, bloodless hands appear at the side of the shaft, gripping tightly to the frame. In another moment, first one, then another withered forearm appeared over the edge of the shaft and there was a grunting sound, as if someone were struggling to climb up.

When the head appeared, Minette and Mignon were snapped out of their shock, and screaming like banshees, bolted for their bedroom; but not before they had each gotten a good look at the face – that of a dead Negro man, its putrid skin blistered and festering, one eye lolling on the bare white of a cheekbone, the lips stretched in a grimace over yellowed teeth in a mouth busy with the scavenging of maggots and beetles.

The shrieks and screams of the girls shocked their parents from sleep and in a moment their father, instructing his wife to wait in the safety of their bedroom, emerged into the hallway and came upon a horrible sight. The animated corpse had pulled itself, or what remained of itself, up so that it now clung, dangling over the edge of the dumbwaiter shaft. Its broken neck creaked as the grinning, decomposing face turned to look at the man, and as he approached the thing a mixture of recognition and fear suddenly came over him. He looked down at the rabbit and gasped audibly, his face white with terror.

"Papa! Papa!" the girls screamed from their room, distracting him. "There is a man in the house!"

The father watched as the corpse released its grip and, apparently, fell back down the dumbwaiter shaft; in a flash, the white rabbit leapt to the shaft's ledge and it, too, disappeared into the pitch black of the hole in the wall. The man rushed to the dumbwaiter and did exactly the worst thing he could possibly have done: he bent forward to peer down the chute. A rattle and the horrible squeal of the dumbwaiter pulley letting go were the last sounds he heard on this earth. In an instant, the dumbwaiter plummeted down the shaft, and the weight of it, combined with the force of it, instantly cut the man in half.

A short time later in a noisy Gallatin Street tavern, a tall Kaintuck flatboatman stood up from his game of cards and stuffed his winnings into his pockets.

"Beaten at your own game!" the Kaintuck said in a heavy Swedish accent. "Try to cheat me, but I turn the tables! Ha!" he laughed triumphantly as the other players waved him away.

"Go away, you fool," growled a wide-shouldered German. "No one cheated you! Go sleep it off!"

"Not until I have my drink!" the Kaintuck replied, swaying slightly. Holding up a bottle of whiskey he said, "Thank you, gentlemen, for emptying your pockets to me!" With that, he put the bottle to his lips and drained it of its considerable contents. "Here is for you!" he laughed. The men grumbled and ignored him; even when he slammed the bottle on the table, no one flinched. "Ah!" he said finally, grabbing at his crotch. "Time to piss!"

The Kaintuck stumbled off through the cluster of women and drunks, and the thick, smoky haze of tobacco and opium, making for the rear of the tavern. He pushed his way down the narrow back hallway where prostitutes were busily working their trade, and, ducking through the low back door, came out into the tavern's yard, really just a festering square of muck that opened onto the river battures. It was almost pitch dark, with only the feeble glow of the tavern lamps and a bare hint of waning moonlight to see by, but a foul stench made the cesspits easy to find. With one arm against a fence pole to help keep his balance, the Kaintuck quickly set about his business. A long night of drinking kept him occupied for several minutes, long enough to be joined by another man whose legs he could just see under his outstretched arm. An overpoweringly foul smell suddenly filled the already-polluted air and just then the man spied a flash of white passing behind him, at the very edge of his line of sight.

"Wha –?" he muttered. His immediate thought was that one or two of his disgruntled fellow gamblers had followed him outside to get back their losses. He fumbled quickly with the buttons on his pants and turned to the man standing beside him. But when he looked - his eyes now accustomed to the darkness - the Kaintuck recoiled from the horrific sight. There was no man standing beside him, but there was, only feet away, the lower half of a body – really just a mass of maggoty putrefaction and decomposition on legs lost in a pair of blousy, striped pants. Sobriety was quickly gaining ground and with it the man's realization that he recognized the pattern of those pants, had seen them before – the parti-colored stripes of a clown's costume!

He gasped and backed away, and as he did so he bumped into someone standing behind him. "Look out!" he warned, and spun around.

Now the man's horror multiplied exponentially as he confronted the top half of the decomposing corpse of Bouqui the Clown whose skeletal grin and grey-green, maggot-eaten face was only inches away from his own. The clown's bony hand, rancid with grey, peeling flesh, gripped a chain that extended down from levers holding up a wooden platform which the tavern used to load in beer, ale, whiskey and wine, and sometimes even food directly off the river docks. The curious sight of a familiar white rabbit moving along the edge of the platform was surreal and only added to the man's now full-blown terror. The rabbit's glowing red eyes held the Kaintuck transfixed when, in a movement so swift, so fast, it seemed hardly to have happened at all, the torso of the clown dropped down to the ground – its hand still gripping at the platform's chain. Overhead there was a heavy groaning as the contraption gave way and swung whistling down in a large arc, pinning the Kaintuck against the fence and snapping him in two.

Paddy had worked a full day with Nunzio the produce vendor and had accompanied him on his daily retreat from the markets. Now he stood listening, even though his mother kept waving him away, as Nunzio shared the grisly details of strange deaths rumored to have happened in the city only a few nights before.

"Dear God!" his mother said, putting a hand over her mouth. "How awful!"

Nunzio nodded deeply. "I tell you the truth, Signora Mainz," he said in his thick Italian accent. "Cut in half!" Here he made a slicing motion across his abdomen. "The sheriffs, they no have any clues!"

"It's a murderer, it is!" Paddy's mother replied in a whisper, noticing her son was nearby again. "Someone's killin' poor workin' folk!"

"Ah! The Kaintuck - aw, sure, sure!" Nunzio said. "But what about that Frenchman? He live in the fine house on the other side of the Carré! Who killa him?" Then Nunzio delivered even more disturbing news. "And someone is still killing de children!"

"No!' Paddy's mother gasped.

"Yes!" Nunzio replied, with a deep nod. "They find a girl dead in the woods on the Bayou Road. A little deaf and mute girl! Tsk! So sad!"

Paddy's mother stood silent for a long moment and stared, not even aware that he had sidled back up beside her. "But how can tha' be? I thought t'ey caught – "

Nunzio shrugged. He took off his little cap and brushed back his thick, black hair. "The clown?" he replied. "No," he said flatly, fixing his cap back upon his head. "The murders, they still happen!"

A heavy silence fell. Paddy looked curiously at the faces of his mother and the Italian vendor. Something seemed to pass between them, something that did not need to be spoken and to which he was not privy.

"Sure I'll be watchin' mine own tonight, like I do every night!" she said, holding out her apron as Nunzio gave her several eggplants and green Italian squash. "Ah! Yer too kind, Nunzi!"

Nunzio gave her a little salute from the brim of his cap. "Is my pleasure, Signora," he said. "More tomorrow! You keep safe, alright? And you, too, Paddy!" he called over his shoulder as he rolled his wobbly cart away.

"Dat we will!" Paddy's mother called back. She turned around and her eyes fell on Paddy. "Well, I suppose ye heard all dat?" she said to him.

Paddy shrugged. "Some," he said meekly. "He told me all about it at the market, anyway."

His mother rolled her eyes and sighed. "Well, be sure ye don't go tellin' yer sister none of it," she admonished him. "I've enough trouble gettin' her to sleep now. I don't need her a'feared of somethin' else!"

"I won't tell," Paddy promised. "Cross me heart!" he added in response to a last stern look from his mother.

"I'll box ye ears if ye do!" she said, and walked off toward the house. "Stay close. It'll be dark soon!"

Paddy watched his mother go in through the low doorway of the house. In a flash, he bolted in the opposite direction, making for the cemetery where he knew he would find Josie. Sure enough, as he came to the old gate, he could see his sister inside, sitting under a tree in the fading sunlight, the now-familiar white rabbit by her side.

Normally when he returned home he would rush over to join her, or at least call out to her if he was late since he knew she had no playmates; but this day he was surprised to see that Josie was not alone. Two little girls were sitting with her, feeding the rabbit, and a small boy, barely of walking age, was standing just nearby; Paddy didn't recognize any of them.

"Josie!" he called as he came through the gate. As soon as he approached, the rabbit bolted. The strange children ran after it, giggling.

"Agh! Paddy!" Josie cried, exasperated. "Ye always scare him away!"

Paddy ran up and stood, hands on hips, looking around. "Who's dat ye were playin' wit'?"

Josie looked down and picked idly at the grass. "Friends," she said quietly.

"Friends?" Paddy repeated. "From where? I never saw 'em before."

"They live over t'ere," Josie said and pointed to the woods beyond the burying ground.

"Wha'? Back t'ere?" he said, somewhat incredulously.

"Uh, huh," Josie replied. "We were feeding my rabbit."

Paddy knelt down next to his sister. "Ah, *your* rabbit," he said, tossing sticks. "So ye don't think he likes me yet?"

"No!" Josie mumbled and threw a few acorns at a headstone. Then she laughed in spite of herself, and Paddy laughed, too.

"Ah well, t'ere's no accountin' fer taste!" he said.

"Wha' did Mister Nunzio say to Ma?" Josie asked offhandedly.

Paddy hesitated. "Ah, nothin'," he said. "Givin' Ma some of those Ital'yun veg'ables he sells. I know wha's fer dinner now." He rolled his eyes. "See'd 'em all day, have t'eat 'em at night!"

Josie laughed and idly tossed a few more acorns. "I think he told her about the dead people," she said quietly.

Paddy looked at her in surprise. "Wha? Ah, no, dey weren't talkin' about no dead people!"

"Oh, yes dey was'," Josie replied.

"I were standin' right dere," Paddy said, lying and feigning impatience. "I heared t'whole talk. Ain't no mention of dead people."

"Uh huh," Josie nodded. "Two dead men," she said. "And a little girl, too."

Paddy stared at his sister. "And how d'ye know dat smarty?"

"The rabbit told me," Josie said.

McAndrew was a burly Irishman well known in the lower strata of New Orleans as a ruthless bare-knuckle boxer and muscle-for-hire. Odd jobs – even very odd jobs – were his specialty and his only allegiance was to whoever was holding the purse strings in any particular situation. He worked mainly on the docks where his strength made him much sought after, but the pay varied so he often took on occasional jobs, and this time the job entailed keeping the night watch at a brickyard in the Rue Dumaine. Locals now and then pilfered a few bricks from the yards under a mostly-blind eye; but when some of the local hoodoo workers began to use the yards for their rituals late at night, the religious sensibilities of the owners were at last offended and they were forced to seek out a deterrent. As deterrents went, it happened that one couldn't do much better than Quinn McAndrew.

For three nights McAndrew had walked the yards with Fred, his bulldog, checking that gates were secure and that no one had been bold enough to sneak inside. On the third night, Fred had some fun chasing a large white rabbit out of the yards, but other than this, the watches had been uneventful. By the fourth night, McAndrew had even abandoned making rounds, leaving it to Fred to patrol the yard while he sat in a little alcove near the entrance, warming himself with whiskey and dozing in front of a small stove. Then around two o'clock in the morning of the fifth day McAndrew was jolted awake by his dog's fierce barking.

Taking with him a lantern and the wooden club he always carried, McAndrew made his way to the back of the yard where Fred was barking frantically and running along the ground in front of several high stacks of bricks.

"Who's dat, Fred?" he said to the dog. "Ye got sometin' dere? Tha' friend o'yern back, eh?" He held up the lantern expecting to see the rabbit again; he was puzzled to see nothing that could be the cause of the dog's anxiety. This made him suspicious.

"Lissen here, boy-o!" he called out in a loud voice. "I ain't in no mood t'be climbing all over dese rocks lookin' fer ye low, thievin' ass! Ye better come out now and face me!"

Fred continued to whine and prance along the brick piles. Suddenly, McAndrew heard the scuttling of falling bricks and the distinct sound of footsteps running into the recesses of the yard on his right. Fred immediately sprinted off in that direction; McAndrew quickly closed the distance between them.

"Hey, ye bastard!" he called out. "This here yard's locked up tight! Ain't nowhere t'go! Ye best come out now if ye know what's good for ye!"

The shadows in this area of the yard were thick and the ordinary brick stacks were interspersed with pallets of sheeted stone; brought over as ship's ballast, the large, flat pieces – mostly limestone – were destined to be hammered into fill for the Carré's ever-sinking streets. Fred ran headlong into the darkness of a long alleyway and soon disappeared from sight, but McAndrew could still hear him panting and barking.

"Sure ye'll be sorry ye made me chase yer ass when I get a hold on ye!" he grumbled, swinging his lantern from side to side to get a better view of where he was going.

Suddenly Fred came running back to him, whining and jumping, then running in circles around him; the dog seemed uncharacteristically nervous, even frightened, and was no longer interested in running ahead. Instead, it stayed close to McAndrew's side and barked at the darkness, its breath condensing thickly in the chill night air. McAndrew held out his lantern and moved forward with caution.

"Wha's dat? Ye come out here now!" he called out to the shadows. "Show yerself, damn ye!"

McAndrew spied a flash of white and just then, after he had demanded it to show itself, he saw the head of the white rabbit peering down at him from the top of the tallest pallets.

"God damn'it!" McAndrew spat. "Ye bastard rabbit! I'd beat ye to a pulp, I would, if I felt like climbin' like a monkey after ye! Make stew of ye, I would!" Fred continued to bark and whine.

The rabbit, completely out of reach, now busied itself with scratching and chewing at something on the top of the pallets. McAndrew could hear its furtive little noises but had to content himself with yelling at it and then at his dog to stop barking. With Fred subdued, McAndrew made one last scowl at the rabbit and turned to walk away. But just then he heard another sound – that of swift footsteps coming from where the rabbit sat, still working diligently.

McAndrew turned back and held up his lantern. He could still see the rabbit there, busily chewing and scratching, but now something else caught his eye – someone was standing next to the rabbit. McAndrew could just make out the striped fabric of the pants, colored with dark patches; the intruder's upper body seemed to be hidden in the deep, shadowy gloom.

"Alright, ye!" he growled. "Come down here, now! Ain't no one here but me and ye, and I've got all night to wait!" He swung his club over his shoulder. "I hope yer as ready to make my acquaintance as I am to make yers!" he added sarcastically.

At just this moment he heard Fred yelping from the front of the yard – he was surprised to find that the dog had not been by his side all this time, and the sound was unquestionably one of fear. McAndrew leaned back and peered down the dark alley, but his attention was suddenly diverted by something lying on the ground near his feet. He looked down and there, crawling just inches away from him, was the fetid upper portion of Bouqui the Clown!

With a cracking of its broken neck that jarred loose a cluster of maggots from its matted hair, the corpse turned its rotting face up and grinned balefully at McAndrew who could do nothing but stare back, struck dumb and frozen to the spot in shock and terror. The corpse reached out slowly and grabbed hold of his ankle with a festering, wet hand. McAndrew dropped both lantern and club, and screamed in abject terror; he shook his foot violently and kicked at the corpse, but it would not loosen its grip. Then, from high above, he heard the popping of rope and the spring of cords giving way.

He looked up just in time to see the rabbit jump, now nothing more than a white wraith disappearing into the darkness ahead of the foul, blood-soaked legs of Bouqui the Clown that rode the shuddering sheets of limestone like the falling crest of a wave: the stones shattered and broke, and crushed the body of Quinn McAndrew to pulp underneath.

Paddy always hated whenever his father came home and announced he had work for him. He never knew what that work might entail: on one occasion he spent five sweltering days repairing roofs in the Carré with his father mostly directing from the shade; on another he had been made to stand lookout while his father and his low friends sold bodies, freshly removed from the criminal's burying ground, to doctors eager for dissection specimens; and once he was put to watch as they pried poor boxes from nearby churches and afterwards was forced to wait outside a Gallatin Street flop alley while his father had his way with both the church's money and a prostitute inside.

"Get ready," Gunder Mainz told his son. "We're leaving after dinner."

"Wha' t'night?" Paddy exclaimed and got a slap on the head in return.

"Yah, tonight, you little bastard," his father growled. "Don't talk back to me!"

"Don't hit the boy!" Paddy's mother protested, gently stroking her son's head. "Wher'r ye takin' him anyway?"

"Not your business is it?" Gunder barked, spitting food everywhere.

Paddy hung his head and sighed.

An hour later he was standing with a few other boys on a lonely dock behind the levee slave markets, stamping against the October chill and keeping watch for a tramp schooner that had gone overdue. His father and a friend, another German named Gand, were sitting under a makeshift shelter nearby warming their hands over a kettle fire and drinking beer. They were talking, or more accurately Gand was talking and Mainz was listening; though the men lapsed in and out of German and English, Paddy caught enough of the conversation to gather that Gand was a frightened man.

"They were all killed, I tell you!" he was saying. "All three of them!"

Mainz made a face. "Why haven't I heard anything about it?"

"It just happened!" Gand replied, his voice pitching higher. There was a thoughtful pause, then, "I'm telling you Gunder, I'm afraid!"

Mainz laughed. "What?" he exclaimed. "Don't be ridiculous, Reinhard! It's coincidence! People die all the time, in all kinds of ways!"

Gand took a long swig of beer. "Gunder," he choked, "every one of them – of us – we all had a hand in it."

Mainz frowned maliciously. "I told you not to mention that," he growled. "Anyway, so did others."

"But it's true!" his friend entreated. "It's true! First LeBecq, cut in half in his own house; then Jorgsen, behind the slanty bar; and now McAndrew. McAndrew!" Gand repeated the name as if he couldn't believe his own words. "Smashed in the brick yard!"

"Keep lookin', you dawdler!" Mainz growled at Paddy, who had drawn near to better hear the conversation. "You're worse than a woman!" Mainz said then, turning back to Gand.

"No," Gand said flatly. "I am not. I tell you, someone is getting revenge."

Mainz considered this for several minutes. "It's those Jew bastards," he said at last. "The Jew scum that tried to save the nigger. They're the ones behind it!"

A hopeful look passed over Gand's face. If Mainz was correct, at least it gave them a natural, human agent to focus on. "Do you really think it's them?" he said.

"Of course it is," Mainz replied and took another long pull on his beer. "Who else? They saw everything."

"But, they don't know any of us," Gand replied.

Mainz gave him a long look. "But I know them," he said. "That Jew doctor, Gottschalk – always poking his nose where he's no business – and that fop Avetante, 'Dr. Cracker' they call him – goes about with the darkies in the Congo Fields pretending to be a hoodoo man. They're rich Jews, is all. They control everything, but they couldn't save one nigger, so . . ." He shrugged. Gand blinked at him. "So," he went on testily, "they put some of those Congo thugs to work on it!"

Gand's eyes widened. "What if that Dr. Cracker put the hoodoo on us?"

Mainz looked at him incredulously. "Why don't you just stop talking? It would be better for both of us. No, there's only one way," he added in an afterthought. "We'll have to take care of those Hebrew dogs."

Paddy's whistle interrupted any reply Gand could make. He and Mainz joined Paddy on the dock in time to see a ragged schooner drifting up with no lights and men scurrying about on deck. By the look of the crew, the lack of uniforms and the obvious lack of coordination, Paddy knew them immediately as scallywags and bootleggers.

Paddy and the other boys, the sons of criminals or budding criminals themselves, secured the lines while his father, Gand,

and some of the crew laid out the gang planks. Mainz whistled to Paddy and snapped his fingers.

"Make it quick, boy!" he said. "We don't need the watch catching us!"

Paddy made fast a line and ran down the dock toward the gang plank. Gazing toward the vessel's bow he saw his father already busy directing the offloading of nondescript canvas parcels onto the dock. But, unhappy with the work of the boys on the stern end, Gand had stepped onto the gang plank complaining in harsh whispers, waving his arms about and making such a spectacle that Paddy couldn't help laughing at the sight. It was just about this time that Paddy saw the rabbit.

There, perched on the forecastle railing, calmly snuffling and grooming itself with its long paws, sat the very same rabbit that Josie had been playing with for days in the old cemetery. Paddy screwed up his brow in wonder; he could think of no reasonable explanation for that rabbit to be there.

"There's Josie's rabbit!" he exclaimed then, realizing what he had said, quickly put a hand over his mouth.

But Paddy's father had already heard. He looked, squinting at the large hare sitting on the railing. All the color flushed from his face in one horrible moment of recognition. He grabbed Paddy and shook him. "What did you say, boy?" he cried. "What did you say? Josie's rabbit? *Is that what you said?*"

Paddy couldn't reply and what he saw next was just one of many things he would see that night that would haunt him until the end of his days.

"God damn it! Who tied these lines?" Gand hollered and jumped onto the dock. "You bunch of slackers!" he yelled and went busily at the lines, cursing in German. All the boys nearby backed away to let him have his fit. Suddenly, two of the vessel's lines went extremely taut and didn't respond to Gand's tugging: in the next moment, all the boys ran away as fast as their feet could move.

"What the hell . . .?" Gand fussed. "Pull *this* one," he said and turned to hand a line to what he thought was one of the crew: with grey, decomposing flesh bubbling and dripping like tree sap and bones showing through bare shreds of skin, the fetid hand of Bouqui the Clown reached out from mid-air and took the line.

Gand screamed and tried to run, but Bouqui's hand pulled the line tighter. On the vessel there was mayhem as the crew ran about or jumped overboard to escape Bouqui's noxious, foul-smelling legs that had suddenly jumped down from the mast and walked, unaided, dripping putrefaction, across the schooner's deck.

In his rush to scold the dock boys, Gand had inadvertently tangled himself in his own lines; now, as the hand of the clown pulled tightly on one line, the feet of the clown fixed firmly on another where it was threaded over a dock cleat. Pulling ever tighter and tighter, the lines sawed into Gand's skin as he struggled and fought, screaming in shrill terror, the face of the dead clown gazing fixedly upon him.

Paddy stood stricken with fear, rooted in place by the supernatural horror unfolding before his eyes. Gunder Mainz, too, stood momentarily transfixed. But he was made of tougher sinew, and in another moment his ferocity and hatred overrode his fear and he rushed forward to help his friend.

Paddy watched as his father, braving both fearsome corpse and ghostly white rabbit, pulled at the vessel's lines, trying in vain to loosen them. He ran back and forth between the ropes and Gand's quaking, squirming body but was defeated and at last could only stand and watch his friend expel one last wail of anguish as his body exploded, splintering bones and shredding clothing, and splattering Mainz with blood and innards. Chunks of Reinhard Gand thudded to the dock and some parts fell with noisome splashes into the dark Mississippi waters. Great catfish rose from the inky river depths, gulping at the body parts with their cavernous mouths; what the fish did not mangle, the swift current carried away.

Mainz stood motionless and a light of wild madness flashed in his icy blue eyes. He was convinced the clown would take him next, and he set himself to face his dreadful fate. But to his surprise, Bouqui only smiled – or so it seemed when the remainder of the flesh around the skeletal teeth stretched even more; and then, lifting a ragged, rotten finger, the ghost wagged it slowly back and forth as if to scold Gunder Mainz like a miscreant child. Then Bouqui the Clown – both halves – disappeared into thin air. Only the rabbit remained. It regarded Mainz with gleaming, knowing eyes then it, too, faded away.

For a long moment Gunder Mainz stood silent and shaking, breathing deeply to calm his shattered nerves. Then suddenly he recalled his son's words and anger drove out all fear: *"Josie's rabbit!"* he seethed. With that he turned on his heel and stalked away toward home.

Already blocks ahead of his father, Paddy burst into the house and fell crying into his mother's arms. It was several minutes before she could make sense of anything he was saying, but the one thing that came through quite clearly was that her husband was on his way and he was angry.

"Now, now, son!" she said, soothing him. "Shhh! Tell me – tell me wha' happened?"

Paddy's sobs came in shuddering gasps. He turned to Josie. "I'm sorry, Josie!" he cried. "I'm so sorry! But he saw t'rabbit!"

Standing in the doorway of her little room, Josie blanched and her eyes widened like saucers. She bolted and scrambled under her bed for safety.

"Wha' is this nonsense, Padraic?" his mother cried, shaking him gently. "Wha' rabbit?"

"T'rabbit," Paddy sobbed, "t'rabbit tha' comes t'play with Josie! It was there t'night, and Mr. Gand was killed!"

She grabbed his face. "Wha'? Wha'? Mr. Gand was killed?"

Paddy wagged his head. "Aye, he was! And the clown . . ." He sobbed anew at the thought of it all, but then went suddenly silent. His mother tensed. Both clearly heard the stamping of feet outside.

"Run! Hide yerself! Go!" Paddy's mother cried, as she grabbed a kitchen knife from off a nearby table. She had a feeling this confrontation would be unlike any she had previously had with her husband. Paddy ran into the bedroom. "And Paddy!" she called after him. "Keep yer sister safe!"

The whole house shook as the massive bulk of Gunder Mainz pounded up the steps and ploughed inside; the light of every candle and even the fire of the hearth seemed dimmed by his very presence. His wife stood up and bravely put herself between her panting, wild-eyed husband and the door of her children's room.

"Where is she?" Gunder growled. "Where's that little bitch? She's been up to witchcraft, she has – and I'm going to beat it out of her!"

But his wife stood firm. "Ye'll stay away from her and from Paddy until ye calm down!" she cried. "Get out! Go sleep it off an' t'en ye can ask me wher' my children are!" Her hand tightened around the hilt of the knife now hidden in the folds of her apron.

"Back away, woman," he growled. "JOSIE!" he called out loudly. "JOSIE! It's you behind all this! You get in here you little hoodoo bitch! I'll teach you a lesson you won't soon forget!" He made for the bedroom door but his wife pushed against him.

"Ye'll not touch her!" she hissed, and in one swift move brought the knife from her apron to her husband's throat. "Ye'll have to kill me first!"

Mainz smiled and gave her a look so filled with malice it chilled her to the bone; but she stood her ground. "And do you think I *won't* kill you?" he said, towering over her at his full height.

She screamed and shoved the knife into her husband's throat with all her might; but he was swifter and turned his head at the last minute so that the blade only grazed his flesh. Now completely enraged, he grabbed hold of his wife's hand and beat it against the door frame until the knife fell from it. Reeling from that assault, she was unprepared for the thundering blow of her husband's fist as it came down against her jaw. She heard a crack and felt teeth loosen, blood filling her mouth and nose, then she fell backward and, losing her footing on Josie's treasure of acorns, struck her head on the edge of her daughter's bed. As she passed out of consciousness she saw the hulking shape of her husband step over her, his shadow filling every inch of her children's tiny room. "Paddy!" she whispered, then all went black.

Paddy had been huddled in the corner of his own bed watching and listening; now he leapt forward. "No!" he cried, angry tears burning his flushed cheeks. "Ye killed Ma! Ye bastard! Ye damned bastard! Ye killed me Ma!"

He had long waited for this day, the day he would confront – and possibly kill – his own father. He jumped off the bed brandishing a club that he had skillfully crafted and kept hidden under his mattress for just this moment. As he gained his footing, he landed a firm blow on his father's shoulder, surprising Mainz and knocking him off balance; his foot slipped on acorns and he came crashing down on one knee. Paddy then landed another blow and was going for a third when his father reached up suddenly and with his thick hand grabbed hold of the club in mid-air. His own grip now tightened over Paddy's; he lifted the club and his son several feet off the floor. As they looked at each other, eye to eye, Paddy saw in his father's countenance such a malevolent and wanton evil it seemed to the boy that he was staring into the face of a devil and not a man at all. He pulled against his father's grip and kicked savagely at the air trying to free himself; but Mainz only held tighter and laughed. Then, his smile faded and his face became set as stone; he came in close to Paddy, eyes burning fiercely.

"So you have the stones after all, eh?" he chuckled. "Well, I have killed better than you!" Then he cursed his son in German and tossed him away with no more effort than he would spare to flick at a fly.

The boy fell back against the wall, gasping for breath as the air shot from his lungs. He slid onto his bed, dazed and unable to move, and yet still conscious enough to know that he could be of no help to Josie now. He moaned and tried to lift himself; a punch from his father's massive fist drove him into darkness.

All this time little Josie had lain cowering under her bed. She dared not make a sound, not even after her mother fell and her battered, bloody face came to rest only inches away on the floor. When Paddy was defeated though, Josie's heart swelled with desperate fear. An ominous silence now settled on the entire house, punctuated only by her father's heavy, labored breathing. She watched his feet move as he shuffled about, kicking the clutter of acorns that crackled under his feet; she heard him cursing under his breath and muttering in his harsh native German.

"Sie hexe," he whispered, "sie kleine hexe!" *You little witch!*

How she hated the sound of him! Then, in an instant, he suddenly fell to his knees beside her bed and the horror of his great, meaty arm was grasping for her.

"Come here, my lovely," he cooed through gritted teeth, trying to mask his anger, and it sent chills through every inch of Josie's body. "Come to your Da," he panted, grabbing and feeling about in the darkness. "You know I'd never hurt you. I just want to talk to you is all. Come out and tell me about the rabbit."

Josie knew better. So many nights – numberless they seemed now – when the rest of the house slumbered, he had come to her in just this way - drunk, wooing, not at all like a father. Sometimes she would hear him coming and slip out of the bedroom window to take refuge among the nearby dead, and these narrow escapes caused him to accuse her of working hoodoo tricks; at other times he would be so full of drink that he couldn't make it across the kitchen to her door. He knew her mother couldn't hear him as she slept, collapsed from sheer exhaustion, on the other side of the house; and Paddy, well, he slept like a pile of stones and even if he had awakened, their father would do to him exactly as he had done this night – knock him out with a punch to the head. But to Josie he would show "kindness," as he described it, calling her "mein hübsches Mädchen" – "my pretty girl" – whenever she awoke in terror to find his hand firmly on her mouth and his body stretched out over hers.

Then one day in solitary play among the dilapidated cemetery stones, as she amused herself with the sound of acorns crunching under her feet, a thought came to her. From that day on she had collected acorns as if they were gifts from the royal treasure trove of a Fairy queen. Each brown nut became, in turn, a little sentry that crackled its warning whenever anything approached her bed. Her nature's legion had worked, and several times had foiled the approach of the horrible night monster that was her father. But sometimes, like this night, her sentries failed utterly. This night, she realized, there was nothing that could save her.

"Dort sind Sie, Hexe!" he roared. *There you are, witch!*

Josie screamed and kicked as her father's hand locked around her tiny leg. He pulled, but she would not come out easily. With every ounce of strength in her, she resisted, holding on with tiny little fingers to the bed – first to the moss and the roping and then clutching the frame. But she was not strong enough. Her father lifted her up and tossed her onto the bed like a rag doll.

"There's my girl," he said, looking down at her, and Josie's blood ran cold. She kicked and screamed, but this did nothing to deter the horrible intent now fixed upon her. The awful, sweaty face, the bulging, bloodshot eyes, the stinking, slavering lips – he held her down with one arm while his hand fumbled with his pants. "I'm going to teach you a lesson," he panted, "that's right! You're in need of a lesson, you are!"

Josie crossed her legs tightly, but his massive hands overpowered her. "Did you send the rabbit out, little bitch?" he whispered harshly, his sweating face next to her ear. "Was it you, eh? How else would it know where to go?"

She scratched at his face, but this only seemed to heighten his evil desire and he leered at her with a hungry grin. She cried, and closed her eyes, and was about to scream the loudest scream she could muster when suddenly everything stopped.

There was silence.

What happened then, in what sequence, Josie never really knew, but she knew what resulted. Was it the rabbit her father saw first, sitting still as stone on the windowsill? Or was it the putrefying legs crawling out from under Paddy's bed? Or did he, perhaps, first behold the remainder of the corpse of Bouqui the Clown as it floated up to the window and into the room?

Josie watched as the monstrous brute that was her father confronted a depth of terror he had clearly never known before. How different he looked now! All the rage had left his face, and Josie could tell by his peculiar cast of countenance, the blinking, fear-filled eyes, and the mouth that yammered but could not utter a sound, that this was a man who was staring into the face of his doom.

The rabbit, glowing with an ethereal whiteness but now quite solid, jumped down onto the bed and snuggled next to Josie, unmistakably protecting her as together they watched a fantastic drama unfold: the clown's bodiless legs stood to full height and circled behind Josie's father, blocking his path to the door – there would be no escape; slowly and without a sound, the upper half of Bouqui the Clown floated ever-closer to him. Ghostly, glowing with a sickly green hue, dripping putrefaction and gobs of festering flesh upon the floor, it stopped and came face-to-face with the quaking figure of its killer.

Yes, it had been Mainz who had instigated the murder of the clown, and had done so to protect himself from suspicion and scrutiny: for Gunder Mainz was also the shadowy killer who had violated and killed the children of his friends and neighbors, and who, while burying the battered remains of one of his victims in the lonely criminal's fields, had been spied by poor Bouqui, the much-loved clown of the Creoles, as he passed by on his way to his humble shack on the Bayou Road.

Even if Bouqui had gone to the authorities, confessed what he had seen, no one would believe him, a poor Negro testifying against a white man. The thought had never crossed Bouqui's mind. But the chance glimpse had put a guilty fear into Mainz and so he had worked out and hatched a deadly plan, one that would cast the scrutiny on none other than Bouqui himself! Bouqui had to be got rid of, had to be made to take the blame; Bouqui, the poor Negro about whom no one would protest with any credulity, about whom no one would make much fuss, and whom no one would really miss, would die to hide the crimes of Gunder Mainz.

Once the target was chosen, it only took too much drink and some well-placed accusations for Mainz to rouse from among his like-minded friends a group willing to go the full distance, to take "justice" into their own hands. The result was the beating and lynching of old Bouqui and his poor white rabbit. Now, however, all his friends were dead and Gunder Mainz was on his knees, alone, before the vengeful specter of the decomposing clown.

"No! Please!" he begged, crying and wringing his hands. "Please! Have pity! I'm a ruined man, please!!"

The clown looked down at the man groveling before him. There was no pity in that skeletal visage, no hint of compassion, only anger burning like a fire in the dark orbital recesses where the eyes once had been; the grimacing jaw, with only the barest remnants of skin attached, where wormy sinew made the semblance of a mouth, ground its teeth together in an angry, comfortless sneer. Then the head, now little more than a swiveling object on a rotted neck long-broken by the lynching rope, lolled around until finally it tilted forward, looking directly into Mainz's wet eyes.

Mainz tried to look away. A bony hand reached out and its spindly fingers grasped the man's hair, turning his face up, forcing him to look. Then the jaw of the horrid face appeared to detach and fall open, and there emerged such a scream, more like a howl that started low then rose and rose in an ever-increasing pitch, so that all the room was filled with its timbre; it was a sound so melancholy and hopeless that as soon as she heard it, Josie burst into tears and buried her head against the rabbit's body. In fact, the sound was so loud that it helped bring Paddy back to consciousness, though he immediately crawled into a ball in the corner of his bed to escape the sheer, unearthly terror of it. And under the skeletal hand of Bouqui the Clown the hair of Gunder Mainz went snow white as the banshee-like scream wafted over him; now he was little more than a blubbering mass of fear at the mercy of a dead man.

Bouqui stopped wailing and a ringing silence filled all the space where only a moment earlier the fearsome noise had reigned; it was a silence almost as deafening as the scream itself had been. The ghost regarded Mainz with a steady gaze, then its shoulders heaved, up and down, and what remained of its body shook, and from the gaping abdomen pools of defilement fell like slime upon the floor. A new and horrible sound now replaced the silence; guttural, detached, it welled up from deep inside the fetid torso, as if it came from a great distance: Bouqui the Clown was laughing.

The rabbit jumped away from Josie and leapt over to where the clown's legs stood; it reached up, as if it meant to climb, but instead it pulled out a skein of rope wound around the putrid soup that once was the clown's waist. Silently and swiftly, it worked with tooth and claw, jumping in circles until the rope was wound about the waist of the bent and babbling man.

"No!" Mainz was crying, rocking back and forth on his legs where he knelt in the foul, nauseating mess that had pooled beneath the clown. "No, please, please . . ." he begged, "don't hang me!"

Once again the hollow, cavernous laugh rolled up from inside the clown, like the clanging of the rusty door of a long-abandoned sepulcher. The clown looked at Mainz and let go its grasp on his hair. The words came with difficulty. "*Hang . . . you . . . ?*" it warbled.

The rabbit had waited at the windowsill with the loose end of the rope in its mouth; then it leapt away with preternatural speed. The rope whined out after it in length after length until the section binding Mainz's waist suddenly pulled taut, and his body lunged forward with the rope yanking him up toward the tiny bedroom window. Out there, somewhere in the darkness, he could hear the sound of children's laughter – the ghosts of his victims waiting for him to join them. Fear consumed him.

"Mein Gott!" he cried. "Gott! Gott im Himmel, helfen mir!"

He stood against the window now, resisting with every muscle of his being the supernatural force that pulled him inexorably forward. The rope sawed into his abdomen and he bled profusely as he braced himself with his feet against the wainscoting, his hands clutching the window frame. His jaw jutted out in a mix of defiance and pain, teeth gritting, face swollen and red.

"No!" he choked. "No! You won't take me, you bastard!"

The detached legs of the clown sprinted forward in a smooth, surreal motion and planted one firm kick against the back of Gunder Mainz. A loud, shuddering "crack" sounded out and his hulking mass broke suddenly in two.

"Aaaaaahhh!!" he cried in hellish agony, his body bending backward upon itself.

A final yank of the rope from somewhere in the darkness outside and Mainz at last disappeared through the little window like a leaf being sucked down a drain. Then, all again was silence.

While their father's horrible death drama played out, Paddy had jumped over to Josie's bed and now he held her tightly there, blinking and looking back and forth between the dark window and the figure of Bouqui the Clown. Now the specter slowly turned to face the children and, remarkably, where there had before been two festering body parts, both a mass of rot and putrefaction, there was now a single figure – the ghostly body had become whole again. Moreover, where there had lately been the frightening visage of a fetid skeleton, now the face, and indeed the entire aspect of the clown appeared exactly as it had in life; the flesh appeared completely restored, and the bright eyes and warm smile that had been so familiar to all the children of the Old Carré had returned.

The clown faced them fully now and a smile lit up his countenance. Then he nodded and tipped his worn yellow top hat as slowly his luminous figure began to shimmer and, wavering slightly, like a patch of mist under a full, pale moon, finally faded and was gone.

"The boy appeared at my door in the hour between midnight and one o'clock, knocking feverishly and crying something about his mother having been killed.

I brought him in and immediately attempted to calm him, but he resisted my every effort and pulled at me until I agreed to accompany him. Of course, I suspected nothing of the boy – a thin, will-o'-the-wisp of a youth, weeping and shaking:– It was obvious to me he had experienced some kind of trauma. But I was concerned about venturing into the night after him – where had he come from? – And so I roused my valet, Henry, to accompany us with a lantern. I do not hesitate to add, I placed my pistol in my vest.

We ventured into the Rue Conti and though the boy attempted to lead me toward the unwholesome edges of the Rue

Dauphine I convinced him that we should walk the Rue Royale for the fact that there was more light to see by.

'I live off the Esplanade, sir,' he said to me, and his accent was as thick as Irish stew. Talking seemed to calm him, so as we walked along I encouraged him to convey to me every speck of detail he could about what had happened to his mother. Imagine my shock when the boy responded, 'I think my "Da" killed her!'

'Who?' I asked. 'Do you mean to say your father has killed your mother?'

'Aye!' he responded.

'Then it is the sheriff you need and not me, son,' said I.

He grabbed my arm. 'No, sir,' he cried. 'You must come! My Ma might not be dead,' and here he crossed himself in the Catholic fashion, 'but it's just me and my sister, you see, we're alone.'

Henry and I exchanged glances. It seemed very possible we were heading into some sort of entrapment. But then the boy said an amazing thing, and the words stopped me in my tracks.

'I came to you, sir,' he said, 'because my Da said he wanted to kill you. That's how I remembered your name: Doctor Gottschalk. But now the clown's killed him instead!'

We had just reached the corner of the Rue d'Orleans and in the smoky yellow light of the large oil lantern burning there I could see nothing but earnestness in the countenance of the boy. He was telling the truth. In my troubled mind I now wondered what rent in the fabric of the unseen, what dimly-lit corner of mystery could have placed this child upon my doorstep, for such is the way of the preternatural. But there was no time to ponder. 'Let us hurry!' I said to him. 'Come! Lead the way!'

We passed through the narrow streets that bordered des Ramparts and emerged upon the Esplanade not far from the Rue Dauphine. Here we crossed onto the common lands adjacent to the criminal's burying ground. Among the darkened shacks and shanties there was one in which a light still burned:– This was the home of the boy, Paddy.

As we entered I found the scene altogether as he had described it to me. His mother lay prone upon the floor, her head in a pool of blood that had congealed in her hair and on her face. She seemed lifeless, and I feared Paddy might have been correct in presuming her dead. The poor lad! He burst into tears upon seeing her again; Henry, bending over us with the lantern, shook his head. Then, unexpectedly, Paddy jumped up and exclaimed, 'Josie!' I took this to mean his sister, about whom he had hurriedly told me, and could only watch as he frantically searched a little room nearby. 'I told her to wait here, but she's gone!'

'Help me,' I said to Henry and together we lifted the mother to a small bed. Paddy stood in the middle of the little room wringing his hands and crying. I went over to him and took his hands, asking if Josie was his sister. He nodded wildly. 'Now, I need to see to your mother,' I told him calmly, 'her condition is very grave, and I need your help. In a few moments Henry will take you outside to look for Josie.'

This did much to calm him and he was able to assist me in getting hot water and tearing cloth for bandages. I reassured him that his mother yet lived and he made such a pitiful sight sitting on the floor tearing shreds of sheeting and crying for joy that my heart broke to look at him. I nodded and he smiled at me.

But the mother was in dire straits. I wiped the blood from her face and with my finger reached into her mouth and pulled out several teeth that had been knocked loose by a tremendous blow. Her left eye was swollen shut, her cheekbone was compromised, and her lips enormously swollen; also her right hand was broken. I had my work cut out for me and focused all my attention upon it, yet in the back of my mind I could still hear Paddy saying to me '. . . now the clown's killed him instead . . .'

'Whiskey!' I called and young Paddy produced a jug. I poured a scant amount into a small cup and pressed it to the woman's lips. Nothing. I pressed again and this time there was coughing and the eyes fluttered open. 'Her name?' I called to Paddy before he burst into tears again.

'Adelaide!' He wailed the name and it was as if all the weight of the world fell upon his shoulders in uttering it. His

face puckered and his body shook with weeping. 'Ma!' he cried. 'Ma!'

The woman's eyes opened wide at the sound of her son's voice; she looked around wildly but I held her face gently and spoke to her consolingly. 'Adelaide,' I called, and her eyes came to rest on me, 'Adelaide, I am Doctor Gottschalk and Paddy has brought me here to see to you. Do you understand? Ah! Do not try to speak.' But try she did.

'Josie –?' she choked.

'Josie is nearby,' I assured her, 'and Paddy is about to take my manservant to bring her in.'

At this the woman relaxed and laid back, content to let me move forward in my ministrations. 'Henry,' I said calmly, with a mind to not show any alarm in my voice. He came near to me. 'Will you take Paddy now and bring Josie in?'

Henry nodded gravely. Of all my men I now know I can rely upon him to be the bravest. There is an unpredictability that surrounds me in all my works, but Henry has always faced the unknown with a stout heart, and never more than in that moment, for he went out into the dark of that night not knowing what he might find or what might confront him.

'Wait!' Paddy cried and I watched him searching his room, I could not guess for what until at last I saw him pull up a small club from beside his bed. He and Henry then passed out into the night and I was left alone with Adelaide.

Though she winced at first, she accepted a pain tonic admirably well and I was able to finish all the bandaging. I pondered what to say.

'I know it is your husband who has done this to you,' I said at last, and she started at the comment. I shook my head and held her unwounded hand. 'He is nowhere here,' I said. 'He cannot hurt you any longer.'

Adelaide looked directly at me and I knew she understood my meaning; then in the depths of her sea-green eyes I saw something I did not anticipate – hope. Yes, hope, and I believe also a great thankfulness. Then she closed those faceted, cathedral-windowed orbs and, sighing, rested.

The house had been the scene of some dramatic event that seemed mostly to have occurred in the tiny bedroom, which was disheveled and the air noisome. I stepped about carefully – acorns littered the floor and there was something else, something darkly familiar and with a foul smell:– Curiously, it was not fresh blood, which, if Paddy were to be believed, would logically have been found there. This was putrefaction, the foul emissions of advanced death. I laid a blanket over the spot and this made the fetid air more bearable.

Along the rim of the tiny window, however, I did find new blood, and also scratch marks whereon my first thoughts were that an animal had clawed its way in. But on closer inspection I marveled to find a human fingernail embedded in the wood and saw that the scratches started on the inside *of the frame, then appeared to drag outward. Something had been pulled through that window, and with tremendous force. Outside I could see Henry's lantern bobbing up and down like an aimless specter in the darkness of the nearby burying grounds. Every now and again Paddy's smaller figure passed in front of the light and it cast him in a strange silhouette. I settled down to wait in a chair near the hearth.*

I must have dozed because Henry's bursting into the house startled me from the throes of a strange dream. 'What is it?' I asked, shaken.

'You need to see this, boss,' Henry replied. He had a strange look and just stood there, shaking his head. 'I ain't see'd nothin' like this ever!'

My first thought was to check on Adelaide; I found her sleeping soundly. My next thought was a dark misgiving that the findings somehow foreshadowed something awful had happened to Josie. I quickly pulled on my coat and followed Henry out the door.

Night was passing. It was the hour before dawn and the late-October chill had settled in a bare frost on house, tree and land. I buttoned my coat and plunged my hands into its pockets, and doggedly followed Henry into the confines of the derelict cemetery. As we passed the gate he stopped and pointed to the ground with a knowing look upon his face. I looked but saw nothing except a freshly-trodden path through the thin frost. I shrugged and Henry pointed, indicating that I should walk ahead of him.

Some yards up, in the cold shade of a spreading oak, I saw Paddy sitting on the ground with his arms around a little girl. Both he and Henry had taken off their coats and had placed them around her and when I came upon her it seemed to me her head was peeking out from the folds of a many-layered Bedouin tent. Her hair was red and her eyes green like her mother's, and she smiled at me as I knelt down beside her.

'So you are Josie?' I asked, as I pressed my hand upon her forehead feeling for any hint of fever. She nodded deeply. 'I am glad we have found you,' I said, 'but what on earth have you been doing sitting out here in the unwholesome night air?'

She turned to me, her eyes wide with wonder. 'I wanted to watch!' she said.

I looked at her and smiled. 'Watch?' I chuckled. 'Watch what, my dear?'

Just then something moved under the heap of coats and as the child Josie reached down and pulled at the covering I could clearly see, snuggled in the crux of her crossed legs, a large white rabbit. I must have gasped aloud, in spite of myself, because Henry and Paddy both looked at me. I recognized the rabbit immediately. I saw Henry nod slightly; he had recognized it, too.

'Josie,' I said now, 'that is a beautiful hare! Where did you find him?'

The rabbit's head poked out from the folds of the coats and Josie stroked it lovingly. 'It was given to me!' she said.

Somewhere in my mind I had known that would be her answer, but this did nothing to prepare me to hear it. I thought for a moment. 'You said you were watching something, my dear,' I asked her now. 'Tell me, what is it that you could see here, in this sad place, at night?'

She looked at me again with those emerald eyes. 'Oh, this isn't a sad place at all!' she said. 'It's where we play.'

I looked to Paddy and he only nodded. 'And you have watched . . . ?' I said, turning back to Josie.

From out the warm embrace of her coated tenting Josie extended her thin, white arm and pointed, indicating something ahead of her and as yet out of my sight. Henry touched my elbow and I followed him, leaving Josie safely in the watch of her brother.

The path was slippery beneath my feet and I had frequently to look down lest I lose my footing. It was then that I recalled Henry's actions at the cemetery gate, how he had pointed down at the ground. A sudden realization illuminated his behavior:– It was no ordinary path we walked. Yes, the grass was beaten down and looked well-trodden – I even noted tiny footprints that I assumed to be Josie's going to and fro – but the shape of the path, and the manner in which it was pitted with ridges and small clefts put me in sudden mind of feet not walking, but dragging on the mud, and of fingers . . . I recalled the fingernail in the window frame.

Henry had stopped as I pondered these thoughts. Retrieved from my musings by his nudging, I nodded to him. 'Lead on.'

We went a short distance more and I now began to notice something strange about the frost; here it was heavy and undisturbed but it did not have the crisp whiteness of an early winter's kiss. No, instead, all about us was a frost tinged with pink and red – the colors of freshly spilled blood. The growing light of morning cast the gruesome scheme all the more plainly in that disheveled place.

Now we approached a lonely stand of broken stones leaning at odd angles in the boggy roots of a cypress tree. I could clearly see their grey façade as we drew nearer and at first they appeared as nothing more than ordinary markers. Henry bent and picked up a spindly tree branch that lay nearby and walked a few steps ahead of me. As he came nearer the stones he stepped carefully around to one side and, using the tree branch, pointed to something clustered there. I drew closer and peered into the area at the end of Henry's stick; it was a hole, but something was blocking it. I moved in closer and Henry accommodated me by gingerly moving aside a patch of grass with the stick.

I had no words then, and still struggle to describe it, nay, to encompass it within my mind! What I saw that cold morning in that humble burying ground is a sight I would not wish upon any other man, and one I pray to God I never witness the likes of again:–

There, jammed into a hole barely the size of the mouth of a wooden bucket, were the remains of a man – or what had lately been a man, for now this human was reduced to little more than a corrupted mass of shredded skin and sinew, crushed and splintered bones, and blood – copious amounts of blood:– He had been drawn, pulled by some incredible force that cannot but have been supernatural in nature, so that he went into the hole by his spine, *that had somehow been broken, and bent in half, his form a grotesque nightmare smashed in upon itself. Too large to fit completely down the hole, some parts of his body remained unconcealed and were juxtaposed at such garish angles that reason cannot explain it, nor my darkest fantasy conceive it: and yet, there was the sight!:– The large, booted feet, broken at the ankles and bent against the edge of the hole in opposing directions; the thick, bloodless hands, disjointed from the wrists and twisted savagely like the fetid blooms of flowers in some daemon's garden; worse, the head – torn off at the neck, it sat wedged between the crumbled limbs, bloodless, eyes wide and fixed, mouth gaping in a death cry that was never meant to be heard, and – the oddest thing – stuffed with acorns:– It seemed hundreds of the small brown nuts had been jammed into the open orifice! The imprint of a small heel, a child's shoe, bruised the furrowed brow and, more horrible still, the frighted hair, snow white, was knotted tightly round the bare, bony fingers of a skeleton's hand!*

I recalled the words Paddy had spoken to me – '. . . now the clown's killed him . . .' – and knew he had spoken the truth. This bloody, tangled mass had been Paddy's father.

I shivered at the thought, and then the cheerful, lilting words of sweet Josie rang again like a death knell in my ears: 'I wanted to watch!' "

J.V. Gottschalk, *Notes.*

"*I again found myself before the large fireplace of our dwelling on the street 'des Ramparts' at New Orleans, where in the evening, squatting on the matting, the negroes, myself, and the children of the house formed a circle and listened, by the trembling fire on the hearth . . . for the hundredth time to*

the marvelous adventures of Compe Bouqui (the clown of the negroes) and the knavery of Compe Lapin . . . [and] cast fearful glances under the old bed with its baldachins, and drew close together by creeping the one between the other . . ."

Louis Moreau Gottschalk, **Notes of a Pianist**

The Vampire

The legend of the vampire runs deeper in New Orleans than almost anywhere else in the continental United States. And this is not just an affectation taken on in modern times. The waves of immigrants that came to call New Orleans home throughout the eighteenth and nineteenth centuries originated from a variety of cultures, mostly European, and represented nearly every walk of life. They came with the courage to start a new life in a strange, unpredictable place, and they also brought something else: a wealth of traditions and beliefs about the supernatural. In their European homelands these people were well-acquainted with the various monstrous beings haunting their folklore. Witches and ghosts, werewolves and other devilish animals, and even the wily, evasive folk of Faery were all familiar to them in one form or another. But one evil creature was known to people of every European country, the fear of it crossing all boundaries of culture and dark memory: this creature was the vampire.

If asked, the European settlers of early New Orleans would have described the vampire as a local peasant, someone of their own social rank who had recently died and not - as might be expected - a long-dead aristocrat from the distant past. Their vampire was not repelled by religious symbols or relics, could not be dissuaded by religious rites, had no need to sleep in its native soil or a coffin, and reckoned nothing of bats or wolves. It was believed to travel in spirit form while its corpse remained safely entombed; those whom it attacked always died, and usually stayed dead – although having been victimized by a vampire did sometimes make a person more likely to become one in the death state.

Settlers in New Orleans and other areas of south Louisiana would have understood that it was not hard to become a vampire. Excommunication by the Church was a condemnation that assured one would walk with the undead; likewise, failure to honor the Holy Days of Obligation, indulging in the Seven Deadly Sins, and failure to regularly confess also put one dangerously close to becoming a vampire, or a vampire's next meal. Murdering someone, practicing sorcery, being overlooked by the Evil Eye, and committing suicide could also condemn one to the vampire state. In fact, there were so many ways by which one might become a vampire that even when natural death claimed a victim the corpse still remained suspect. Observing the body until sure signs of decomposition were present was one way to be certain that a corpse would not awake in league with the unholy dead, a custom that gave rise to the rowdy "wakes" of the Irish, and the all-night vigils of the Italians long-familiar to generations of New Orleanians.

The now-popular belief that vampires physically leave their graves and stalk the night seems to have been held in disrepute by nearly all cultures that comprised the population of early New Orleans. Instead, most people believed that what leaves the grave is a hungry, predatory spirit that must depredate the living in order to survive. However, opinions did vary about the activities of vampires.

Some people – the French, Spanish, and English, for instance – held onto European beliefs that vampires kept at least a remnant of their physical form and fed on blood. Others, such as the Germans, the Italians, and the Greeks, held that the vampire was a ghostly creature with piercing red eyes that emerged from its resting place and floated from victim to victim, until at last, torpid and swollen with blood, it returned to the grave and burrowed back inside.

Every culture agreed that a new vampire will first seek out and prey upon members of its own family; it will then move on to friends and neighbors, until at the last it will attack and feed upon anyone it can find. It was also widely accepted, especially by those immigrants from the original homelands of the vampire, that these creatures feared sunlight and running water; that garlic, onions, and lilies were effective in keeping the vampire away; and that a vampire could be wounded or even killed by any sharp, metal object – though iron was preferred above all other materials. People understood that cremation of the vampire's corpse – with or without the stake – was the only sure way to kill this most dangerous of supernatural predators, and that nothing short of annihilation would do. The vampire must be destroyed, spirit and body, or it will live on to kill again and again and again.

Perhaps the oldest vampire legend in New Orleans is associated with a group of women known as the Cassette Girls, or sometimes the Casket Girls. These girls – it is generally believed they were twenty-eight in number – were daughters of the French aristocracy chosen to be groomed as wives for French gentlemen who had already immigrated to the Louisiana colony. The girls received the finest secular and religious education the French Catholic Church could provide and were under the constant tutelage of the pious and devoted Ursuline nuns. When the time came for the girls to depart for Louisiana, the Church issued to each of them a stunning jewel-encrusted chest – "cassette" in French – crafted by Church artisans to be part of the girls' dowries. Each chest contained a Bible and illuminated Book of Hours, a rosary, a reliquary, and a wedding trousseau, and represented the Church's blessing on these most pious and outstanding young women. Accompanied by their devoted Ursulines, the beautiful French maidens arrived in New Orleans in 1728. Each of the Cassette Girls eventually became the wife of a suitably high-placed Frenchman, and the few old-line New Orleans families who can trace their heritage back to a "Cassette Girl" are proud to do so.

Yet over these innocent young women the devilish shadow of vampirism lies long, and in the generations following their arrival at New Orleans a deplorable fable was popularized casting them as bloodthirsty sirens with the Ursulines their knowing protectors. Their elaborate "cassettes" were transformed by superstitious memory into caskets, the horrible beds of the living dead, and the tale of the "Vampire Casket Girls" was passed far and wide.

But in fact, the arrival of the Cassette Girls is wound up in the concurrent arrival of another group of French females – criminals, prostitutes, and excommunicates known to local folklore as the "Correction Girls." They, too, arrived under the supervision of Ursuline nuns – though these, it was said, were the iron-handed, sadistic nuns of the ruined and debased convent of Loudun – and they descended upon the city with every kind of nefarious intent. Exclusion from the Church being at the time a true form of living hell, and a prerequisite for vampirism, this latter group apparently went out to actively serve their debauched and possibly supernatural desires. The deeds of these godless French women were so reprehensible that the memory still lingers; and although it blackens the name of the righteous Cassette Girls, the mystery surrounding this dark sisterhood leaves one to ponder whether or not vampire girls really did prowl the streets of old New Orleans. In answer, the record is silent.

Vampires were also believed to haunt the country surrounding New Orleans, and one area was particularly feared as the domain of this supernatural being: a place known as the Marais Tremblement, the "Trembling Marshes" east of the city. A vast expanse of wilderness and swampland between Lake Pontchartrain and Lake Borgne, the Trembling Marshes were so called because of the way in which the tall marsh grasses billowed like waves in the lake breezes. Here and there small encampments of Native Americans, and sometimes the occasional hunting camp established by sportsmen taking holiday from New Orleans would break the brown monotony of the landscape, but for the most part the Marais was simply uninhabited wilderness.

Only one community truly thrived there: Hidden in the marshlands along the shore of Lake Borgne was a small fishing village of Filipinos known as St. Malo. Established around 1763 by a group of Filipino slaves on the run from Spain's galleon trade, St. Malo is the earliest established settlement of Asian people in the New World. To avoid the vengeance of their brutal Spanish masters, St. Malo villagers kept the community's location a closely-guarded secret for many years. It wasn't until 1883, when famed Louisiana journalist Lafcadio Hearn discovered and wrote about them, that the existence of the "Manilamen" and St. Malo was revealed. Until this time, the Manilamen were a people of rumor, a part of the all-encompassing mystery of the vast Louisiana marshlands.

Folklore of the Trembling Marshes confirms that the Manilamen preserved the rich supernatural tradition of their homeland. It was a folklore filled with weird, fantastic creatures, some of which were very much like the traditional vampire, and most of which had apparently followed the Manilamen from their native lands. In the evenings, when their palmetto hut rooftops and the spindly masts of their little Oriental boats were cast in stark silhouette against the ruddy colors of the sunset skies, the Manilamen would gather together and light the fat stumps of tallow candles in empty oyster shells; peering into the close darkness of the Louisiana night, they would tell tales of a horrible creature that might lay in wait for them just nearby.

She was called the Tik-Tik, a vampire-like ghoul that took the form of a woman from the waist up; but from the waist down she had the shape of a deformed octopus. Using a long, otherworldly tentacle to navigate the narrow waterways of the deep swamp, the Tik-Tik emerged from its hiding place at night to slake its unquenchable thirst for human blood. When it found its unlucky prey, the Tik-Tik would feed by extending a long, mosquito-like tongue from its mouth, inserting it into the victim's chest to lap the blood directly from the heart. Sometimes the Tik-Tik – which earned its name because of how it clacked its teeth and clicked its long claws together when it approached its victim – would even dig up the bloated bodies of the dead and steal them away into the darkness of the swamp where it could feed on them at leisure.

According to the elderly Filipino shamans of St. Malo, the Tik-Tik could shape-shift into the form of an animal or even an insect, and a favorite habit of the creature was to conceal itself in the swamp water, hiding among the tree roots and undergrowth, where it would lay in wait to snatch unwary fishermen from their lugger-boats. The Tik-Tik could also possess a living human being: according to the lore of St. Malo, if you saw your reflection inverted in a man's eyes it meant that he had been taken over by a Tik-Tik. Another favorite ruse of the Tik-Tik was to take the form of a child pretending to be lost or abandoned in the swamps. Sitting hunched over by the side of the bayou, its shoulders heaving slightly with its mournful cries, it could easily lure an unsuspecting victim who, drawn near out of pity, would suddenly find himself the unwitting prey of a horrible bloodsucker.

Some old tales indicate the Tik-Tik sometimes traveled with a familiar, a companion creature that it sometimes used as a decoy. The Manilamen called this second creature the Sigbin. When on the hunt, sometimes the Sigbin would engage a victim in order to distract it from the Tik-Tik approaching nearby. Eyewitnesses and survivors described the Sigbin as a foul-smelling, goat-like creature that went about on four legs, with matted hair, yellow eyes, and a mouth full of sharp fangs. Once the Tik-Tik attacked, the Sigbin would join in and together the bloodthirsty creatures would tear the victim to pieces.

Like the traditional vampire, the Tik-Tik was repulsed by garlic and onions, and although it traveled the murky, slow-moving waters of the swamp, it avoided the open waters of the nearby lakes. The Tik-Tik also feared anything sharp because this posed a danger to its long, tentacle-like tail. For this reason, the Manilamen would line the entrances of their huts with broken bottles, strewing shards of the glass around. They also encouraged brambles and thorn bushes to grow around the huts, hoping the prickles would entangle the prowling Tik-Tik and hold it captive until the light of the morning sun could destroy it.

St. Malo and the Manilamen are long gone. The wild lands once known as the Marais Tremblement still lie between the lakes in the uninhabited areas east of the city of New Orleans, changed by decades of development and hurricanes, and now known by other names. But many believe that in some deep, as-yet undiscovered pocket of the ancient marshes, the Tik-Tik and its servant the Sigbin still prowl the dark, impenetrable night.

As has been shown, legends of the vampire are not limited to the city of New Orleans alone. Perhaps the most enduring legend comes from the Parish of St. Bernard, from an area once known as the Terre-aux-Boeufs, or the "Oxen Lands," after the long practice of using oxen to plow the rich plantation fields. Located down past the Barracks and the place of the English Turn, St. Bernard's Parish keeps its own rich store of supernatural legend and folklore.

In a remote, overgrown corner of the Terre-aux-Boeufs, where the meandering Bayou Boeuf flows into the Lost Lakes, there long stood a ruined old home. The air hung heavy about the old bricks in every season of the year, it was said; and although the name of the once-beautiful plantation has long passed from memory, an antique tale of romance and supernatural tragedy still lingers there – a cautionary tableaux about a mysterious nobleman, a mystical potion, and a woman recalled only as . . .

The Bloody Lady

She exhaled a deep gasp and awoke. Chthonian night. Stifling, humid air, a burden to the lungs. The sickly-sweet smell of moldering earth. Silence, all-encompassing and profound, magnified her every movement in the narrow confines of her coffin. Waves of nausea came upon her; she wretched, but brought up nothing. Sweat broke upon her brow. Her mind raced. Her situation was immediately plain. She thought of her Chevalier. He had betrayed her! She had rejected him and married another man; he resented her for this injustice and had killed her. But he had not *killed her! This had been his plan all along, to punish her, to make her suffer, so that she would sicken and appear dead, and awaken here, buried in the fetid, smothering confines of a grave – buried alive!!*

A scream that came from the very pits of her desperate soul now escaped her lips; it rattled her ears in the abysmal silence, but no one in the wide world could hear her – nor would ever hear her under the cold, consuming earth: this is what he had wanted! This was his revenge!

She tore wildly at the lid of the coffin, now her prison, in which she knew the moments would tick away interminably, the air would be consumed, and she . . . !

She screamed and screamed and screamed!

"I emerged from my hiding place, spade in hand, and immediately went to work. The wait had been painfully long. The sexton – a sloth! – had moved so slowly that many times I considered jumping from my cover just for the sake of frighting him! Now I had not even the benefit of twilight! I knew I must work quickly if I was to reach Alexandra before the poison wore off and she awoke. I worked without regard for convention or respect for Alexandra's, shall we say, neighbors. Soil and old bones went everywhere, but time was of the essence.

"A sudden noise distracted me: the arrival of Adeluse, Alexandra's maid. 'You are late!' I admonished her, and immediately set her to work – on her knees, with her own bare hands – commanding her to dig if she ever wanted to see her mistress alive again!

"And so we dug, and as we swept the earth away I could hear the muffled sound of Alexandra's wild screams. I whispered reassurances and knew it was hopeless – locked inside that gloomy prison she could perceive nothing but fear. But at last the lid of the coffin emerged under the soil and Alexandra's screams were plainly audible. I hammered at the lock and Adeluse pried at the lip of the lid until her fingers were bloody. At last, mercifully, we had it open."

Here the Chevalier hesitated in the telling of his tale; he shifted uneasily in his chair. Abbe Sistrenatus, a man of seemingly infinite patience, sat nearby as he had for the last quarter hour, listening attentively, saying nothing, barely moving.

"I recoiled in terror at the sight of her," the Chevalier continued, "screaming hysterically, her face contorted in wild spasms of abject, irretrievable terror. Blood covered her, streaming from her fingers and from a wide gash on her forehead where she had pushed against her prison lid; tufts of her beautiful dark hair had lost their luster altogether and gone white with fright. She fixed me with a lunatic's gaze and in an instant was upon me shrieking that I had meant this all along – that I had meant to kill her out of vengeance."

The Chevalier looked up sheepishly at the Abbe. "Well, what could I do?" he then exclaimed, as if in answer to a question Sistrenatus had not even voiced. "What could I do? I held her, of course, reassured her that all would be well, and with the help of Adeluse lifted her from that rank, narrow cell. But she was inconsolable and in the instant I feared that her screams and cries, proceeding as they did from the midst of that field of death, would attract attention and defeat our purposes altogether.

"I had with me a flask, one that I am accustomed to carry and which contained some of the decoction. What else could I do?" he asked again, but knew the question had no answer. "I bade her drink and, compelled by some notion that I was attempting to remedy the unfinished poisoning, she at first fought against me. At last I commanded her: 'Drink or you shall die!'"

A long silence ensued, broken at last by the steady voice of the Abbe. "And did she drink?"

"Yes," said the Chevalier, and looked away. "Yes, she drank. Within moments I could see the vitality returning to her body. Her stiff, cold limbs were warm and pliable; her heartbeat was vibrant, her face flushed with renewed vigor. I could tell it was the most profound sensation she had ever experienced." The Chevalier smiled in spite of himself. "I said, 'I restore you, and I restore to you everything you have lost.'"

Sistrenatus frowned. "Is this pride I see? You presume much, Señor," he said, lapsing into his native Spanish.

"I did not mean . . ." the Chevalier started.

"Only God can restore life," Sistrenatus replied gravely. "It is He who chooses those worthy to inherit resurrection."

The men were seated in a long gallery of the Diocese cloisters where once the Ursuline nuns had softly tread, carrying out the humble tasks of their daily life; three stories up in that cavernous old building Abbe Sistrenatus kept a solitary cell. It was spring and the Abbe had opened the lower windows of the room that let on to a secluded garden. Now and then a gentle breeze wafted over them, heavy with the scent of jasmine and new roses, dispelling the musty air of the old interiors. The Abbe had set out candles and a simple meal of bread, cheese and fruit; he had also opened a bottle of the heady wine laid down by the Jesuits when the Spanish yet held sway over New Orleans. The bottle was now nearly empty. On the table between the men lay a large book, the uneven edges of its thick pages stained and yellowed, its complicated leather and metal binding worn with age; and the whole held fast under a doubled length of chains secured with an antique padlock.

The Chevalier rubbed his eyes wearily. "I know, I know," he said in response to the Abbe's admonishment.

"How did you come to bring her to New Orleans?" Sistrenatus asked, pouring a little wine into the Chevalier's empty glass.

"Her husband yet lived," the Chevalier sighed, fingering the stem of the glass. "To him and everyone else who knew her Alexandra was dead; the sleeping philter had done its job. It would have been folly to have remained anywhere in Europe. Certainly I could not take her back to her home in Russia; nor, indeed, could we linger long in France." He shrugged and took a sip of wine. "Here, in this barely charted place we could disappear, become one with our surroundings, begin a new life together. So, appearing outwardly as husband and wife, I settled Alexandra on the plantation in the Terre-aux-Boeufs and for the purpose of conducting business with the locals I obtained for myself the townhouse here in the City.

"Alexandra had her Adeluse, of course, whom we brought over with us, but we had need of others to service the house and work the lands, and so I acquired Negroes and thus it was that occupied in the purchase of these I discovered Dr. Joseph Gottschalk to be living here as well. I was happy to recognize another member of our Society here, and also in Avetante, whom he later introduced to me."

Sistrenatus nodded. "Yes of course, I know them both."

"Of course," the Chevalier replied sheepishly, "of course you do." He drained his glass of wine. "Ever since she had awakened in the darkness of her 'grave,' Alexandra had continued to experience bouts of hysteria. Although I thought it would help settling here, the natural isolation of the plantation, and only Adeluse for company, did little to improve her condition. She was nervous, filled with vague fears, and slept less and less. The nature of my business often required me to stay overnight here in the City and when I would return to the plantation Adeluse would confide in me the depressing details of Alexandra's ever-increasing woe.

"By this time she had taken to wandering the empty house at night, wringing her hands and talking to herself. Sometimes when the nights were close and the house stifling, she would wander the fields in only her chemise. It gave the field hands an awful fright when they saw her figure drifting like cobwebs in the shadows of the pecan groves. It was not long before they began to whisper about their mistress, and it is never good to incur the mistrust of those whose job it is to serve you.

"She had no appetite and Adeluse confided that she fought her viciously whenever she encouraged Alexandra to eat. I did not see it clearly then," he sighed, "but her maid was all the friendship and companionship she had. Surely, if I could return to those days and undo the harm that trust has caused, you know I would."

Sistrenatus nodded soberly. "How came Alexandra's access to the decoction?" he asked.

The Chevalier sighed again, heavily. "I am to blame, yet again," he said. "I thought to introduce it in only trace amounts, merely to entice her appetite, to prevent her from becoming an

invalid. I had brought over a full cellar and among it a store of
the liquid that I had already decocted in France."

"And this was kept where just anyone may have access?"
Sistrenatus asked, alarmed.

"Not anyone," the Chevalier replied. "No, I alone had the
key to the keeping room and I would remove a single bottle,
only when necessary. I had to, don't you see?" he added
quickly when Sistrentaus shifted testily in his chair. "I had
prescribed that a set amount be given to Alexandra in a day,
and I could not be there at every moment. I relied upon
Adeluse to make certain Alexandra received her dosages."

Sistrenatus frowned, lost in thought. "And, of course, you
trusted this maid," he said softly, almost as if speaking to
himself. "Did Alexandra improve?" He asked this last more
directly.

The Chevalier went silent. The heady breeze, bolstered by a
gust from the river, shook at the trees and low palms outside
the cloister windows. A pear tree scraped and tapped at the
window frame, its branches full of fat, new buds. Somewhere a
distant ship's bell was pealing in a thin metal voice.

"Yes," the Chevalier said slowly. "Yes and the change was
almost immediate. This was encouraging, and the dosage so
small . . ." His voice trailed off. He looked at Sistrenatus and
shrugged.

The Abbe sighed and, standing, paced up and down before
the windows. "Forgive me, my friend, but I must be frank," he
said at last.

"But of course!" the Chevalier replied.

"It seems to me that you are not treating this matter with the
severity it deserves," Sistrenatus said now. He gazed at the
Chevalier. "You seem incredulous? I do not see why. Had you
approached this with even a hint of responsibility, we would
not be here now, discussing," here he hesitated and gave the
Chevalier a long steady look, then, "anything at all." The
Chevalier straightened in his chair and narrowed his gaze at the
Abbe. "I believe this change in Alexandra fostered a growing
curiosity in the maid," Sistrenatus continued. "I believe she
wondered about the liquid she herself mixed into the medical

philters her mistress took each day. It must have been tempting."

The Chevalier considered this. "Yes," he said. "But I doubt there was any malice on her part, at first. She seemed to dote over her mistress. Nothing in her manner gave me any reason for suspicion."

"But you could not be sure?" Sistrenatus sighed.

"No," said the Chevalier. He shook his head, "I could not be sure – until now."

Sistrenatus cocked an eyebrow and looked intrigued. "So you know the circumstances?"

The Chevalier nodded. "Sitting here, now, this night," he said, "yes, I know the circumstances." The Abbe took his seat again and listened as the Chevalier went on.

"The maid, Adeluse, had indeed become curious about the strange enervating elixir that had revived her dying mistress more than once, and which she herself saw me ingest on occasion. I believe one day, alone, in the kitchens, perhaps, or at least out of sight of everyone, she tasted it – very likely by drinking what was left in Alexandra's cups. The taste, ah! – it would have repelled her, as it always does when first sampled – sweet, like boiled molasses or burnt treacle with a hint of rancid wine, the herbs, and that other taste – metallic and oddly familiar.

"Naturally she would feel the sensations in her body, the warmth flowing through her veins and the immediate heightening of the senses. It must have amazed her. I can imagine her now, licking the glass and her fingers like a gluttonous little child devouring its favorite candy. Though she had tasted only a bare amount no doubt it was enough to make her crave for more. But how to get it? A bottle, maybe only one in more than a month, was all I would allow to be used because it was meant to restore Alexandra not to recreate her, not to make her into . . ." The Chevalier fell silent, gazing at the floor. Sistrenatus waited, patiently.

"It was the attenuation of Alexandra's health that gave me my first clue," the Chevalier resumed. "Where it had thrived seemed to be the peak, the time I suspect Adeluse became exposed to the elixir, and afterward Alexandra began by degrees to decline. Oh, the maid continued to give her mistress the prescribed tonics and palliatives, but these were made less potent by the fact that Adeluse was slaking her own addiction from the same doses. I know this now, but I was confounded then, and out of love, or fear of loss, I know not which," he sighed, "I did exactly the wrong thing: I increased the dosage."

Sistrenatus also sighed. The Chevalier looked at him, expecting a judgmental look, even a comment, but the Abbe remained silent, inscrutable.

"I can only imagine the insatiable hunger now growing inside Adeluse," the Chevalier went on. "It must have obscured almost every other thing, except her loyalty to Alexandra. I do not think she entirely deprived her mistress, but I know now that she was pilfering away the greater amount of the elixir for herself. The dregs of each bottle were hers, as well, and in this way she became the stronger of the two. And now in Alexandra I noted a waning, a hollowness about the eyes, a gaunt face, and this puzzled me. Even if Adeluse was stealing some of it, the decoction ought to have been of some help. Even so, she seemed not to be responding."

"You did not increase it again?" Sistrenatus asked suddenly.

The Chevalier shook his head. "No indeed. But I was confounded by her failure to thrive and ultimately I could only assume this to be the progression of a natural death process, something undiagnosed but clearly advancing."

"Was it then that you called for Gottschalk?" Sistrenatus interrupted again.

"Yes," the Chevalier replied, "I asked Dr. Gottschalk to assess her and his conclusion agreed with my suspicions that Alexandra was succumbing to natural consumption. Three months," he added, "that was his estimate of how much time I would have left to spend with my beloved."

A long, heavy moment passed then Sistrenatus said, "I cannot even imagine how you must have felt."

"I could not condemn her," the Chevalier said quickly. "I could not live with myself or her in that condition, that Godless suspension that is the unavoidable result of the addiction . . ." His voice trailed away, he was lost in thought.

"So you withdrew doses of the decoction?" Sistrenatus said quietly and with more than a little relief, but the Chevalier made no reply. "Jacques?" Sistrenatus called.

"Yes, I withdrew it," the Chevalier said quickly, roused from his dark musings. "But the damage was already done, and not only to Alexandra.

"As you might imagine, Adeluse was stricken by the cessation of the medications. Her excessive protestations and appeals, ostensibly on behalf of her mistress, alarmed me and confirmed all my suspicions with a ghastly suddenness. When at last I discovered her and my most trusted slave looting the keeping room, I knew for certain she had become ensnared by the elixir. I inspected the stock and was shocked by the depletion – the two had been there more than once. I suspect now that, in her hunger, Adeluse was willing to do anything . . .

"It was John, my slave, who confessed it all, that she had used her," he coughed and shifted in his chair, "sensual skills to allure my blacksmith into forging a key to fit the keeping room lock and also to coerce the loyal John into a nefarious partnership."

"Lust," Sistrenatus said quietly and the judging look which the Chevalier had previously thought to see now passed over the Abbe's face.

"John I put in chains," the Chevalier continued, avoiding the gaze, "Adeluse I put out onto the road."

"You let her go?" Sistrenatus gasped.

"I put her out," the Chevalier replied, "I wanted her away from me, out of my sight, away from Alexandra and our lives. Yes, in my wrath, I turned her out of my house."

A sudden rain began to fall and drifted in on the breeze. Sistrenatus rose and closed the windows. The Chevalier watched in detachment, and continued his tale.

"That was months ago," he said, "more than three. And I must add that our dear friend Gottschalk was, thankfully, slightly askew in his prediction: Alexandra remained with me for five months."

"Then she is . . . ?" Sistrenatus asked softly.

The Chevalier nodded and was silent; then suddenly he reached out and pushed the large, ornate book toward the

Abbe. "You take it!" he cried. "I do not want to look upon it again! I never want to see inside or feel the skin of its pages on my hands again!" He wiped his hands on his breeches as if to wipe away some awful stain or smell. "All my troubles began there! I wish I had never seen it!"

Sistrenatus pulled the volume toward him and set it at his elbow. "But you have," he said solemnly. "You cannot change that."

"No!" the Chevalier cried. "No, I cannot! And do you not think I know this?" he cried. "Every word, every formula is burned into my brain! I need not that book!" he laughed bitterly. "I am well corrupted!"

The Chevalier now paced up and down, panting, running his hands through his hair. He stopped to fill his glass with wine and quickly drank it down. He gripped at the windowsill and stood staring out at the rain.

"I am like a trapped man, Sistrenatus," he breathed, "I carry the bars of my prison about me wherever I go, invisible to all, save me alone. Once, once in all the long years since I brought this curse upon myself have I ever dared to love, ever *had* love," he almost whispered these last words. "And it was shorn away from me! Better to have taken an arm or my legs! But to make me give *her* up – that is but the cruelty of a wanton God!"

Sistrenatus wanted to speak, wanted to scold the man for cursing God and to tell him how he alone was the author of all his sorrows. Under other circumstances that would have been his swift rebuke. But when at last he did speak all he could say was, "Please, come sit down."

The Chevalier collapsed into his chair with a melancholy sigh. "I buried her in her favorite place," he said at last, "in the pecan grove, under the spreading branches of the largest tree. I can just see the white tomb from the gallery of the house . . .

"I would go away, I decided," he went on, rousing himself, his voice now steady and firm. "I would pack up, perhaps spend time in Cuba and the islands, and then go back to France. I would have gone immediately, but for the loose ends. The most immediate of these was my slave, John. When she addicted him to the decoction, Adeluse had no way of knowing the weakness for drink lying dormant inside the man; deprived of the elixir, his drinking became worse.

"I wish you could have seen him, Sistrenatus. What a specimen! He is enormous, almost seven feet in height with a good humor and a loyal nature. Adeluse ruined all that, of course. After I put her out I had to keep John chained most of the time because he was so unmanageable; whenever he was loosed he would seek out whiskey or the home brew and drink his fill. But his humor had fled entirely, and he had become so extraordinarily strong that none of my other men could match him. I had no desire to take the man away with me, in fact, I feared it; yet neither did I have the heart to send him to the auction block, nor indeed did I desire that his condition be thus exposed. So I hesitated.

"You cannot imagine, Sistrenatus, how my constitution was affected by all this. I had to take more of the decoction myself simply to shore up against the current of troubles and grief that buffeted me daily. At night I tossed and could not settle; when at last I did get to sleep the dreams would come: Alexandra, always Alexandra, looking as she used to in the golden days, those long summers spent in the gardens of the Czar. So peaceful, these dreams, and everything so serene, and yet I awoke from them exhausted, with barely the energy to face each new day."

Sistrenatus leaned forward. "Jacques," he said, but the Chevalier held up his hand.

"I know," he replied. "It was my thought immediately. I inspected Alexandra's grave and found nothing obviously suspicious. Of course, my thoughts then turned to Adeluse. It was not beyond reason to assume that she had somehow concealed herself nearby and was returning in the frightful night hours to exact her punishment upon me, to torment me in the form of the woman I could no longer have. So I began to attune myself to the gossip and whisperings of the slaves; where normally I would dismiss their talk as groundless chatter, now it was my chief way of gleaning information.

"As you well know, wherever slaves are found they are always a superstitious lot, but seldom is the fear expressed without there being some seed of truth at the root. My slaves, I discovered, greatly feared the pecan grove and Alexandra's grave. I thought, 'This is a normal superstition of death.' The slaves then came to me greatly aroused by fearful sightings of a 'misty white thing' that appeared in their hovels late at night, sometimes shrouding the cots of infants or the elderly. Whenever it was approached, it would drift away through a window or a key hole and disappear entirely.

"Then the cattle began to suffer and word spread among the hands that the same white mist had been seen moving over the pastures; there was also a rumor of it preying on the carcasses of slaughtered animals in the abattoirs upriver. But when at last the pecan harvest began, and the first nuts of the tree that covers Alexandra's grave were opened, a horrible discovery was made: the meat of all those nuts was stained a bloody red!"

"Then it was Alexandra all along?" said Sistrenatus gravely.

The Chevalier shook his head. "It was both."

The night was wearing on and the weather was abating, and the Chevalier, who had a berth awaiting him aboard a seagoing vessel docked behind the market, now hurried to finish his tale.

"In my recollection of all the events leading up to that night, I was struck by how melancholy and lethargic John had become. He was suffering a great malaise and this immediately put me in mind of the prior compact he had made with Adeluse. Therefore, I devised a method whereby I sought to use him to lure her, and hoped that this might also draw out my beloved Alexandra. I had only thought so far as how to dispatch Adeluse." He looked at Sistrenatus, "I prepared my sword – the old ways are the best in situations such as this."

Sistrenatus nodded, knowingly.

"I secured John in the keeping room," the Chevalier continued. "I had need of chains to keep him because his mood had become so unpredictable. Nor did I want him to steal away and defeat the purpose of my ruse. I took up a secret place in a nearby antechamber where I could easily observe the room, and there I waited. I knew it was only a matter of time.

"At around the first hour past the middle night I was aware of a change in John's breathing. I peered into the keeping room and there, emerging from a crack in the mortar of the brick wall, was a thin coil of white smoke. It hung there momentarily and grew in mass as it curled down to the ground where, propelled by nothing ordinary to this world, it advanced upon the sleeping John. As the mass reached John's feet I watched it draw up, taking on the shape almost of a wave as it rises when it comes near the shore, and then it bowed forward, covering the man with a rippling blanket of glowing, white mist."

"Amazing," Sistrenatus whispered, intrigued.

"Indeed," the Chevalier replied, "and although I wanted to rush forward and save John from the predations of the entity, I was nonetheless fascinated to observe it at work. John writhed under its influence and tossed about gently, more like in the throes of fever than of fear, and as his disturbances increased, it seemed to me the luminance of the mist increased also until finally the whole chamber was filled with its baleful light. I had seen enough and was just about to move when suddenly I was aware of another presence: something else had entered room."

Sistrenatus sighed. "Alexandra," he said with a hint of sadness in his voice.

The Chevalier nodded. "Alexandra," he repeated flatly. "You can imagine my alarm, and the shock was greater when I realized she, by which I mean her corpse, had entered the room quite normally, had walked right past me through the keeping room door – within feet, and I did not hear or see her! There she stood, in death as in life, but with only the rotting shroud of her grave to cover her; her long tresses, once rich and luxurious, now matted and with the familiar streaks of white, hanging lank about her shoulders and swaying as she walked; her muddy, bare feet tapping in timorous step across the stone floor.

"I moved again, but now the misty entity was also aware of Alexandra's presence. It drew itself up, at first only a ghostly mass in imitation of some form. Finally, it coalesced into a human shape, taking on every aspect of the exiled Adeluse! My ruse had worked, ah! – only too well! With one prey, I had drawn both women to one place. I steeled my heart, knew I must act quickly. I abandoned my hiding place, taking every care not to move so swiftly that I frightened them or awakened John. But no," he said, and sighed, "your God, or whatever fiend is set to make a particular mockery of my life, had deigned I should wait and watch, like Dante in the reaches of Hell, as every act of this drama was played out!

"The women stood over the prone figure of John and I knew immediately they were posturing to fight for the prey. Adeluse, though appearing solid in form, to my amazement floated upward and hovered like a winged harpy over the timid shape of Alexandra. Adeluse's face was gaunt and contorted with evil, her eyes bulged, and the fangs where once her teeth had been now clacked together with a frightful noise. Even her long, blonde hair floated up around her head, as if it was a thing unto itself, watchful and alive. She was naked, too, but her body had lost its youthful firmness and in the grip of the living death that now had hold of her she was changing, transforming into something inconceivable and no longer human.

"She hissed in challenge at Alexandra who, it broke my heart to see, hissed back and lifted her arms to defend herself. It seemed to me that Adeluse was cognizant, exact, and acting swiftly. But Alexandra acted as if in a daze; she was weak, her movements desperate and reactive. Indeed, I was instantly put in mind of what the slaves call 'zombies' – Alexandra was nothing more than a revenant in search of the only thing that had given it vigor in life. Adeluse, though, had completely transformed into a monstrous, greedy, otherworldly thing – in truth, a vampire.

"With a shuffling gait and that strange detachment, Alexandra advanced upon John; she bent over him like an automaton and fumbled about apparently unaware of how to proceed. John moaned but did not stir. In another moment, Adeluse fell upon Alexandra like a great, hovering bird desperate to preserve its prey. Half spirit, half solid in form, she grabbed at Alexandra from the air, hissing and snapping with her foul mouth. Alexandra waved her arms, not even landing any blows upon Adeluse; when the hellish she-creature backed away, Alexandra went right back to the slave. Again

Adeluse swept down, this time knocking her away; even so, Alexandra aimlessly crawled back toward John's body. The she-fiend then alighted on the ground. Now completely solid, or so it seemed, she grabbed at her former mistress, locking her clawed hands around Alexandra's throat and shaking her furiously. The scene was macabre: two corpses – for surely that is what they were! – enthralled by a hunger so horrible and a thirst so unquenchable that even the grave could not hold them, now stood fighting over a living human being!

"I withheld myself no longer. I ran into that room, sword drawn, crying out I know not what command, and for an instant I had the element of surprise. But I had awakened John and, suddenly aware of his plight, he jumped up, cowering against the wall. I commanded him to help me and to lay hold of his mistress so that I might more easily dispatch Adeluse. But weakness and fear, and perhaps an awareness that his life had been in danger, outweighed any word of mine; John stood motionless, wide-eyed and gaping at the unearthly scene: his dead mistress and the possessed Adeluse spinning like unearthly dervishes, shrieking, hissing, locked in grotesque combat."

The Chevalier rubbed his eyes wearily. "I tried to grab Adeluse," he continued. "I grasped her arm but she had such devilish power that she shook me off with merely a shrug, and I fell against the nearby wall. In a moment I was up; I rushed forward and grabbed again. Then I raised my sword and swept out. This shocked them both, of course, and for a moment they ceased their struggle; but in that horrible instant I realized my blow had fallen foul. Adeluse drew back, panting and hissing. Alexandra stood there, her face a mix of disappointment and pain, and as she fixed her eyes upon me I saw there the look of the eternally betrayed. She reached out her arms to me and, though I knew the danger, I reached out to her. But even as our hands touched, I saw the cut and watched as her head slid from her neck and tumbled away into the shadows at John's feet. Her body crumpled before me as if it were made of nothing more than shroud and mist. I had struck and I had freed her, but oh! – the pain that overwhelmed my heart!

"Suddenly John cried out, 'Watch out, boss!' and before I could even turn around, Adeluse was upon me. She clung to my back, grabbing at my neck, a shrieking, mournful thing, angry and envious of life, but desiring it above all else. John was my help, I must admit, for at last he overcame his fear and, grabbing Adeluse about the waist, was able to pull the harpy from me. She kicked and fought and I knew that at any moment she might dissipate into the foul ghost form.

"'Hold her!' I commanded John, and I looked him in the eyes and said, 'Trust me,' as I raised my sword. He nodded and I saw his great dark hand go to Adeluse's hair; he pulled back her head, exposing her neck. I dealt the blow, but she was wily and already dissipating and because of this my sword only injured her, yet that blow kept her from throwing off her solid form. As long as she was manifest, we could continue to fight her. She let out a devilish shriek and kicked backward; John cried out and winced from the pain, and in that moment Adeluse was free – and I delayed by having to fumble with keys to free John from his chains!

"Together we chased her out into the open. She made for the pecan groves and it suddenly became clear to me that she had been hiding there all along, laying with her dead mistress, and sharing in that bed of foulness and decay! And worse, I knew instantly: as they lay together in their common grave, Adeluse had loyally continued to serve her mistress, feeding Alexandra with the blood she had pilfered from her own prey, yet always keeping the lion's share for herself!

"But I had no time to ponder that horror. John, with his great height and stride, ran past me and, catching up to Adeluse, had grabbed hold of her again, bringing her to the ground before she could reach the safety of the grave. I saw now that blood ran thick and dark over her bare breasts and clotted in her hair: I had definitely wounded her. But as I stabbed at her again, she only laughed; and while he still fought with her, I knew I was in danger of harming John. Hold her down!' I ordered him, but suddenly saw his face come alive with a flickering glow.

"'The house, boss!' John cried, and I spun around to see my home engulfed in flames. In the rush to recapture Adeluse we must have overturned a lamp, or maybe several, I do not know; but next I saw that dozens of slaves were emerging from the darkness of the back fields, some bearing water buckets. But these would be of no use - the house was already roaring like a bonfire.

"Again fate had conspired against me and worse still, in the confusion Adeluse was able to slip John's hold. When I looked back again, she was bolting for the road. John was after her in a flash and his great stride made up four of her steps. She must have been aware of this, for she chose this time to reveal a new horror: as she ran she leapt up, holding out her arms as if to fly, and there underneath each of her arms was a flap of membranous skin – wings! This hell fiend now had wings!" The Chevalier paused for a moment and shook his head.

"John hesitated at the sight," he now continued, "and he stood still for a moment as if trying to decide if his heart was still in the pursuit. Adeluse had put a slight distance between them, and I could see her, bloodless and white, fleet but clearly suffering from her injuries, and trying with all her might to gain flight. 'After her!' I cried, and this seemed to rouse John from his fear; then, too, other slaves had come running to us in the confusion, willing to join in the chase.

"I rushed after them. I had earlier secreted a pistol in my vest pocket and now I pulled it out. I ran on, unsteadily, panting, my breath cold and slicing in and out of my lungs. I knew I had only this one desperate move left to me – to shoot Adeluse down. As I came up behind the men, I called out for them to stop, but they did not, or perhaps they did not hear my cries over the pounding of their own feet and hearts. I took the chance and shot into the darkness. But my aim was hindered by my haste – the shot meant for Adeluse struck John instead."

"It seems in every aspect of these events fortune has crossed your deeds," Sistrenatus said to the Chevalier as they walked together to the outer doors of the cloisters. "You have done your best; take comfort in that."

Sistrenatus threw back the heavy bolts and the great, old door squealed on its hinges as it opened wide. The sky was lit with dawn. A mass of humid air, made heavier by the night's steady rain, enveloped them like great, unseen arms. The song of birds was everywhere, from the rooftops, to the branches of the budding crepe myrtles, and all among the azaleas. In the distance, from deep within the narrow streets and alleyways, that other song of the Old Carré could also be heard – the rattle of milk wagons, the clip-clop of the water cart horses, and the cries of the many vendors on their way to the market stalls. The Chevalier loosened his cravat and threw his coat over his shoulder. He turned to the Abbe.

"I embark within the hour," he said. "Everything of importance that I kept at the townhouse has already been packed and loaded in anticipation of my boarding. Except, of course, what I am leaving with you . . ."

Sistrenatus nodded deeply. "You may rely upon me. Leave everything in my hands," he said, patting the Chevalier's shoulder as they walked to the exterior gate. "And," he added, slightly hesitant, "do not think that I seek to instruct you, seeing that you are a peer in matters of the supernatural, but I would suggest that perhaps you might take away from this tragedy a lesson – maybe that of acknowledging one's own limitations."

"You mean God's limitations, do you not?" the Chevalier replied.

Sistrenatus shrugged. "We are limited, Jacques, for imponderable reasons and for purposes that we cannot begin to comprehend. We must accept that nothing happens that is not part of a greater design, and in some circumstances at least, the hand of God bars us and the voice of God tells us 'Thus far, but no further' for a very good reason. Have you the bottle?"

The Chevalier nodded and pulled from his coat a heavy bottle of cobalt blue glass filled with a thick, dark liquid and sealed with layers of wax about its neck. "It is enough, I suppose," he said wryly.

"The Lord giveth, my friend," Sistrenatus said, tapping the bottle with his finger. "He has not left you altogether wanting. Rejoice, and be glad."

The Abbe threw open the gates to the Rue Chartres and the Chevalier passed through. Sistrenatus looked at him solemnly and held out his hand. The Chevalier looked down at the empty palm and then back up at the Abbe. "Alms?" he said, half-jokingly.

"Keys," Sistrenatus replied, unmoved.

"Ah!" The Chevalier reached into his vest pocket and drew out two keys; both were elaborate and ancient. He dropped them into the Abbe's hand.

"But alms would be an extreme kindness," Sistrenatus said now, plain-faced as ever and holding out his other hand. The Chevalier, smiling, drew out his purse. He placed two gold coins into the Abbe's open palm.

"Safe journey, my friend," Sistrenatus said now, and reciting a blessing in Latin, made the sign of the cross over the man. The Chevalier, out of ancient habit, mimicked the movements, and for the first time in a very long time felt a note of sincerity rise within him. He embraced the Abbe quickly and rushed away, disappearing around the corner of the garden wall.

Once inside again, Sistrenatus carefully bolted the heavy exterior doors. He walked back into the silent gallery where the sunlight beaming through the high windows cut long, dusty swaths through the lingering shadows. He gazed over the friendly desuetude of the dining table and leaned forward to blow out the sputtering remains of the last few candles; he covered what was left of the bread and corked the wine, then came around to where the ornate old book lay and sat down, regarding it.

In his mind he recalled the end of the Chevalier's tale and how, having shattered the arm of the loyal slave John with the gunshot, he had declared him free on the spot hoping for his help. But John quickly ran away and the other slaves with him, leaving the Chevalier alone to find and face the vampire Adeluse. Sistrenatus shook his head at the thought then, rising, hefted the huge volume under his arm and left the chamber.

A rattle of keys filled the empty cloisters as the Abbe unlocked an otherwise insignificant door under the rear stairs and passed inside, locking it behind him. More keys and

another, inner door was opened; this, too, he locked as soon as
he passed through. He stopped to light a candle in a nearby
sconce and, taking it in hand, now descended a short flight of
stone steps that led down into a long, earthen passageway
carved out long ago when the foundations of the convent were
laid. It extended to an incalculable distance, losing itself in the
shadows to the left and right of the stairs.

But Sistrenatus knew this place well; indeed, he could travel
it in total darkness if need required. He turned to the left and
walked on some distance until he came to a low alcove set with
a heavy iron door. The lock gave noisily against his key; the
door had not been opened in many long years. Sistrenatus bent
and passed through the low doorway; the light of his candle
fluttering up and down cast fantastic shadows on the dank, old
walls.

He had entered a hidden chamber that was at once library,
repository, reliquary, and prison. Shelves upon shelves filled
with books, parchments, and papers of all sorts leapt out of the
abysmal darkness as he walked on into the forbidding recesses
of the place. A line of shapes, columns of holy statues, their
blank eyes staring out from the gloom, formed a long corridor
at the end of which was a low arch. This led into a further
chamber where the ceiling was high and the space more open,
but the air a hundred times more oppressive. Here even the
light of the Abbe's candle seemed subdued and no longer
danced, but burned steadily as if its elemental spirit was wary
and on guard. From here and there in the heavy shadows
flashes of gold and of fantastic jewels sparked – emeralds,
rubies, sapphires set in the tooled spines and covers of the
books they adorned. But these books were not on shelves.

Hanging in mid-air from heavy chains whose bitter ends
were lost in the smothering darkness of the ceiling overhead
were books of all ages, all kinds, all sizes, all weights, their
bindings enriched with designs from the wildest imaginings of
saints and madmen, or plain and unadorned: yet every one of
them was bound, wrapped tightly in heavy chains and set with
complicated locks of every possible make and intricacy. As
Sistrenatus advanced into the room, some of the ancient books
began to move of their own accord; some were drawn toward

him, others seemed repelled and drew away, or spun around in mute protest. The room was charged with the overwhelming presence of living, sentient beings, watchful, curious, and malevolent.

Sistrenatus set his candle down in a stone niche and reached up for a length of loose chain. Slowly and with the greatest of care he wrapped it several times around the Chevalier's discarded book and threaded it through the lock on the volume's face. He secured the whole with another lock already hanging idle on the chain and, certain that the book was completely bound, he again took up his candle. He stopped for a moment to hang the first of the Chevalier's keys on a peg beside the doorway then he walked from the chamber. In the pitch blackness behind him, the volume he had just imprisoned began to swing and shake, rattling against its fetters. The Abbe walked on, unmoved.

He left that grim repository and padded along, retracing his steps back toward the staircase but passing it by on his way into the darkness at the opposite end of the passageway. The walls were wet and moldy, and here and there the blank spot of a locked door loomed fantastically in the shuddering candlelight; sounds came from behind them – slithering, low growling, muttering – a constant reminder to Sistrenatus that he was not alone in that dark labyrinth.

The long passage ended abruptly at an open metal door that led into a neatly-finished chamber. Its walls and ceiling were covered in stucco, though water trickled down one side and formed a wet, moldy pool on the earthen ground; a single chair and a primitive table were the room's only furnishings. On the table an enormous, ancient and elaborately decorated Bible sat open, resting on a low, wooden podium. There were no windows but near the eaves of the rafters was a single, grated opening that let in a narrow beam of sunlight; it shone directly down upon the Bible's pages. Against the far wall of the room, sitting in a deep, hazy shadow exactly across from the table was a heavy iron cage. Slender openings between the bars of the cage were barely wide enough to fit a finger through. It, too, had been brought by the Chevalier, and like his book, it was also secured with chains and several giant padlocks.

Sistrenatus stopped at the table and thumbed through the Bible; the crinkling of the old parchment pages echoed loudly as he flipped them backward, then forward, then back again in a desultory, unhurried way. At last, having searched out the passages he felt proper, the Abbe turned the podium and pushed it forward toward the edge of the table so that the great book faced the metal cage. From his pocket he drew out the second of the two keys which the Chevalier had given him and laid it down in the crease of the Bible's binding. Then he approached the cage. He could hear a rustling inside, like the sad and mournful quivering of the dead when decay is busy about its business; and there was another sound – the wanton slap of large, fleshy wings. The air was tense, like a stretched cord ready to fray apart at any moment.

A furtive, rapid panting arose from the darkened confines of the cage. There was a long hiss and the thing inside moved, and for an instant Sistrenatus caught a glimpse of an emaciated leg, its flesh leathery and green; a foot with pale webbing between the toes and long, clawed nails slid momentarily into the light and was swiftly drawn back. As the Abbe drew in closer, a single, bony finger poked at him through the narrow bars; it felt around with a long claw, scratching at the metal as if to test it. In the pitch blackness at the back of the cage, two gleaming yellow eyes darted about warily, watching in fearful anticipation.

At last Sistrenatus spoke, addressing the thing locked inside the cage. "Sins are insidious things," he said solemnly. "But they cannot hide forever. Since the moment you came within my sight, I have been plumbing your heart for its hidden truth; now I see it bare before me. It is sin that has ruined you.

"In your life with the Monsieur Chevalier and his mistress you left no sin untried. Sloth, pride, gluttony, lust, wrath, greed, envy," he said solemnly. "These are deadly sins, loathsome to God and proscribed by His church, and for you the worst of these was gluttony: The gluttony of your wanton appetites, hidden from your mistress, misapprehended by her as care and loyalty. Now gluttony has trapped you, the gluttonous thirst for the Chevalier's elixir and for the immortality it conveys. What you did not know, could not know was the true magic of the potion – its even more amazing ability to discern, to become, indeed, to manifest the innermost nature of its user. So, your mistress, timid and frightened in life, remained so in her living death, which pleased you greatly. But you," here Sistrenatus hesitated and peered again into the watery orbs of those panicked yellow eyes, "in you it found every awful sin forbidden by the wisdom of God. Thus, you have become your sin, your very worst self; the elixir has made of you the monster you carried inside."

The Abbe now moved toward the chamber door; he pulled its key from the lock and, turning back, held it up so that the thing could clearly see it. "This is but one key to your earthly prison," he said. Then he pointed to the key that lay upon the open Bible. "That is one other. But therein," he went on, indicating the Bible, "are the only keys that matter now, the ones that shall free your soul. Remember, the Lord is merciful. He may be inclined to save that spark of Himself yet abiding within you, however terribly you may have corrupted it.

"Yes," he went on, moving into the doorway, pausing in thoughtful reflection, "the Lord may give, may shed His mercy to save your soul. But your spirit? That is mine. And I am he who taketh away." Thus saying, Abbe Sistrenatus left the chamber. The metal door groaned on its hinges and the clanking of the key in its rusty lock reverberated throughout the nether reaches of that gloomy place.

Yet neither sound was loud enough to drown out the hellish shrieking, the unearthly wailing that now issued forth from that secret prison where inside her iron coffin the creature, the vampire Adeluse screamed and screamed and screamed . . .

The Monster

Along the banks of the Mississippi River where it runs south from New Orleans, great plantations built on crops of citrus, sugar, and cotton provided some order in an otherwise wild and tractless land. Away from the river, the Louisiana swamplands form a half-solid, half-fluid area of forest growth dense with cypress, tupelo, and gum trees, water oaks, ferns, palmettos and a web of ancient vines that in some areas give it the appearance of a primordial jungle. Dispersed along this network of interior waterways, hunters, trappers, and fishermen lived in palmetto huts and rudimentary houseboats. By the early 1800's only sparse numbers of a once-thriving Native American population lived in the more remote areas of the swamplands.

The hundreds of years of European tradition that silted up in the founding of the city of New Orleans were easily lost amid the thick foliage and heady night air of the deep Louisiana swamp. In that wild place, amid its labyrinth of watery byways, one can drift for hours through tunnels of cypress and moss and not see another human being or hear a completely recognizable sound; normal sensibility can be obscured and old superstitions and folk beliefs come readily to mind.

Swamp residents shared many of the same fears as the plantation slaves and at the setting of the sun all retreated to the safety of their respective shelters, locking fast the doors against the encroaching night. In humble houses and bare slave huts the air was thick from smoking wax myrtle candles; even on the most humid nights a slow fire burned upon the hearth to aid in driving off the terrors that lurked in the darkness. Wise bayou country folk knew that out in the shrouded night fearsome creatures were busy, going to and fro about their godless tasks.

Civilized New Orleanians could not even imagine the monsters haunting their swampland neighbors. The people of the swamps knew the She-Hag, a horrible old crone of a woman who hid in the cool hollow of a cypress tree by day; emerging at night, she would shuffle up and down the network of narrow footpaths that criss-crossed the deep places of the swamp. On the lookout for the unwary traveler and those foolish enough to stay outside in the tangled swamplands after dark, she would suddenly appear in the darkness of the road ahead as a hunched old woman, hobbling slowly along. Try though they might, frightened travelers could never catch up to the hag; by the time she rushed from behind them, looming out of the darkness, it was too late. Those taken by the She-Hag were never seen or heard from again.

Swamp folk also greatly feared the "fey follet," swamp fairies that danced like little flames over stagnant marshes and deep, overgrown pools. Like their ethereal European cousins, the "will-o'-the-wisp," the fey follet posed a great danger to night travelers who often mistook their wavering flames for the lights of a distant shelter. Those who strayed toward the "death candles," as locals called those lights, often found themselves trapped in a spongy, sucking mire that soon became their final resting place. Fear of the fey follet spread well beyond the pathless darkness of the swamp and those who lived nearby often suffered from their malevolence. Livestock, the elderly, and children were always in great danger of attacks from the swamp fairies. The fey follet most especially loved infants whom they often fed upon by sucking the clear liquid exuded from the newborn's teats; and like their fairy family the world over, the fey follet sometimes simply stole babies directly from their cribs. But swamp fairies left no changeling in place of the kidnapped child and parents who lost children to their depredations knew the precious innocents were lost forever to the world of the living.

Recalcitrant bayou children were kept inside with tales of Johnny Fatchupas, a terrifying ghoul who jumped about the darkened swamp on one leg peering into huts and houses where lights were left burning after dark. According to legend, wherever Johnny found children awake after their bedtime he would jump in through the window and whisk them away. Despite his handicap, Johnny Fatchupas moved with deadly speed and was apparently capable of amazing acrobatics; he often jumped to great heights, disappearing into the trees where he would swing from limb to limb with the aid of his strong arms. Some swamp residents claimed to have seen Johnny loping away with a child under his arm and one grasped tightly between his teeth, jumping and navigating the tall cypress trees like a one-armed monkey. This was a sight no one wanted to witness and something no child wanted to experience. As a result, bayou children were well-behaved; proud swampland parents boasted that the manners of their children could match those of a well-to-do New Orleans child any day. But if the legend of Johnny Fatchupas didn't frighten them, children of the swamp learned early to live in healthy fear of another fearsome beast – the dreaded Loup Garou.

Only a very few who have studied the history of the Louisiana swamps are not familiar with some story of this terrifying, shape-shifting wolf creature. Like its Lycan brethren of Europe, the Loup Garou is believed to be a human who walks the earth, whether by doom or desire, in the form of a ravening wild wolf preying indiscriminately upon men, women, and children. A person might deliberately pursue this accursed life, such as the dreaded Atta'kapas Indians of southwest Louisiana who prayed for the ability to shapeshift out of desire for revenge against their enemies. And, as was the case with so many other creatures of Louisiana legend, a person could easily fall under the werewolf curse if he or she were to backslide or abandon his or her Catholic faith. Not attending Mass regularly, failing to confess every sin, or not fasting during Lent – any of these transgressions might bring one under the shadow of the werewolf's curse. But the folk of the Louisiana swamplands were a wily stock; preserved in their cultural memories were any number of ways to elude and kill the werewolf. Indian tribes such as the Chitimacha and the Opelousas knew "medicine" strong enough to defeat their enemy, the Atta'kapas, in their werewolf forms; and the lore of southwest Louisiana is full of tales of the bravery of common folk in the face of this horrible beast.

But in the lush riverlands stretching out south of the City of New Orleans, below the labyrinth known as Barataria, where the pirate captain Jean Lafitte once hid with his hordes of scallywags and bootleggers, a people with strange customs – and a slave population with customs stranger still – took root and flourished. These people were the Isleños and their slaves, who were brought from a place in Africa that once boasted a fabulous ancient civilization and who practiced strange magic – or as the swamp Indians would say a "bad medicine." Deep in the darkened swamps of the Mississippi river plains, in a place known as Plaquemines, the slaves of the Islenos created something more terrifying than all the other fearsome denizens of bayou country. And in the blazing heat of a Louisiana summer, with a hurricane upon the doorstep and nowhere to run, three highly-placed and well-educated New Orleans men came to learn more about that monster than anyone could ever want to know.

The Swamp Golem

Maxim Truxille, a doctor of New Orleans, stood in the doorway of the Barbazon house squinting at the heat shimmering in a mercurial haze along the brown horizon. A stiflingly hot wind shook the parched trees that ranged along the nearby levee; they seemed to squat against it helplessly, already stunted by the blistering rays of the August sun. The end of a long, humid Louisiana day was coming, though at a snail's pace. Truxille pulled out his handkerchief to wipe the sweat where it ran down his neck and puddled along his collarbone. He felt a tap at his elbow.

"Something to drink?" said a familiar voice. It was Dumiot, a friend and fellow physician. He held out a glass of lemonade and shook it a little so that the floating slivers of lemon peel swirled around hypnotically. Truxille accepted it thankfully.

"Detestable heat," Dumiot said now, between sips of his own drink.

Truxille nodded, but said nothing. The hot wind gusted closer, creating a little whirlwind of dried leaves that skittered about the porch steps for a moment, then dispersed and was gone. A passing cloud momentarily shrouded the sun's blaze.

"Looks like the weather might change," Dumiot remarked offhandedly.

Truxille squinted at the sky, roused from his lethargy. "Yes," he said in his quiet, measured voice. "Perhaps we should break away earlier?"

Dumiot shrugged. "Barbazon has invited us to stay for supper," he said. "I think the skies will hold."

Truxille was not so sure, but he had no time to make reply as Borqa, their host's manservant, appeared in the doorway.

"Supper, gentlemen," he said in his thick Isleños accent.

Four men sat down to dine at a long table in an otherwise sparsely-furnished room, darkened to spare the heat; indoors was barely less stifling than the afternoon outside, so no candles or lamps had been lit. Overhead, a faded canopy fan, its aged pattern bespeaking a medieval whimsy of unicorns and maidens, swung back and forth, slicing the hot air with a monotonous thumping; a small, black boy sat in a nearby corner, staring blankly as his hand mechanically pulled each slow stroke. Tall, French doors stood open wide on two sides providing a breeze and a view of the elaborate gardens – now mostly wilted – at the rear of the Barbazon home. In the distance, a bare wooden fence against a wedge of tall sugar cane stalks and a dark, unbroken line of trees sloped down to the edge of a tangled swamp.

Defying convention in the face of the summer heat, the four men sat in shirts and breeches as servants moved around passively, setting out the meal – cold fish, tomato aspic, stewed greens, fruits, wine, and coarse yellow bread served straight from a black skillet.

"Not much of a meal," Barbazon, the host, said apologetically, just as he had for six nights prior. "My wife would be appalled! But this late in the summer and with this heat . . ." He shrugged.

Sósthene, a doctor of homeopathy whose pursuits had brought Truxille and Dumiot there, held up a hand. "Not at all, Barbazon," he said, through a mouthful of bread. "We appreciate your hospitality!"

"Yes," Dumiot chimed in, "you have been an impeccable host; though I am sorry we had not the opportunity to meet your dear wife. Thank you for providing one last supper!"

"Humh!" Barbazon snorted. "I do not think I like the sound of that!" he joked, and the others laughed.

At the far end of the table, Truxille raised his glass but said nothing, having a natural aversion for the forced genteelism so often found among Creole society.

"Bah!" Barbazon went on. "It is the very least I could do! I only hope I have been of some help to you in your studies?" He looked inquiringly around the table.

"Yes, indeed!" Sósthene replied; it had been, after all, his study. "I have collected some amazing specimens, many of them completely unknown, I believe. Of course, I cannot wait to return to New Orleans and study them at length."

Sósthene was referring to botanical specimens, botany being the work that had formed the impetus of the little expedition into the parish of Plaquemines. A welcome – and necessary – break from New Orleans where the dual plagues of yellow fever and Asiatic cholera had raged since the late spring, the trip to Plaquemines had not been without purpose. Through his work with local Indian tribes, Sósthene had promulgated a theory that a treatment of the diseases might be found in the native Louisiana flora; Truxille and Dumiot had seen enough merit in the proposition to accompany him. Barbazon, an acquaintance of Sósthene and the owner of a large plantation on the edge of a navigable swamp, had generously provided the team with lodgings, food, and experienced guides to assist them in their efforts. But the summer was hot, and the heat that August week had been almost unbearable. Now, as they sat down for their last meal together, it was all any of them could do to stay attentive and keep civil; the exhaustion in the room was as palpable as the humid air outside.

For his part, Truxille ardently desired to be away both from the suffocating heat of Plaquemines and from Barbazon, a man whom he found so detestable that even the noxious air of New Orleans seemed preferable. His dislike had been quickly cultivated, almost from the moment when a river-going barge deposited the three physicians at the levee dock opposite the Barbazon house. They were met by the redoubtable Borqa, accompanied by several slaves brought along to handle the luggage. Once debarked, they had climbed the levee and followed Borqa along a blinding-white stretch of shell road that unfurled toward the house, winding through a neatly-tended grove of citrus trees. Scores of slaves toiled there in the sweltering heat, picking the early fruit and stacking bushels; those nearest the road stopped for a moment to swipe the sweat from their brows and gaze curiously as Borqa and the men passed. The breeze off the river rustled through the grove, rattling the leathery, emerald-green leaves and bouncing the young lemons about playfully. It was idyllic, in every way pleasantly redolent of summer; but then, at a turn in the road that plunged into the deep shade of a brace of oaks, the reverie was abruptly shattered. With sobering immediacy, the men came upon a horrible scene: an old Negro woman, bent and crippled, lay cowering and sobbing upon the ground, a basket of lemons scattered about her; a tall, gangly white man stood over her, brandishing a long whip, and clearly still in the process of using it.

Borqa let out an audible gasp at the sight, and the slaves who carried the luggage bent their heads down and walked doggedly on, doing their best not to become involved. "This way, gentlemen," Borqa coughed, pointing along the road, trying to draw them away.

But Truxille and the other physicians stood transfixed; to their horror, the tall white man, with barely an acknowledgement in their direction, lifted the whip and bent to strike again. Truxille moved upon the man then, pushing him to the ground and pulling the whip from his hands. For a moment he considered using it, but instead stepped over to where Dumiot was already busy helping the aged woman to her feet.

She lifted herself gingerly between the two men, leaning with her bony, bloodied arms on their strong frames. Gasping in labored breaths, shoulders shaking with quiet sobs, she let them help her to a makeshift seat on a shorn log nearby. Blood stained her shredded cotton dress where the whip had mercilessly swiped her back. But when Dumiot tried to get a better look at the cuts, the old woman shook her head and gently pushed his hand away. A group of disheveled-looking slaves standing nearby looked on in wide-eyed amazement, glancing back and forth between the old woman, the physicians, and the gangly man who had lost his whip but apparently not his nerve.

"Ain't no harm to that ol' bitch," he spat, wiping his chin and his red, sweaty face on a filthy sleeve. "Whassa matter? Ain't dey no slaves where you from? Nigger needs to larn to lissen is all!" He opened his mouth to speak again but was met with a look of such withering contempt from Truxille that all he could think to do was skulk away.

Suddenly, Truxille felt a cold, bony hand slip into his own; he looked down into a gaunt, yellow face and cloudy blue eyes, and the old woman spoke. "Thank yo," she whispered hoarsely. She pulled his hand toward her face and, gently patting, kissed it. "Thank yo!"

Mumbling apologies and excuses, Borqa stepped up and pulled the woman's hand away. "The boss," he said, almost apologetically, "he not like if we interfere."

The old woman was left in the care of the other slaves who gathered around her and carried her away to the slave quarters where, Truxille was later told, she had despondently taken to her bed. The gangly man was the plantation overseer whose ruthless treatment of the slaves, they all learned, was endorsed wholeheartedly by Barbazon. And to their great disillusionment, when told of the incident, Barbazon had only laughed and asked if Truxille had returned the whip . . .

"I say, Truxille!" It was Barbazon, his voice raspy, strangled by the fat clustered at his throat and the food in his mouth. Truxille had cringed each time he had heard the sound in that unbearably long week. "You must certainly be ready to return to New Orleans!" A bare hint of sarcasm.

Truxille turned his brooding, black eyes upon the man. "So ready I would ride bare-backed with the Angel of Death all the way up the Mississippi," he said flatly, and drained his glass of wine. "Excuse me," he added with a nod to no one in particular, and rising from the table went into the parlor to have a smoke.

Barbazon scowled but said nothing. Dumiot, to his left, continued to eat in silence.

"Well!" Sósthene bleated and the others jumped slightly. "This heat can be hard on a man's appetite."

"Yes," was Dumiot's half-hearted reply. He knew what bothered Truxille; it stuck in his throat, too.

A sudden gust of wind blew into the room and drew their attention to the storm gathering outside. While the men dined, a blanket of clouds had silted up in masses of gray and green that filled the sky to the south and east, obscuring the fading sun. Winds now whipped the trees, blowing leaves and small branches across the clipped grass of Barbazon's gardens; gusts swept into the dining room, puffing out the window curtains like billowing white sails.

"Looks bad," Dumiot now observed.

Borqa came to the door with his usual perfect timing. "Pardon me, sir," he said nervously to Barbazon. "But I think this storm might be very bad." Another strong gust blew into the room, this one wet with rain.

Barbazon jumped to his feet. "Gentlemen, please excuse me," he said. "I must see that all is secure." He bowed quickly and ran toward the door, barking something at Borqa in a Spanish dialect.

"Boy!" Borqa hollered to the black boy who had all the while sat silently by, pulling at the canopy fan. "Look lively! Close up the house! Get moving!"

The boy jumped to life, running about the room shutting the windows and glass doors against the ever-increasing winds.

Dumiot rushed to help him. Interested, Truxille had wandered back in; Sósthene chose this moment to confront him.

"How dare you be so rude to Señor Barbazon!?" he blurted. "The man has been hospitable, has helped us greatly in our research! I cannot fathom your behavior!"

Truxille stood still, regarding Sósthene with a look somewhere between perplexity and exasperation. Then turning to Dumiot he said flatly, "We should have left earlier."

Dumiot nodded deeply. "Maxim, I know. But there is nothing we can do about that now!"

"This is just wonderful, Alexis," Truxille replied. "And no telling how long we will be delayed now!"

Dumiot let out a weary sigh. "Maxim, I am as eager as you to get away from here but we cannot debate this now," he pleaded. "What is one more night?"

Thunder clapped overhead. Lightning flashed. Gusting winds rattled at the windows and blew open a pair of glass parlor doors. Truxille rushed back into the room with Dumiot on his heels.

"This is no ordinary summer storm!" Dumiot cried, as he helped shutter the doors. The sky outside was roiling, a sea of grays and blacks; inside, the house was as dark as if night had fallen. Trees everywhere were bending in the constant assault of the winds, casting debris here and there in random disarray.

"I am ready to get out of this place!" Truxille growled and hammered against the shutter pane as if to press his point. He stood still, listening to the rain and the low wailing of the wind, gusting, building to small crescendos then falling into a tense silence. He gave Dumiot a defeated look. "Very well," he said. "You are right. What difference if we stay one more night?"

Dumiot smiled wanly and was about to speak when a sudden crash sounded from the second floor of the house. They rushed to the foyer in time to see the house boy bounding down the stairs, his eyes wide with fear, leaves and raindrops in his hair. "De tree, mistah!" he said. "It done broke tru de howse!"

Just then, Barbazon and Borqa returned and, together with Dumiot and a shaky Sósthene, bounded up the stairs; the house boy followed quickly after them. Rain pounded the rooftop and swept by in great gusts, blown from all directions by the feckless winds. Wet and windblown, the house servants were busy on the porch, closing and reclosing the heavy wooden shutters.

Truxille watched gloomily from a parlor window until its shutters, too, were slammed and fastened. Then, an inexplicable feeling came over him, and he felt the hairs on his neck rise slightly. Something told him he was no longer alone. He turned quickly and there, in the near-impenetrable shadows of the foyer, was the outline of a woman; he could just make out her dress and the feminine shape of her hair as she stood there, silently, regarding him. Truxille could hear her breathing, ragged and thin, and feel her eyes upon him. The door had not sounded, he had not heard her enter the house. Disconcerted, he called out, "Who is there?"

The figure moved slowly forward, hobbling, hunched over, as if walking was a difficulty. Undaunted, Truxille moved toward it as it shuffled into the dim parlor light. He was surprised to see the bent, shriveled figure of the old Negro woman whom he had saved from the overseer's whip. Truxille looked at her curiously. She gazed back in silence, staring at him with wide, watery eyes. "May I help you? Are you unwell, m'am?" he asked, suddenly uncomfortable. "Are you afraid of the storm?"

At last she smiled, not broadly, but in a way that was reassuring and kind. "Yo' already done it," she said, her voice soft and strangely melodious. "Yo' hep'd me, mistah," she said, obviously recalling the horrible scene in which Truxille had first come upon her. "Yo' an' t'other doctor – ya'll both hep'd me when no one e'se would." She drew closer now, her arms outstretched, hands making grasping motions at the thin air.

Truxille felt his cheeks burning; he wanted to look away. "It was only right," he coughed. "It was the right thing to do."

"It were a brave ting yo' did," she said quietly, musically, "yas, it were! An' I ain't gwon't fo'gets it now," she added, and reached out a shaky hand toward Truxille's flushing cheek. Shaking his head, he stepped back with a start, yet he could not avoid her eyes and for a moment stood as if frozen by the intensity of their gaze.

"Dat's why I is gwon't saves yo," she said now, squeezing her hands together as if in prayer. "Ain't gwon't let no'ting happen to yo. Yo's gwon't gets away from heah, yas, an' t'other doctor, too!"

Try as he could, Truxille could not disconnect from the woman's clouded blue eyes, shining like marbles in the dimly-lit room. He had heard of this, remotely, how the slaves of the countryside possessed the power to fascinate with looks, to hypnotize and bend others to their will, and had dismissed it as fancy: in this moment that felt like folly. He heard her speak again, her voice the only sound, as if they were locked together in a vacuum. And something else fascinating – though torrents of rain swept by outside, and she must have entered through the front door – this ragged old woman was entirely dry.

"Dey all gwon't *die*," she said now, almost spitting out the last word. "All 'cept yo' an dat other kind man. It comin', yo' see, it comin' an' it gwon't *kill* dat man what make us suffer! Gwon't kill dat man what whupped me and hurts us all! But yo' is safe! Yas! Safe in de storm dat be comin'! Yas, indeed!"

Monstrous thunderclaps shook the house. Chandeliers and glassware tinkled everywhere as each clap sounded then rolled away into the distance like the drums of a great army. Truxille was taken aback by the sound, and at first he did not comprehend why. Suddenly, he realized that it was not merely the thunder he heard, rolling like drums, but drums, indeed! He heard them at a distance, rolling, thumping, and following on from each peal of thunder. The sound immediately put him in mind of the drums of slave rituals and the "bamboula" dances he had witnessed in the Congo Fields of New Orleans. But to hear them there, miles from the city, indeed miles from any other habitation, and with that ancient woman standing there, staring at him, was disconcerting in the extreme. Then, just as suddenly as they had started, the drums fell silent.

The house shook again, but this time it was the blast of real thunder followed on immediately by a fearsome flash of lightning that charged the air. Distracted, Truxille looked away toward the shuttered windows; when he looked back, the old woman was gone and he was alone in the darkened parlor. The strange mood was broken when Barbazon burst into the room, pursued by Borqa and Sósthene; Dumiot followed dejectedly behind.

"Everything is secured! We have prepared as best we could!" Barbazon cried, and fell into a long chair, wiping his dripping wet brow. "All we can do now is wait, and ride it out! Yes, wait, and ride it out! Borqa!" he barked. "Brandy!"

The rotund little Isleño hurried over with a decanter and glass, pouring as he ran; Barbazon downed a full two glasses before he spoke again. "Yes, ride it out . . ." he said with a sigh, and everyone there detected more than a hint of fear in his voice.

Barbazon continued to drink, Sósthene paced nervously about, and Dumiot retreated to a chair in a dark corner of the room; a flash of tinder followed by a steady stream of pipe smoke was the only indication he was there. Truxille turned his weary gaze back to the window where a chink in the shutter allowed him a narrow view.

Day had passed into a dusky twilight of storm, but there was still a hint of light left, just enough for Truxille to discern, against the shaking, tormented tree line, the shadowy silhouette of a tall, broad-shouldered black man. At least it appeared to be a man. Impaired by distance and the rain-laden winds, he could not make out any features, nor see any eyes, but for some reason the sight unsettled him. It was as if, more than man-like, the figure was a living shadow standing straight and rigid in the cover of the trees, where it wished not to be seen; and like the old woman when she stood in the foyer of the house, its gaze regarded only him. In another moment, a stark flash of lightning illuminated the tree line; Truxille looked again, but the shadowy man was gone.

Time wore inexorably on. The storm continued to rage. Inside the house, the heat was stifling. Truxille sat alone in the parlor trying to occupy his mind with reading a tattered old number of the New Orleans _Bee_ by the dull light of an oil lamp, but he was having little success in concentrating. The words of the old woman still lingered, ominously prescient, in his ears; neither could he erase the sight of the shadowy figure from his mind's eye. He suspected these strange occurrences were connected, and that the shadow in the trees had *wanted* him to see it; yet his rational mind could not reason it out completely, and this bothered him.

The others fought boredom by undertaking a desultory exploration of the possessions of Barbazon's library and study – an admirable collection of books – some old, some new; family portraits; the trappings of the avid horsemen; small statuary; and the odd memento of the Canary Islands, Barbazon's ancestral home.

"We are Castilian, originally, you see," Barbazon explained, "and in the days of Ferdinand and Isabella the horrible lie took hold that we Castilians were the descendants of heathen Moors. A lie, yes, of course, as has been proven over the generations! We were Spaniards, and always good Catholics!" he added quickly. "But, like so many other people of the time, our lives could nonetheless be disrupted at the whisper of rumor and the whim of royalty. This is one reason why my ancestors came to find themselves deported to the unforgiving Canaries."

Life in the Canary Islands was hard, Barbazon told them, but because they had been among the peoples of Castile whom Queen Isabella held dear when she was yet a princess there, these castaways were allowed to keep the major portion of their wealth and possessions. "All that was required in the islands," Barbazon explained, "were workers to help rebuild our society, and to serve us, of course."

Truxille, overhearing from the next room, snorted. Dumiot hid a wry smile at the sound. Thunder roared and flashes of lightning crackled across the sky in jagged white arcs; the wind flailed on, unceasing.

"They sent us Greeks!" Barbazon said, shaking his face so that his heavy jowls wobbled. "Have you ever tried to get work out of a Greek?" he added, though no one ventured to answer. "It was an appalling condition to be in. Because of it, we appealed to the King and Queen and at last were allowed to bring over slaves from Africa to compensate for those lazy olive-eaters."

Though he was discussing an old history, Barbazon nonetheless spoke with the urgency and conviction of a man who had personal experience of the events, as if it had all just happened and directly to him. "But," and here he held up a finger, "we *did not* want those slaves to be from the west of Africa."

There was a silence. With the exception of Truxille, the men had returned to the dining room where a solitary oil lamp now burned. Borqa sat in a low chair next to a sideboard, ready to keep the men's brandy glasses filled, their apparent reward for patiently allowing Barbazon to drone on and on.

"Wh-?" Sósthene blurted after some thought. "Is there a difference?" Dumiot blinked at him in astonishment; in the parlor, Truxille snorted again.

"Oh, yes," Barbazon replied emphatically, nodding deeply. "Yes, indeed! You see, the blacks of western Africa have not the sense," here he put a finger to his temple, "the smarts, as it were, for certainly one cannot call any native of Africa intelligent."

In the parlor, Truxille rattled the newspaper noisily. Another clap of thunder and the drumming peal over the lightning flash. The rain swept over the house in new torrents. Barbazon continued, undaunted.

"Not for us, those Congoese or the darkies of the White Man's Graveyard," he said, wagging his finger at his listeners. "We Castilians required that at least our slaves could lay square bricks end to end!" He laughed uproariously and downed another glass of brandy; he was now quite drunk, but nonetheless Borqa rushed up from the shadows with a refill. "Instead, we looked to the east of Africa, to Ethiopia. At least there the Africans had learned some hint of civilization!"

Dumiot coughed. "Yes," he said at last, "I have heard that contention before. It is supposed, by some anthropographers, that the Ethiops are – in some of their practices anyway – connected to the Hebrews of old."

Barbazon snorted. "Well, that would not surprise me. But we Islenos found them agreeably intelligent, if that can be said. Then, when Spain sought to check the spread of the French colonials here, it was we Isleños that they sent to settle these lands for the empire." Here he held up his brandy glass in a toast. "They know we are industrious, and that we know how to keep the ignorant in line!" To this last, no one made any reply.

The storm continued to roar ferociously, but inside the stuffy dining room Barbazon was losing his fight with drink; and when at last it overcame him, he collapsed onto a chaise lounge. Borqa came to the table and sat down with a deep sigh. Dumiot laughed and pushed the brandy bottle toward him. "Go ahead," he said. "You have earned it!"

Borqa relaxed and laughed nervously in his turn. He filled a glass and drank the brandy straight down, his face contorting in strange acrobatics at the sting. He gasped and coughed while Dumiot firmly slapped his back; then, his composure regained at last, Borqa told his own tale.

"I do not like them," he said in his thick, heavy accent, "the Ethiops. They scare me. They keep secrets; and the boss, he never bothered to bring them into the church, to baptize them like other masters do their slaves. He let them keep their own religion. I do not like *that* very well at all!"

"Oh? And why is that?" Dumiot asked, his curiosity piqued. Borqa had sounded almost frightened.

"It is strange, you know?" Borqa replied. "Their practice is dark, a mystery – not like the Congos with their spirits and their roots and candles. These Ethiops, they worship some other gods, I do not know which; and they go out there," he waved a hand in the direction of the swamp, "and they make themselves idols to worship." He made the Sign of the Cross and fell silent.

"Do you mean fetishes?" Truxille asked. He had stepped in from the parlor when Barbazon passed out. "They build fetishes and worship them?"

Borqa shook his head. "I do not know what they are called, doctor," he said. "They take the swamp mud, moss, and strange plants – even, I have been told, hair and fingernails and bits of dead men's skin, and they make of these things the figures. Some are little, like holy statues but with the looks on the face like the Africans," he pulled his lips to demonstrate. "Some I have seen are big as men." He paused. "Mud men, or heathen gods, maybe, and these they worship in the empty places chopped out back in the swamp. They dance and sing, and play their mongrel drums . . . " He trailed off and downed another glass of brandy.

The others waited, then when there seemed to be nothing more forthcoming from the man, Dumiot said, "Surely that is not all?"

"Yes," said Sósthene, leaning forward in interest, "certainly there is more."

Borqa looked at each of them in turn. For the first time they were aware that the man's fear was genuine; they could see it in his dark, watery eyes. He moved to speak, but suddenly a horrible rattling jarred the stuffy air. Borqa jumped, startling them all. Only Truxille kept his head about him. He put a finger to his lips and directed their attention to where Barbazon lay, sprawled out on the lounge, cradling a brandy glass in his arms and snoring loudly. This was the sound that had startled them.

Sósthene put a hand on his heart and pushed his empty brandy glass forward; laughing softly, Dumiot obligingly refilled it. Truxille sat down as quietly as he could, his finger still to his lips; the very last thing he wanted was for Barbazon to wake up. Borqa sat shaking his head and smiling; Dumiot filled his glass, too.

"Go on, tell us," Truxille said, as Borqa watched the liquid trickle and roll over the faceted crystal of the glass, glowing amber in the wavering lamplight. Clearly, he was hesitant.

"What do they do with these fetishes, these 'mud men'?" Dumiot asked, now very interested.

"The little ones, I don't know," Borqa said with a shrug. "But the big ones, they worship them with wild dancing and singing. I have heard this! It is horrible, straight from the darkest jungles of that awful place." The others knew he was speaking of Africa.

"They dance," Truxille replied. "That is all?"

Borqa drank deep of his brandy and shook his head. "You do not understand," he sighed. "I have been here many years and watched them. Yes, they dance, yes, they sing and drum, and they talk to the thing and ask it favors and they – they keep this up until the thing it . . ." there was an anxious pause then Borqa said flatly, "wakes up."

"Oh, indeed!" Sósthene snorted incredulously, breaking the stunned silence.

Dumiot laughed and shook his head. "Well, old man," he said, "you have earned another glass! You certainly had us on with that story," he added, as he reached to top off Borqa's brandy.

Borqa was resolute. "It is no fantasy I tell you, sir," he said, but took the refill anyway.

Dumiot and Sósthene exchanged glances. "What do you think, Maxim?" Dumiot chuckled and turned to Truxille. "A good tale for a stormy night, eh?" But Truxille did not reply. Instead, he sat up straight, listening intently.

"The storm," he said at last. The others listened. The wind and rain had ceased; the house no longer shook. There was a brooding silence.

"It has stopped," Sósthene said, brightening up a little.

"So it has," Dumiot added.

Truxille got up from the table and walked toward the foyer, making for the front door; the others crowded after him. Truxille opened the door carefully and peered out. Reassured by what he saw, he opened the door wider and stepped out onto the porch. Dumiot and Sósthene followed him, but Borqa hung back, wavering inside the doorway.

It seemed the storm *had* ceased. Debris was everywhere – tree limbs swathed with grey Spanish moss littered the front lawn; wide fronds of "Spanish blade" plants and spindly branches of the rain-beaten azaleas cluttered the porch steps and choked the nearby fountain; a low palm tree close to the house appeared to have taken a strike from lightning; and the banana trees nearby had been ripped to shreds by the punishing winds. Only a light, gentle breeze blew now, rustling through the park and woodlands. A few bare clouds scudded in the distance, east and west, but overhead a great, clear dome of deepest blue had opened, the distant stars twinkling brightly in its rain-washed chasm.

Borqa still hesitated in the doorway. He looked out to where Truxille, Dumiot, and Sósthene stood talking softly together a few feet from the porch steps. He saw Dumiot reach into his pocket and pull out his watch to check the time. He looked behind at the close, stuffy darkness of the house, then back to the men. He was just about to step out when suddenly a great, wailing gust of wind swept over everything, buffeting Truxille and the other men with sticks and leaves. They all looked up at once to see the clouds returning, swirling together out of the clear sky and blotting out everything overhead. Rain began to pelt them and they rushed back to the porch for shelter. Thunder rolled in the distance once again.

"Take cover!" Truxille cried as they all crowded back into the house.

The storm had returned with new ferocity. Its winds blew and roared against the door like a thing alive and Truxille could not close it alone; he and Dumiot fell against it while Sósthene fumbled with the locks. The thunder, too, had returned with a vengeance; or so it seemed. Truxille was the first to recognize the rolling as the reprise of the drumming he had earlier heard; and the realization now became jarringly clear to them all. But they had barely a chance to think when suddenly another cacophony of sound filled the house: wood splintering, glass breaking, and a shriek so wild and bloodcurdling just hearing it riveted the men in place.

"What in God's name - ?" Sósthene cried.

"My God – !" Dumiot exclaimed at exactly the same moment. His blood ran cold.

"Barbazon!" Truxille said and ran off toward the dining room.

He, Dumiot, and Sósthene gained the door of the room just in time to see the bulging form of Barbazon, legs kicking, arms flailing, being pulled up and out of his chair. A great, dense shadow filled the entire frame of the demolished French doors just behind where Barbazon had been sleeping. It appeared to wrap itself around Barbazon's body, and he hung there for a breathless moment, but then was pulled whole through the gaping doorway.

The men rushed forward; blood soaked the remnants of the doorway and pooled, inky black in the darkness at their feet. Rain and wind assaulted them all as they crowded into the doorway to look out, and each could clearly see the bloated white form of Barbazon, screaming and kicking as *something* carried him away toward the swamps: *something* had him, something hulking and dark, and powerful – more powerful than any man. They could just discern the shape of the thing, its broad shoulders and what looked like an arm gripping Barbazon's waist, holding him suspended, so that he appeared to float above the ground. They could see his arms flailing and hear his wild screams; his swollen face was visible in the flash of the lightning strikes, its eyes popping from their sockets, and the round, opaque hole of his mouth fixed in a howl of terror.

"Madre de Dios!" Borqa cried, and crossed himself.

Instinctively, the compassion and courage of the physician overcoming both his loathing of Barbazon and his fear of the unknown creature, Truxille began to push through the window's splintered remains. Dumiot and Sósthene grabbed him.

"Maxim! Are you mad?" Dumiot cried.

"You cannot go out there!" Sósthene wailed.

But Truxille knew he must. He broke free of his friends and bolted like a shot, across the porch and out into the rain, in pursuit of Barbazon and whatever monstrous thing had stolen him away. He could not, as a man who had dedicated his life to healing, simply let the man be dragged away to his death. In an instant, Dumiot and Borqa were behind him. More fearful of being left alone in the house than of following the others, a reluctant Sósthene climbed through the window and ran off screaming after them into the windswept night.

Truxille raced across the dark, disheveled gardens; stalks of sugar cane slapped him like ragged wet rods as he bounded through the back fields toward the swamp. The wind howled at him belligerently, now and then casting up stray branches and tufts of leaves that fixed onto his saturated clothes. When he reached the mire of the swamp he hesitated, uncertain which way to go. Then a powerful gust of wind, like great, unseen hands, bent back the tree line and Truxille could clearly discern the spot where the massive creature had passed through, stamping down trees and underbrush that stood in the way of its onslaught.

"Maxim!" Dumiot cried, coming up behind him and grabbing his soaking wet shirt. Truxille fought his grip. "This is folly! Whatever that – that *thing* is, we cannot hope to win against it!"

Truxille held Dumiot fast by his shoulders. "You saw it?" He cried to be heard over the wind gusting and howling around them, and knowing he sounded like a madman. "What did you see? For surely that has to be some natural beast we saw – else I am mad, and you, too!"

Dumiot shook his head, confused, and then admitted, "A hulking form, a moving shadow, squeezing the life out of – dear God, that *can't* be . . . !"

"No!" Borqa cried, and crossed himself. "It is the man-thing! The monster of the Ethiops!"

"Maxim! Alexis!" Sósthene cried breathlessly as he came running up. "Come back to the house! We can get weapons, and then we can follow it! We'll all be killed out here!"

Truxille was about to speak, but his heart fell in him and a shadow passed over his face. "Look!" he cried, pointing to the cane fields behind them. They looked and there beheld a cadre of shadowy forms, like silent standing sentinels, straight and unmoving amid the waving stalks, indeed unaffected in any way by the fury of the storm.

"Are they men?" Dumiot cried. Thunder rolled and lightning cracked overhead, but the flashing white light only cast the shadows more starkly; they looked for all the world like statues.

This was more than Borqa could take. "Mudmen!" he wailed, and dreadful terror at last overcame him. "What shall we do? *What shall we do?*"

"No," Truxille said in a voice hollow with hopelessness, "they *must* be real men." He turned back toward the swamps and there, just beside the path, he spied something else, something utterly surreal: the old Negro woman was standing there, silhouetted against a hole that yawned like a pitch-black maw in the midst of shredded trees. The old woman raised a thin, frail arm and pointed into the gaping hole, and Truxille knew that she was showing him the path that the creature had taken. But he hesitated, puzzled and more than a little fearful, until he heard Borqa cry out from behind: "Dear God! *They are coming!*"

Truxille turned around just in time to see that the shadowy forms dispersed throughout the cane field had started to move toward them.

"Maxim!" Dumiot urged.

When he turned back again, Truxille was puzzled to see that the old woman was gone, but he had no time to stop and consider how or why. "This way!" he cried, and ran like a madman into the trees. Dumiot, Sósthene, and Borqa did not hesitate, and were fast on his heels. None of them wanted to face the terror of those shadow forms out in the open field.

They ran on and on. The wet branches of low palms and ferns slapped against them, as if trying to bar their way. All around, they could hear the limbs of the cypress trees groaning, wrestling with the merciless winds; distant cracks sounded out loudly from trees losing that battle. At times their feet caught and sank into the sucking, saturated earth, but they helped each other and carried on in search of Barbazon. Before long, over the howling storm, they heard again the rolling drumbeats; to their horror these were punctuated by shrill screams: Barbazon wailing for his life somewhere on the path ahead of them. They knew he must be close by, and the shadowy beast, as well.

Then suddenly, unexpectedly, the line of trees thinned, and the men ran out into the open. They found themselves exposed on the edge of a clearing where the land sloped suddenly down to the low grass of a man-made circle, one of the ritual places of the Ethiops. Though reason was fleeting this night, competing with terror and disbelief in their minds, the sight of the man-made clearing now seemed to confirm to them their greatest fear: the creature they had seen was indeed supernatural, one of those created by the black magic of the Ethiops; and it made sense that it had returned to the place of its making, the root of its power.

Truxille held out his arms protectively, barring the others from entering that ring of blasphemy. They looked and saw that the ground on the edge of the clearing was beaten down in a circle, stamped down by the march of many feet during inscrutable rituals meant to draw up the power that would bring their mudman, their avenging golem, to life. The smell of wet, bloody earth filled the air, an earth saturated by sacrifices that not even a hurricane could wash away. The winds whipped, throwing leaf, branch and moss against them, obscuring their view. Then the air seemed to suck away, to draw back, and in a moment of stillness they could again see, standing all around them outside the circle, the black shadow forms they had glimpsed in the open fields.

"Ah! We are doomed!" Borqa cried.

"Wh -?" Dumiot blurted. "How did they . . . ?"

At the opposite side of the circle, directly across from where Truxille now stood, the brush and ferns shook violently in spite of the lowering wind; it was as if something was inside there, thrashing about. He was struck with the fearsome realization of just what was coming at them through those trees; just as he and was about to cry out, suddenly, with a horrifying immediacy, the trees on the edge of the circle seemed to explode, belching forth a monstrous and fearful sight.

As black as the mud of the Mississippi River from which it was made, the being, the man-thing of the swamp now towered over them. In shape and style it mimicked man, and yet it was only a crudely made shape, a husk in man form, a golem animated from within by supernatural power. Its face was an exaggerated rendering of its Ethiopian followers, a broad brow and nose, and wide lips that curled up in a menacing grin as soon as it caught sight of the men; a baleful flame of counterfeit life shone as a green glow in the hollows where its eyes ought to have been. Under its left arm, as easily as a child might hold a rag doll, it held the squirming, bleeding form of Barbazon. His face was torpid, red with blood and wet with tears and rain, and his eyes bulged as much from crying as from the sheer power of the grip of that awful creature.

The men stood fixed in place, half in disbelief of what their eyes were seeing – *wanting* not to believe – and half in resolute acceptance of the supernatural event unfolding before their eyes. The golem stared back, regarding them with glowing eyes that seethed palpable malevolence. Perhaps sensing him to be the most resolute of the men, it fixed its eyes upon Truxille, as if it wanted him, in particular, to watch what followed. With one hand, it extended the broken, bleeding body of Barbazon toward them.

"No," Truxille whispered, and shook his head. "No." With a demonic grimace and a low, guttural grunting that made a mockery of laughter, the golem tightened its grip on Barbazon and began to squeeze.

Barbazon's unearthly shrieks of pain filled the night, drowning out the golem's malicious laughter, and the grumblings of the storm. His bones popped, his skin ripped to shreds in the monster's stony clutches; blood shot forth from the tangled body and ran like red juice through the giant fingers of the thing. The ground where the golem stood was littered with pulverized organs and body parts; and Barbazon, in the awful circumstance of still being alive, bellowed woefully. His painful, otherworldly cries rose in an ever-more-chilling crescendo until finally, unable any longer to withstand the pressure of the creature's massive fist, his head exploded. A sound like a dropped melon, but many times magnified, reverberated through the little clearing; Barabzon's eyes burst from their orbits, his teeth and jaw bulged from his gaping mouth, and what remained of his brain oozed like bloody custard over the creature's hulking hand and spewed forth in a great arc toward the men.

They had all stood transfixed by terror, as if frozen in place by some awful, unuttered spell, holding their ears against the sound of Barbazon's piteous screams; and now, covered in the dead man's flesh and blood, they were confronted again with the golem's menacing stare. Its lips curled in a horrible grin, and the glow in its eyes was smoldering low, its anticipation growing with every passing second. The men knew upon instinct that it had every intention of dispatching them exactly as it had done poor Barbazon.

Truxille had watched the murder of Barbazon with a strange detachment, as that of someone who observes something from a great distance and without any hope of affecting the situation for good or ill. Now, with a frightening suddenness, he was back in the moment, and a heightened sense of awareness suddenly overcame him. He knew in an instant that to try to fight the creature would be folly, and there would be no shame in running away. He spun around wildly, looking in every direction; the shadow forms still surrounded them, though they had hung back while the great fiend was busy about the dispatch of Barbazon: the killing done, they now began to move.

"Maxim!" Dumiot cried. "MAXIM!"

"I know!" Truxille cried. Then, somewhere in his deep consciousness, he heard another voice speaking to him. Rasping, vaguely familiar; it was the voice of the old woman! And it barked at him with utter urgency: "Go, NOW!"

"This way!" he cried, and broke to the left of the clearing, plunging back into the wet, tangled swamp. The others leapt behind him, and as they disappeared into the trees, an angry, howling roar erupted from the golem. When the trees behind them began to rend and shudder, they knew the monster had taken up the pursuit.

Truxille squinted in the rainy darkness. He could see the bare outline of a path winding away ahead of him and he followed this, not even certain where it led or what his next move would be. Behind him ran Dumiot, Sósthene, and finally Borqa, struggling to keep up; but then, in another moment, horrible, wild cries let the others know the beast had caught up to the little Isleños man. They did not have time to react, and could only be glad of it, for Borqa's capture had delayed the thing's pursuit of them.

A brace of black-leafed castor trees now loomed up in the path ahead, and when Truxille looked, to his amazement, he saw the familiar shape of the old black woman standing in it. She held up a spindly arm and pointed – without a moment's hesitation, Truxille ran in that direction. After many minutes, confidence began to grow in the men that they had perhaps evaded the creature while it was occupied with killing Borqa; but with an awful suddenness it was there again, pounding along the path behind them. They could hear the roaring breath of the thing and feel the ground shaking with its heavy footfalls; now in the rear, Sósthene was clutching at the empty air and shrieking like a banshee as the golem swiftly closed the distance between. Then, when all hope seemed lost, a great clap of wind and lightning struck the trees immediately above them, and lit the branches with white flame. A rending, grating sound told them a tree limb had been hit and was falling away.

"Above you!" Truxille cried. "Look out!"

They ducked down and looked back in time to see fortune, fate, or the whim of God intervene for them: the broken branch flew down and, caught in the tangled web of a goat's tongue vine, became a natural battering-ram. Cast with almost perfect aim at the golem, it struck the thing with so much force that it sheared the creature's head right off its body. That head, its eyes still glowing with malevolence, flew over them where they cowered on the ground, and landed with a powerful thud, like a huge cannonball, in the center of the path ahead. Behind, the now-headless body of the golem fell to its knees, groping around, helpless and lost.

Truxille looked back at the head and was amazed yet again to see the fragile form of the old woman. She stood beside it, pointing down at the creature's mouth which had opened slightly when the head hit the ground. In another moment the woman was gone, as if she had vanished into thin air. Truxille was amazed, but with no time to wonder, he quickly got to his feet and called out for Dumiot; together they ran over to the decapitated head.

"Look!" Truxille cried, and there, sticking out of the golem's gaping lips, were bits of knotted rope. Something was in its mouth, and the old woman had meant for him to take it.

"Do not touch it!" Dumiot said, and pulled Truxille's hand away.

Behind them the scene had turned for the worse yet again. The body of the golem had righted itself and, guided by the eyes of its severed head, was hovering very near the spot where Sósthene now lay crying on the wet ground. Clustered in the path behind it, like a spindly black thicket swaying in the silvery shafts of rain, the shadow men were moving to the aid of their fallen champion.

"We must!" Truxille cried now, and he reached for the rope, pulling with all his might. The golem, suddenly aware of what was happening, clenched its mouth tighter; worse, the headless body had now abandoned Sósthene and was making its way toward its head!

"Here!" Dumiot cried. He fumbled in his pants pocket and pulled out a long jack-knife. "You pull, and I will push!"

Dumiot fixed the jack-knife blade and, kneeling down, shoved it between the great lips of the golem in an effort to pry them open. Truxille fixed a foot over the creature's eyes, hoping to hinder its sight; he pulled hard at the rope. The thing's face contorted with anger, and it was suddenly aware of what the men were trying to do. It grunted savagely, and seemed to be calling out urgently to its body – and its body heard. Truxille and Dumiot were suddenly aware of great steps pounding closer; and if they had not heard, the shrieking of Sósthene was more than enough to alert them. They fought with every bit of strength left in them; the mouth was relenting, but slowly. At last, a string of knots came free of the massive jaws; a bladder-like pouch was visible just inside.

"Push!" Truxille hissed through clenched teeth.

"Pull!" Dumiot grunted.

Truxille fell, sprawling backward onto the soaking ground with a look of surprise on his face. The grimacing mouth had suddenly loosened, and the rope and pouch were free! The golem's eyes glowed angrily, and for a moment flared with blinding brightness, casting all the surrounding swamp in a surreal green glow. A cry came up then and although the men knew it originated in the head, it seemed to them that it came from somewhere deep under the ground, as if the earth itself were groaning. The green light flashed one final time, and then winked out; the great head began to stiffen, its face fixed in a look of confounded, unrequited anger. The body of the golem, deprived of both the head and the mysterious pouch, was now nothing more than an inanimate object, an imposing headless statue glistening in the pelting rain.

Truxille and Dumiot sat breathing with exhaustion; Sósthene, still crying, crawled over to them. "Is it dead?" he wailed.

Truxille looked from the head to the body of the golem, and then down at the pouch in his hand. "I think so," he said, sighing heavily.

They passed a long moment in silence, listening to the steady rain and the wind whipping around them, rustling through the swamp. Or so it seemed. The men exchanged knowing glances. The wind still blew fiercely, but the low rustling took on the steady, measured pace of marching feet – perhaps hundreds of them, and all around! The shadowy figures of the golem's army were still moving out there; some had already reached the body of the fallen creature.

"We must go – NOW!" Truxille cried. Whether the shadows were men or not, Truxille knew that he and the others must move quickly if they were to make good their escape. "Back to the house!" he cried. "Run!"

Once again, the men were running for their lives: first Truxille, with Dumiot beside him, and both of them pulling the wavering, crying Sósthene. The trees around them began to grow sparse, no longer choking the narrow path; soon the roiling expanse of the cane fields and the house, more distant, came into view. But now a sudden roaring sound welled up all around them: angrier than the crashing thunder, more shuddering than a landslide, a sound like the howl of a fallen god roared in their ears. Truxille strained to get a glimpse behind him as he ran, and what he saw stopped him in his tracks. A look of awe and wonder came over him.

"Maxim!" Dumiot cried, grabbing at Truxille and pulling at him as Sósthene ran past them both.

"Look!" Truxille cried out, pointing upward.

Dumiot looked and from out of the overarching night sky a swirling tornado was reaching down. It spun like a mighty dervish, and wherever its tail touched there was a tremendous thrashing and a rending sound, as throughout the swamp ancient trees were churned out of their roots. Movement filled all the dark gaps between the trees as tangled roots and vines were braided by the tornado's searching fingers. Roiling, roaring, it bent down and, seemingly possessed of a sentient will, upon sight of the men it moved toward them.

"My God! Come on! We must get to the house!" Dumiot cried, and ran on.

Truxille moved to follow, but his legs felt leaden; suddenly, he was overcome by the same inexplicable feeling which he had felt just before he saw the old woman in the darkened house – a lifetime ago, it seemed. The hair on his neck and arms stood on end and he felt compelled to turn around; this he did, and what he saw amazed him.

Just inside the shuddering treeline, clustered in the path Truxille and the others had beaten down in their retreat, were the shadow men, the minions of the great golem. More amazing still, standing before them, blocking their path, Truxille was shocked to see the diminutive form of the old woman. He gasped in alarm, and might have moved to help her, but emotion went far from him in that moment and made of him a transfixed spectator to the unfolding scene. He saw the black shadows move eagerly forward, as the old woman lifted her arms up to the sky. She mouthed words that Truxille could not hear, but then, as if in answer, peals of thunder sounded from the very heart of the monstrous tornado. Lightning flashed and illuminated the vicious countenance of the clouds as the thing roiled forward. The old woman clapped her hands together over her white head and held them there: immediately the tornado swept down, chewing along the edge of the trees. At last, when it reached the spot where the shadowy soldiers of the dead golem were clustered, it bent low. In another instant it righted itself, and lifted again toward the sky: the shadowy shapes were gone, sucked out of the world of men.

Finally, the old woman turned, and facing Truxille – who still stood gaping and fixed in place – she smiled benignly. The trees still thrashed all around her, even as the tornado was moving away, and debris that, in his awe, Truxillo saw as suspended in the air, now rushed upon him. The sound of Dumiot's voice then intruded and caused him to look away. When he did so, he felt a terrible blow to the head; something pitched by the storm had struck him. He lay where he fell, sound and sight fading, and aware of the old woman now close nearby. She bent over him and in his swoon Truxille saw her face looming before him, large like the moon and lit by a strange white light that blinded but did not hurt to look into. She smiled, or so it seemed to him, and as she bowed lower her great moon-face appeared to move pendulously, to and fro, until finally it whirled out of sight. Everything went irresistibly black and Truxille let go as nothingness flowed in, and his consciousness winked out.

"He's coming around."

Truxille heard the soft voice of Dumiot fall into the fainting darkness that had engulfed him. That darkness was slowly retreating, fading to a luminescent grey which he perceived through tightly-shut eyes; then, sunlight. He found that he was laying on a long chaise lounge in the parlor of dead Barbazon's house. Sunlight streamed through the open windows, shooting into the room like spears; a hot, humid breeze tossed motes of dust in and out of the glare, and fluttered in the gauzy folds of the window curtains.

"Thank God!" The nervous pitch of Sósthene's voice jarred Truxille's throbbing brain.

"There you are!" Dumiot said with a heavy sigh. He smiled. "I don't hesitate to say, you've had us more than a little worried."

Truxille rubbed his eyes, and tried to sit up. Dumiot reached to help him. "Careful," he said. "That was quite a blow to your head, Maxim."

The pounding in his head compelled Truxille to agree: it must have been quite a blow. Slowly, the events of the night came back to him. He grasped Dumiot's arm. "Barbazon?" he said hoarsely. Dumiot shook his head.

"Then it is true," Truxille sighed.

"Yes," Dumiot replied. "I am afraid it is all true."

Just then, Sósthene, who had stepped out of the parlor, returned carrying a decanter of brandy and a glass. "I am of a mind to think," he said, as he poured out a good measure and handed the glass to Truxille, "that we have been the victims of an awful phantasm." The other men looked at him incredulously. "Well," he replied, "it has been known to happen, to individuals as well as to whole groups of people."

Truxille coughed at a swig of brandy. "What I saw happen to Barbazon was no phantasm or fevered delusion!" he said at last, and instinctively glanced down at his blood-stained clothing.

"Yes," Dumiot added thoughtfully, "there can be no doubt but that something extraordinary has occurred, some . . . *thing* reached into this world – maybe, indeed, a product of heathen magic – but something came alive and into our reality, bent on murder and destruction. And like it or not, we have had a very close call, a very close experience of something unexplainable and preternatural."

While Dumiot was speaking, the realization stole over Truxille that he still clutched in the fist of his hand the noisome bag that he had pulled from the golem's mouth; despite all that had happened, he never let it go. He held it up for the others to see. "*This* is no phantasm," he said.

Dumiot nodded that he agreed, and Sósthene's eyes widened. "What are you going to do with that?" he asked nervously, and perhaps a little eagerly.

"I will see it destroyed," Truxille replied flatly, eyes flashing with the terrible memory of the horror of the previous night. He stuffed the awful pouch deep into a pocket of his breeches. "But now, we are getting out of here!"

⚜⚜⚜⚜

The three men wasted no time in assembling their belongings in preparation of leaving. The young house boy who had fled in terror the night before was found and sent to the riverside docks to flag down, as Dumiot chided him, "the first thing floating in the direction of New Orleans."

Dumiot took it upon himself to check on the field workers; all had survived the storm intact, though their bare little cabins had been no match for the storm's ferocity. The overseer, Dumiot learned, had been killed when a huge oak tree was uprooted and crashed down into his cabin. When he heard this news, Dumiot went in search of Truxille and the two walked out to inspect the scene. Deep holes that looked like giant footprints surrounded the cabin and, rather than falling, the tree appeared up-ended, as if it had been pulled up at the roots and shoved, branches first, into the cabin. The men exchanged a knowing look.

"But there is something else strange," Dumiot added as they walked back toward the house. Truxille eyed him curiously. "Last night, while you suffered through the delirium, you kept insisting," Dumiot hesitated, then, "you kept imploring us to save the old woman, that she would be lost in the storm if we did not act. Did you," he went on, wavering a little, "actually *see her?*"

Truxille nodded. "Yes, and I am amazed she was out in such a storm. Didn't you see her?"

Dumiot shook his head. "No, and I'm afraid she is nowhere to be seen; I mean to say, that is, that there is no way you could have seen her either."

Truxille stopped walking and gazed at Dumiot. "My head is pounding, Alexis. Please speak in something other than riddles. Was she injured in the storm?"

"No, not that," the other replied.

"Well, what is it?" Truxille was confused.

"Maxim," Dumiot sighed. "She died three nights ago – by her own hand."

Truxille gave Dumiot a dark, disbelieving look. "That can't be," he said thoughtfully.

"It is true," Dumiot replied. There was a silence then, "She was buried that evening. I can show you – "

"No," Truxille said sharply, and took a few steps back toward the slave quarters. Then he stopped and put a hand on Dumiot's shoulder, and said, more kindly, "No. I have had enough. Leave this place to the slaves and their magic. I am ready to go!" He did not say that he thought the old woman would not want them lingering over her grave – a grave he could only believe she had abandoned, body and soul.

They found Sósthene sitting at a desk in Barbazon's study. He gave them a weary, sad look as they entered. "I have sent to town for the authorities, and have written all the necessary papers," he said solemnly. "Barbazon, Borqa – I account them lost to the storm – and the deaths of the old woman and the overseer . . . " He fell silent and looked away, downcast..

Within the hour, the sound of horses' hooves and the grate of wheels on gravel announced the arrival of the local authorities. Sósthene went out to meet the men, and was shortly joined by Truxille and Dumiot who were bringing out the last of their luggage.

"Looks like ya'll got it a lot worse than we did up in Bizot," said a short, chubby man who then introduced himself as the overseer from a neighboring farm. "This here is the sheriff," he added as a thick, dour-looking man stepped up beside him.

"Yes," Dumiot said in a perfunctory manner that belied his own thoughts at the recollection of the previous night's horror. "It was very bad here."

Sósthene led the two men inside where he provided them with the paperwork and certificates that he had earlier prepared. Truxille and Dumiot sat together on the porch steps, squinting at the sun and talking very little until at last Sósthene and the others emerged from the house.

"We'll move 'em all over to Montego Bend," said the overseer, referring to Barbazon's numerous slaves. "They got a doctor there can look 'em over and keep 'em 'til Miz Barbazon gets back down here from Cuba. This will go hard on her," he added, and shook his head. The sheriff broke away to begin securing the property.

Dumiot drew in a little breath. "I had not even thought of that," he said. "How awful for her," he added thoughtfully, looking down at his feet.

"Yes, regrettable," Truxille echoed the sentiment.

Sósthene had a pained look and was sifting his rattled brain for something to say when they all suddenly caught sight of the house boy running up the shell road toward them.

"Dey's here, boss!" he cried, panting as he ran up to the porch. "Dey's gwon't takes yo's back to N'awlins, but yo's gots to come right now!"

The overseer gave them a startled look. "New Orleans?" he said inquisitively. "Surely ya'll don't mean to go up there now? I mean, the fever's still running there, or so I heard."

Truxille gave him a miserable look and said flatly, "We will take our chances."

✽✽✽✽

The three physicians, with their luggage, arrived at the riverside to see a long, wide produce barge tethered to the dock. Truxille negotiated briefly with the Spanish captain who agreed to take them aboard; for the price of a few American coins, they would be dropped as near as possible to the Picayune Pier. The arrangements made and agreed upon, Truxille and the others were soon settling in among stacks of bananas and piles of Spanish limes.

The heat was fierce and the men languished with the spare shade provided by a few dried palmetto leaves found on the deck of the barge. The going was slow at first.· The river was littered with the debris of the woods and swamps, and noisome with the run-off from farms and pasturelands along its banks. But before long the barge joined a swiftly flowing current and was traveling at a good speed. When they had passed the better part of an hour without much speaking, each man lost in his own thoughts, it was Sósthene who finally broke the silence.

"Maxim," he said, and Truxille squinted over at him, shielding his eyes from the blistering glare of the sun on the water. "Have you looked inside that bag you took from the mouth . . . from its mouth?"

"Ah! No, I have not" Truxille replied, and now reminded of it he reached into his breeches pocket and pulled out the knotted pouch.

They each examined it in turn: it was leathery, like the tanned bladder of a small animal, and was bound with knots that were quite clearly animal intestines – on the whole it put them in mind of innards taken from a cat. It was next opened and the contents scrutinized: a mass of common roots and mosses, some herbs and seeds, noxious-looking powders, something that looked like lard or animal fat, and in the midst of it all a tiny roll of what appeared to be parchment. Truxille picked this free of the other materials and studied it, and was then disgusted when he realized what he took for parchment was actually a piece of dried skin – skin of what, he did not wish to ponder. With the greatest of care, he unrolled the abominable little scroll. He frowned.

"What is it?" Sósthene asked eagerly.

"Yes," said Dumiot, "what does it say?"

Truxille displayed the skin. There, written in an ink that looked disturbingly like blood, were two Hebrew letters. Dumiot and Sósthene looked puzzled.

"What does it mean?" Dumiot asked, as Truxille put everything back into the pouch and tied it tightly.

"It is Hebrew," Truxille replied. He shook his head and hefted the little pouch in his hand; with a quick jerk, he threw the whole thing over the side of the barge.

"No!" Sósthene gasped, but reached for the bag too late. The others looked at him curiously. "I should like to have had a better look at the contents," he said meekly.

Truxille shook his head. "It is better left alone, my friend," he said, patting Sósthene on the shoulder. "Trust me." He did not tell them what the letters symbolized, that written in blood upon the scroll were the Hebrew symbols for "chaos" and "harvest."

⚜⚜⚜⚜

The men talked only occasionally and mostly dozed as the barge made its way steadily up the Mississippi to New Orleans. A crewman roused them when, in the early evening, they came within sight of the battures and the little makeshift settlements that lined the river just below the city. The docks and the great sugar and cotton houses of the riverfront grew steadily in their view, and as the barge maneuvered through the growing press of downriver traffic, the Place d'Armes and the markets of the Rue du Quay were clearly visible. The men's spirits lifted in pace with their approach to New Orleans; they gathered their belongings and anxiously prepared to debark.

"I think I have never been so glad to see the old Carré!" Truxille said as he pulled a bottle of Florida water cologne from his grip. He dampened his handkerchief, and those of Dumiot and Sósthene in turn; these they tied over their faces, covering their noses and mouths. Every man on board had done the same, for although the fever was now abating and people were returning to the city, there was still a danger of infection from the necessary press and commerce of the populace.

Dumiot nodded. "I agree," he said, his voice muffled. "But Maxim, you must come to see me soon. It is not every day a man can say he has walked in the preternatural world and returned! We must record every detail of these fantastic events! And you, as well, Sósthene," he called over his shoulder.

"Indeed!" Sósthene replied, fumbling with his kerchief. "You may rely upon it!"

Truxille was silent; a brooding shadow clouded his eyes. He shook his head. "I am sorry, Alexis," he said quietly. "I cannot oblige you."

"But – ?" Dumiot sputtered.

Truxille shook his head emphatically. "I do not ever want to relive these past several hours, nor indeed, any of this past week. I want," he said, looking away, "I want to forget every scrap of it!" Dumiot nodded and put a hand on Truxille's shoulder, squeezing slightly to show he understood. No words were necessary between them.

"Well, I shall come," Sósthene said as he watched Truxille and Dumiot scramble up onto the pier.

Dumiot shrugged. "Very well," he said. "Let us plan to meet in a week."

Truxille and Dumiot now cast weary glances down at Sósthene's copious baggage which the bargemen were slowly offloading. Truxille shook his head.

"Do you need help?" Dumiot asked, half-heartedly.

"No, of course," Sósthene replied. "Do not trouble yourself! I will arrange a dray."

"Ah! Farewell, then!" Dumiot said quickly, more than a little relieved. "I will send a post to confirm our meeting!" He waved over his shoulder as he and Truxille hurried away, and were soon lost from view in the press of activity in the market and along the piers.

Sósthene waved after them and returned to gathering up his bags. He made his way gingerly along the deck of the barge, then suddenly he stopped – something caught his eye. He had to crawl over a pile of limes to get to it, but when he reached down he brought up, to his surprise, the golem's pouch which Truxille had cast away: it had fallen short of the river, and had lodged in a narrow crevasse among the fruit. Sósthene's heart was pounding and he clutched the greasy pouch with a grip of iron as he carefully climbed off the barge. At the street, he secured a dray and a driver willing to take him with all his baggage.

"You will take me to the Rue l'Amour," he said to the swarthy Creole driver as he settled among his luggage in the bed of the cart. "I will tell you where to go from there."

Sósthene looked about warily as they got underway. When he was certain he could not be observed, he reached down and unbuckled a plain leather valise that he had secured between his feet. In it were some of the strangest specimens he had collected during the Plaquemines expedition, the ones he must handle with the greatest care. He tucked the little pouch deep inside among the jars of swamp water, flora, and insects, taking extra care to keep it separated from his most prized specimen, a thing he had thought to take only as a souvenir of his trip, but which had now taken on new significance: a small, crudely made, mud statue that he had found half-buried among the roots of a cypress tree. He closed the valise securely and clutched it tightly on his lap. The cart lurched away into the hinterlands of the old Carré.

The Ghoul

The idea that the dead could return to the living was commonplace among late medieval and Renaissance Europeans, and there are a surprising number of historical references about wandering corpses engaging with those left behind. The physical resurrection of the holy dead, body and soul reunited at an end of time that was always about to occur, was central to the Christian faith as the resultant inheritance of Christ's own death and resurrection. This faith informed both the core beliefs and the folklore of the peoples of Europe; where God could affect a holy resurrection, the Devil might produce the "unnatural marvels" of unholy resurrection in an attempt to mimic the Almighty and undermine the natural order of things.

It was also widely believed that the spirits of men and women, and frequently children, returned all the time, and were allowed or compelled to do so by a need to communicate something important to the living. Often the dead brought information that was of benefit to survivors, such as the location of wills or lost treasure; other times the dead might return to shame or avenge themselves upon those who might have wronged them in life.

The Church encouraged the saying of masses for all the dead, and taught that "good works" ought to be performed in the names of those who had preceded the faithful in death. More prosaically, the Church also taught that any unsettled grievances between the living and the dead should be remunerated through the confession and penance of the living, so as to ensure the dead stayed dead, and had no compelling reason to return or seek vengeance.

The physical return of the dead was consistently reported throughout the late Middle Ages and the Renaissance, and it continued to puzzle the reasonable and scientific minds of the seventeenth and eighteenth centuries, none of whom could conclusively prove the existence or non-existence of the revenants of popular belief. This history would have informed the beliefs, folklore, and superstitions of the Europeans who were the first settlers of early New Orleans.

Mariquita

"When my body dies,
Then let my soul behold,
The sight of your first-born."

The Stabat Mater Speciosa (15th Century)

Laron, a portly, unkempt Frenchman, stuck his head in at the door of the blacksmith shop and smiled at the sight that met his eyes.

"Hey, Rodrigo!" he called out to the man occupied with shoeing a horse. "Every time I look for you, I find you bent under a horse's ass!"

Rodrigo righted himself and peered at Laron through the pungent smoke wafting up from the horse's hot shoes. "That is better than being a horse's ass, like you," he replied flatly and with a straight face.

Laron made a face. "So funny – a king somewhere is missing a jester," he said, and smiled. "Come on! Come and have your lunch!"

"Alright," Rodrigo chuckled, wiping the sweat from his forehead with his apron. He threw aside his tools and, signaling to a stable boy to lead the horse away, bent low over nearby a wash basin from which he splashed his face and arms. Stepping out into the work yard, he caught sight of Laron busily setting up lunch in the shade of a spreading yaupon tree; he held out a cup of wine as Rodrigo approached. The board was simple fare – olives and pickled onions, cold chicken, cheese, and coarse bread – with fat, red strawberries for dessert and good, purple port to wash it all down. Weary from a working day that at noon was already nearly nine hours long, Rodrigo gratefully accepted the cup from Laron; he cast his large frame to the ground and settled his back against the tree, sighing as he drained the cup dry.

It was a fine April day in New Orleans, and although the sun was already nearly as hot as any day in June, the air was still refreshing under the little tree. Rodrigo and Laron ate in silence, for the most part, enjoying the respite from the hot and dusty confines of the blacksmith shop, and thinking, each in turn, about the remainder of the work left in the day. Rodrigo leaned back and had just closed his eyes when he heard Laron snort.

"Humpf!" the Frenchman grunted through a mouth full of food. "Here come the peacocks!"

Rodrigo opened his eyes just in time to see the small troop of Spanish soldiers as it turned out of the Calle de Santa Ana. Some went on foot, others mounted, and as these latter broke away toward the stables on the Calle de San Felipe, Rodrigo could see the glint of the sun on their high hats and gorgets. He sighed. The return of the Spaniards from the parade grounds of the Plaza de Armas always portended more work.

"And here come the pea hens!" Laron chuckled.

Clusters of Creole beauties that had followed the garrison were breaking into lines along the Calle de Borbón, jostling for better views of the higher-ranking soldiers atop their robust Spanish steeds. Rodrigo sat up, and strained in spite of himself to get a better view. A blue parasol suddenly came into sight, and Rodrigo felt his heart jump as he watched it bob up and down amidst the crowd. Under that parasol, he knew, was the loveliest of all the Creole belles – the dark, mysterious Mariquita. Tall and shapely, with skin the color of new honey, it was said that one look from Mariquita's coal black eyes could melt the heart of any man, whether green youth or whiskered father. Rodrigo had fallen under that gaze only once and from that moment he, too, became one of the envied and pitied whom Laron laughingly called "ceux perdus dans la joie," *"those who are lost in joy."*

They both watched her now, moving through the press of people, her rosy cheeks and delicate nose shaded coyly behind the lattice of her fan, her luxurious black hair glistening through the fine lace of her Spanish mantilla. Here and there she encountered someone whom she recognized and then the fan would lower, and her garnet-colored lips would part in a smile so luminous it seemed to dim the sunlight; and slowly, surely she was making her way up the Calle de Borbón toward the blacksmith shop and the yards of the Spanish meadow.

"My friend," Laron said quietly, addressing Rodrigo, "you should tell her how you feel in your heart." He had watched Rodrigo watching Mariquita on more than one occasion, and indeed had been present on the day the young blacksmith had fallen into her gaze.

Rodrigo's eyes fluttered as if waking from a pleasant dream; he looked downcast. "No," he said quietly. "I couldn't . . ." His voice drifted away to join the part of his heart that was still dreaming.

Laron considered this; he shrugged. "Why not?" he said, stating a point he thought was obvious. "You are a fine man – young, handsome: you could match any suitor!"

In fact, Rodrigo was very handsome – tall, broad-shouldered and muscular, with the dark eyes and hair, and golden skin of his Spanish heritage: he was rugged and young, and might have had any woman he wanted, if Mariquita had not already taken command of his heart. But Laron did not go much out of his way to encourage Rodrigo, because a part of him suspected that Mariquita had stolen more than her share of hearts in her young life and had cast them aside, empty shells. He did not want Rodrigo to be one of those. Nor was it likely, he thought, that she would give even a second look to his stoic young friend; just as it was clear that in every aspect she had won Rodrigo over, so Laron could also clearly see that Mariquita had already cast her eyes and her heart elsewhere. And maybe this time it was she who would lose, he thought; the evidence was now before him.

Paulo was a fine, though vain young soldier who cut a handsome figure in his fancy dress uniform and riding atop his magnificent horse. He always distinguished himself in the trooping and marching that occupied the Spanish garrison at least two or three times a month in the parade grounds of the Plaza de Armas. This day was no different, and Laron watched as Paulo urged his horse to trot out in front of the rest of the cavalry, the better for the swooning women to see him. Then, he checked the horse's gait and slowed as he passed Mariquita; he acknowledged her with a slight nod and she, trying to be demure, fluttered her fan across her face, though behind it her cheeks went crimson. Laron glanced over at Rodrigo who was casting crumbs to a few tiny sparrows and so did not see what had just transpired; Laron was glad for this, because, though not exactly friends, Rodrigo and Paulo recognized a casual rapport.

The stables that fronted the Calle de San Felipe adjacent to the blacksmith shop had been designated by the Spanish for the keeping of their horses, and all the open fields lining the Calle de la Delfina were where the horses grazed; the men of the garrison were housed nearby at the barracks in the Calle del Arsenal. The area had exploded into activity as soon as the soldiers had reached the Calle de Borbón; stable boys were running to and fro, unsaddling the horses and moving them into their stalls, while military attendants checked the general welfare of the animals. It was rare for a shoe not to be loose or to need some attention after traveling over the unreliable city streets. Rodrigo stood up and stretched.

"Back to work," he said, and sighed.

As he crossed the porte-cochere to the shop door, Rodrigo just caught sight of Mariquita in her beautiful blue dress, under her blue parasol, walking away toward the Calle Reál and closely followed by her mulatto maid. So it was that he did not see Paulo coming up behind him, but heard him instead.

"There you are!" Paulo called, removing his gloves and extending a hand as he approached Rodrigo.

"So I am," Rodrigo replied, taking Paulo's hand firmly in greeting.

Paulo smiled, hesitated, and kicked at the dusty ground. "I was wondering – " he started, feebly.

Rodrigo laughed in spite of himself. "Oh, not again, surely?" he said, and here the basis of their friendly rapport was recalled: Paulo's penchant for the ladies frequently depended upon Rodrigo's discretion, and also upon his keys to the stables. "Who is it this time?" Rodrigo chuckled.

"Ah, ah, ah!" Paulo replied, playfully wagging a finger at Rodrigo. "It is something best left to cupid and his playmates . . ."

Rodrigo smirked, and pulled a set of keys off a knob by the door. He pitched them to Paulo. "Just put them back when you are done," he said. He didn't approve of Paulo's illicit liaisons, most especially because he knew the man had a wife in Cuba, but having once agreed to the accommodation, felt he could not easily refuse.

"You know you may rely on it," Paulo replied brightly, throwing the keys into the air and catching them again. "But I must go, or I shall be missed!" And thus saying, he ran off swiftly in the direction of the barracks.

Rodrigo worked until the last light of the setting sun finally faded; the shadows of gloaming were lengthening in the yards when he shut the shop door. The April evening was cool and freshened by the scent of a nearby honeysuckle vine in its first bloom of spring. The little house on the corner of the Calle de

Borbón was already lit by the amber glow of hearth and lamp; the light wavered at the dusty doors and windows, and cast itself like will-o-the-wisps onto the ground outside. Night was settling over New Orleans and everything was quiet and calm. All the noise of the day had faded and only the occasional movements of the horses in their stalls broke the pervading stillness.

Rodrigo and Laron both kept rooms in the second story of the little house, but tonight as he entered, Rodrigo found Laron deeply-involved in a card game with several friends, other Frenchmen who often visited and stayed well into the night. Rodrigo served himself a plate of stew from the hearth – "Do not worry, it is something French!" Laron had said in his offhand way – and grabbing a half-empty jug of port wine, made his way up to his room.

Sometime later, the card playing in the kitchen gave way to a dice game in the small courtyard beside the house, and as Laron and his French compatriots played on, the new wine was spent and the old rum tapped until finally Laron could hold no more.

"Je dois pissér!" he announced to all within earshot. "And don't touch my dice! Especially you, Pierre! You think I don't know when you touch my dice, but I am smart! Oui! Laron is smart!" He mumbled this and many other things as he staggered out of the courtyard in search of the privy.

"Oui, Laron is smart!" the gamblers laughed behind him and the man named Pierre exchanged Laron's dice with a weighted set of his own.

Minutes later Laron emerged from the privy feeling much lighter and slightly less inebriated. He had just crossed the yard and was nearly to the courtyard gate, when movement near the stables caught his eye. He stopped, swaying a little bit so that he had to put his arm on the gatepost to steady himself; nonetheless, he had an excellent view of the stables and his sight was clear, so he was certain of what he saw.

A small door set within the larger stable gate slowly creaked open and Paulo the Spaniard stepped through. Realizing that he had caught Paulo in one of his infamous liaisons, Laron hung back in the shadows to see what more might be seen, and also if what was seen might be worth gossiping about in the morning. But Laron's levity was quickly replaced with feelings of shock and disappointment as Paulo's companion came into view: the woman was none other than the beautiful Mariquita!

"Mon Dieu!" Laron whispered, and instinctively put his hand to his mouth to stifle his exclamation. He watched as Paulo began to kiss Mariquita, first on her hands, then on her neck, and finally, luxuriously, on her lips. He saw Mariquita turn away reluctantly and dash toward the outside gate; Paulo replaced Rodrigo's keys on their peg inside the smithy door, and then he, too, disappeared into the night. All of this dismayed Laron, and he hesitated, thinking in his slow pate what he should do, and whether or not he should tell Rodrigo.

"Rodrigo!" he thought, and instinctively looked up toward the little windows in the second story of the house. His heart fell. There, leaning against the window frame with his head buried in the crook of his arm, was Rodrigo: he had seen everything.

So it was a sober Laron who went up to his room that night, and who reached for but did not grasp the handle of Rodrigo's closed door. When Laron came down to breakfast, he heard Rodrigo already busy in the smithy; when he looked in at the shop door, he saw Rodrigo hammering at a piece of metal that glowed and sparked upon the anvil. At lunch, Rodrigo was no more or less impassive than usual, though Laron, harboring his secret knowledge, felt as if a gulf had suddenly opened up between them; if Rodrigo found Laron's silence unusual, he did not acknowledge it. When it was night, again Rodrigo took his meal and his portion of wine and retired to his room; and Paulo returned to welcome Mariquita into the rustic bower that Rodrigo was now knowingly providing for them. And thus the days went on, and the nights passed; and summer grew, with the heat of the days lingering until well after the sun had set: the upstairs rooms of the little blacksmiths' house grew humid and close, but Rodrigo's window was never opened.

Mariquita lived her days in a kind of ephemeral haze and a feeling that her life only had clarity at night, during the precious stolen moments she spent with Paulo. This was love, surely; and surely, Paulo felt the same: he told her as much when she lay in his arms and he treated her as if she were already his wife. She was a dutiful lover who rarely missed one of these passionate assignations, and she was never late. Though she wondered why her liaisons with her companion had need of such complete secrecy, she simply accepted Paulo's flattering explanations that he did not wish to share her with another soul, and that he could not trust himself around her: did she want him to display such intimacies for all to see? Mariquita's young, loving heart believed all this, though had she been completely honest with herself she might have admitted to a hint of misgiving. She allowed herself to rationalize that, despite the urgent physical intimacy, courtships did take time to develop; and at any rate she had not even considered how she might introduce Paulo to her father, a man for whom Mariquita was the whole world, most especially since the death of her mother. Only one other person knew of Mariquita's clandestine affair, or so she believed, and this was her faithful maid; confidante and alibi, she accompanied Mariquita to each rendezvous and waited patiently nearby so that when the trysting was done, Mariquita would not have to travel home alone.

In early May, just at summer's real onset, Mariquita found herself with child, and this greatly increased her joy and multiplied her love for Paulo. She was certain that upon hearing the happy news, Paulo would bring their love out of the shadows and declare it openly, the first step to making her his wife. So, on a warm evening, one deeply-fragrant with the heady perfume of the night flowers bursting forth in every garden of the old Carré, Mariquita revealed her secret to Paulo as they lay together in the sweet hay.

He looked at her and smiled. "Now, why are you playing with me like that?" he chuckled, though his mind immediately began to churn Mariquita's words around like grist on a wheel.

"But I am not," she said, snuggling into his neck and kissing it. "I am past my time, and I have never before been: I know that we have not come about it in exactly the right way, but that will all be settled once we are married."

Paulo peeled her arms from around him and sat straight up. "Married?" he scoffed, glaring down at her where she lay beside him. "Stupid girl! How could you have let such a thing happen?"

Stricken and confused, Mariquita heard Paulo's angry protestations as someone would who, having fallen down a deep well with no hope of escape, might hear the sounds of life echoing down from the light-filled world above. "But, I thought you would be happy! I mean, I - "

"Happy?" Paulo laughed bitterly, reaching for his clothes. Mariquita grabbed at his arms, trying to pull him toward her, but Paulo fought against her. When she persisted, he turned around and, grabbing her shoulders, shook her violently. "Your kind is never satisfied!" he growled. "You have to ruin everything! And then, after giving yourself up, you want to rob a man of what little freedom he has left – as if that were worth the price!"

His rebuke stung Mariquita bitterly. Tears welled in her eyes and she watched, transfixed and distraught, as Paulo hurriedly pulled on his clothes. "But, I love you," she cried. "All this time – I thought . . ."

"I don't care!" Paulo bit back. "I don't give a damn what you think or what you feel! That baby – get rid of it! Or have it if you will, it makes no difference to me! You will not ruin me with your little bastard!"

Mariquita flinched as if Paulo's words were heavy blows. She wept fully now, and tried to catch her breath but it would only come in great, empty gasps. The reality of her predicament suddenly became clear: *she* would be the ruined one! "But you must, Paulo," she begged desperately, her voice breaking higher now. She grabbed for him wildly, but again he cast her off. "You must! This is your child! You must marry me, or – "

Paulo laughed caustically, and now fully dressed, he stood up, prepared to leave. But he could not resist throwing one more insult at her, and this last was the most bitter of all: "Marry *you*?" he said incredulously. "Why would I want your bastard when I have children of my own? And I cannot marry you: *I already have a wife!*"

Mariquita felt all the blood drain from her face, felt her heart beating wildly against her heaving chest; though she wanted to reply, the words were entwining themselves into the knot that was tightening in her throat. She watched, helpless and mute, as Paulo turned his back on her and bolted from the stables, leaving her there naked and in shock. Wracked with a real, physical pain the likes of which she had never known before, it took every bit of Mariquita's failing strength to get dressed and to walk the short block to the corner of the Calle Reál where her faithful maid waited. She fell into the woman's arms, and as the shock of the episode finally washed over her, clutched the poor woman with desperate strength, as if to let her go meant that she might evaporate or be sucked away into the pitch blackness of the night. She wanted to howl, like a wild, wounded thing. But as the two walked along together, and despite the pleas of her maid, Mariquita did not speak, nor did she weep any longer; a strange, brooding reticence stole over her and settled inside her, an interloper bent upon killing her spirit and usurping her soul. And in due time, its voice would be the only one Mariquita would ever speak with, and the only one she would ever truly heed.

Early in the morning of the next day Paulo sent a messenger to the blacksmith shop to return the stable keys that, in his rush to get away from Mariquita, he had forgotten to replace. He also included a note containing a few taut words thanking Rodrigo for his "friendship and indulgence," and announcing an impending transfer to the colonial seat at Havana, Cuba. Because he wanted to get away quickly, Paulo found it necessary to share with his commander the circumstances of his failed love affair: fortunately for Paulo, his commander was also a friend and it was he who proffered the solution of a transfer. Although the cost to Paulo was his commander's friendly but firm reproach, he sheepishly took it in order to get the wheels turning away from New Orleans – and from Mariquita – forever.

In a shuttered room of her home in the Calle de San Luis, Mariquita languished in a state of nervous prostration; she refused all food and drink, and would not speak but only stared blankly and clutched the hand of her ever-present maid. But when in the afternoon the physician summoned by her despondent father arrived, the maid stole away: unknown to any but her mistress, she had been sent on a desperate mission, carrying a pitiful plea from Mariquita to the man who had abandoned her. When he was informed that the maid awaited him at the barracks gates, Paulo sent no reply, and the maid was summarily ordered away by the gate guards. Undeterred, and knowing the sanity and health of her mistress depended upon it, the maid returned to keep her pitiful vigil at the same time each day. Finally, when a little more than a week had passed, the maid was informed that Paulo had taken orders away from New Orleans, and that she should come no more to the barracks gate unless she wanted to be arrested and thrown in the calaboose. Distraught and unsure of what to do, and certainly fearful of how her mistress would react to news of Paulo's departure, the maid decided to say nothing. She left the house at the same time each day, and returned to say that Paulo would send no reply; secretly she wondered how long she could go on deceiving her mistress with such a ruse.

But time was not on Mariquita's side, and before long the regular visits of the family physician uncovered the indignity of her true condition. The news sent her father into a rage, and surmising correctly that Mariquita's maid had played no small part in facilitating his daughter's licentiousness, he sent the poor woman to the auction block. Knowing, obviously, that he could not do the same with his daughter, he nonetheless told her in no uncertain terms that he wished he could so that he might receive at least some compensation for a lifetime of loving care. And with the firm rebuke that if she wanted to live her life in the streets he would in no wise prevent it, he promptly disowned Mariquita and threw her out; within days he had closed up his house and retired in despair to his small plantation upriver.

Heedless of her reputation and disregarding her lover's warning, Mariquita went to the barracks in the Calle del Arsenal, sobbing and calling for Paulo to come out to her. No longer insulated by the discretion of her maid, Mariquita now heard first-hand the news that her lover had been transferred away from New Orleans – and from her – forever. This was more than her beleaguered mind could take: Mariquita went completely insane.

What a sad sight it was over the summer months to see the once-enthralling beauty brought so low. She wandered the streets in the black taffeta gown she had been wearing the night her father put her out; soon it became ragged and torn and stretched obscenely as her belly expanded. Her beautiful long hair hung in a matted mass that looked like a perpetual black cloud around her head; her ever-present lace mantilla draped over the tangles as a sad memoir of her former state. Often she would cover her face with the veil, and this frightened children and passersby who took to calling her the Black Lady. If anyone approached her, she would mutter in gibberish and make the sign of the cross in the air, calling herself the Pope. Her feet were bare – her fine satin shoes traded for little more than a picayune's worth of bread and half-gill of milk – and she took to chasing vendors in the street; mostly out of fear, but also in pity, they would give her an apple or a praline in hopes she would leave them alone. Often long after the curfew had sounded, Mariquita would wander in the streets, humming and waltzing to a tune only she could hear, or singing at the top of her lungs. Complaints from residents would bring out military guards and the scene was always the same, with Mariquita kicking and screaming wildly as they dragged her away to spend a night in the calaboose; not surprisingly, the sight of a military uniform always disturbed her. Sometimes she would just sit beside the ditches near the barracks or in front of her former home, and sob pitifully for hours at a time; often she would stand across from the Spanish stables and stare fixedly as if trying to recall the significance of the place.

All this and more Laron observed and brought back to Rodrigo, alternately in appeals and admonishments: but Rodrigo was unmoved. From the first night he had seen her with Paulo, he had worked hard at putting Mariquita out of his mind; that she had stooped to Paulo's level had greatly disappointed him, and had changed how he viewed her, forever. It was not he who laid her upon her back, he said in reply to Laron's entreaties; she had done that of her own free will.

Throughout the summer and early autumn, Rodrigo's heart remained hard as stone. Laron tried to understand, and by this time had ceased altogether to gossip about Mariquita or to advocate for rendering her aid. But as the bright, temperate days of October gave way to the rains and creeping chills of late November, something in Rodrigo at last relented; on a night of fog and misting rain, he roused Laron from a sound sleep.

"Merde!" Laron barked. "For God's sake, Rodrigo – disturbing a man at sleep!"

"Get dressed," Rodrigo replied. "It is too cold tonight for her to be sleeping outside."

"Her?" Laron wondered aloud and righted himself in bed. "'Her' who?" Grumpily, he pulled on his pants and stuffed his feet into his boots. "What are you talking about?"

"Mariquita," Rodrigo said flatly.

"Ohhh!" Laron moaned, wiping his sleepy eyes and scratching through his hair. "And you choose to do this now?"

But Rodrigo was already downstairs, lighting fat candles in the bellies of two iron lanterns; one of these he thrust into Laron's hand as he came into the room. They passed silently out of the house and into the damp, darkened streets of the old quarter. For what seemed like hours they searched up and down in all the places Laron could recall having seen Mariquita, but found only a few drunks and mongrel dogs. Around midnight they gave up looking and were heading back along the Calle de Chartres when they came upon the object of their search, wet and shivering, and sheltering in the doorway of a shuttered business. She fought them, as they expected, and it was only with tremendous difficulty – and more than a little force – that they were able to coax her into going with them. Perhaps it was that she had become so used to being dragged away to the calaboose that she knew when to stop fighting, or maybe she understood that shelter on a chill night was better than sleeping on a stone step, but by the time they neared the blacksmith shop, Mariquita had become quite calm.

A single horse stall opened into the shop and had a protected corner that was always warm with the heat of the forge fire. Laron led Mariquita to this stall and spread out fresh hay as Rodrigo rifled through the main stables for spare blankets and wraps. Even in her maddened state – she repeatedly "blessed" the men with dramatic gesticulations of crosses in the air around them – Mariquita was aware that her immediate situation had much improved. She no longer resisted and did not try to run, but settled into the warm corner like a bird in a nest. When Rodrigo returned with the blankets, Mariquita ran her hand over each of them, feeling the weave, and chose the softest one to wrap around herself.

When Laron went into the house to get food and drink, Rodrigo realized it was the first time he had ever been alone with Mariquita. He quickly recalled all the times he had watched her, in the days before Paulo, and how he had crafted in his mind careful phrases that he might say if he were ever so fortunate as to spend time with her. The memories of those sweeter days and of the caring words that Mariquita might hear, but could now never understand, made him terribly sad. Now she only watched him warily, peering with dark, vacant eyes through the fingers of her hands stretched over her face – as if doing so made her invisible to the man she knew only as a stranger.

Laron returned with buttered bread and warm milk; he set these within Mariquita's reach and backed away slowly. He turned to Rodrigo. "We have done much for her, even this little bit," he said quietly. "But I think there is nothing else to be done, not tonight at least. If she stays, or goes," he added with a shrug of his shoulders, "at least we did the charitable thing."

Rodrigo nodded gravely as together the two men stole quietly out of the warm little shop, and closed, but did not lock, the door behind them. Neither wanted Mariquita to face a locked door; if she wanted to leave, even if it was not the best thing, they did not want to impede her, and thereby lose her trust. Weary from the long night, both men were eager to get to their own beds, and sleep was not long in coming to them. Whatever the dawn might bring, they both chose to leave it up to fate.

In the morning, Mariquita was nowhere to be found, and although they expected this might happen, both Rodrigo and Laron could not help but feel disappointed. Then at sunset, just as he was closing the shop, Rodrigo heard a banging sound and, turning around, saw Mariquita crawling into the corner of the stall; the sound had been the slamming of the forge's coal shoot door. This pattern was repeated over the next several nights, and even though she did not interact with them, it was obvious to the men that Mariquita had come to trust them. Now was the time, Rodrigo thought, to teach her to trust someone else.

❧❧❧❧

"Ay! Holy Mother!" Francita said when she saw Mariquita crouching in the blacksmith's stable.

Rodrigo had called upon his sister where she worked in the kitchens of a boulangerie in the Calle de Chartres. In addition to baking wonderful breads and pastries, Francita was also a respected midwife. But, confronted with Mariquita, she could only exclaim and cross herself. She turned to Rodrigo.

"What do you mean, bringing her here?" she scolded him in a whisper. "You shame yourself! Everyone knows she is crazy and her father put her out for a whore!"

"Don't say that," Rodrigo replied. "Please. I was hoping you might be able to tell the condition of the child, or how long before it's due."

Francita's eyes widened; she looked back and forth between the black mass that was Mariquita and her brother's plaintive face. "Dios Santo!" she sighed, and crossed herself again. She shook her head at Rodrigo and took a few faltering steps forward.

"Don't be afraid," Rodrigo said. "She won't harm you."

Francita rolled her eyes at him; she wasn't so sure. "Querida niña," she said softly, now addressing Mariquita. "Dear girl," she repeated, "I am here to help you, if you let me."

Mariquita stared blankly at Francita, her eyes so wide and dark they seemed fully opaque; it was unnerving, but Francita gently persisted, moving closer as she spoke.

"Yes, it will be alright," she cooed. "I hope you will let me help you, Mariquita?"

Mariquita stirred at the sound of her name, spoken, perhaps, for the first time in many long months. Francita was now quite close and she knelt down slowly, putting her face even with Mariquita's. Trying to shore up her faltering nerves, Francita crossed herself once more: to her amazement, Mariquita did the same. A tear leapt into Francita's eye.

"It is alright," she said over her shoulder to Rodrigo. "Leave us. Everything will be fine."

Rodrigo stepped out into the stable yard where he was joined by Laron. A short time later, Francita emerged from the shop and gently shut the door behind her. She stepped over to where the two men were waiting.

"Well?" Rodrigo said.

Francita pulled her shawl up around her shoulders and sighed heavily. "Ay, Rodrigo! So sad!" she said. "I am amazed, but she appears to be in good health."

"And the baby?" Rodrigo asked now.

Francita gave him a narrow look. "Just whose baby is that?"

Rodrigo looked astonished, and Laron laughed out loud. "It is not mine!" Rodrigo chuckled. "I swear it!" Francita was much older than Rodrigo and had been as a mother to him since their own mother had died of cholera long years before; she was very protective.

"Well, I'm sure you did not bring me here at this hour to joke!" she scoffed. "Anyway, it will be several weeks, at least, before that child makes up its mind to be born; maybe even after the turn of the year: I will return whenever the time comes. Until then, I will send over some better clothes for her and a few linens to put aside for the birth. But, now, Rodrigo!" she added, slapping his shoulder. "Walk me home. It is late and I work early!"

At last the happy days of Christmas came around and all of New Orleans was as busy as a beehive in anticipation of the holiday. The little house beside the blacksmith shop was decked in Christmas greenery, and a constant flow of friends – and friends of friends – stopped by to raise a cup of cheer to the season. By Christmas Eve, Laron was happily complaining of a sore arm from having raised so many toasts, but he was also quick to point out that he suspected this was the reason God had provided man with two. Work in the smithy and around the stable yards had ceased at noon that day, and by sunset the house was aglow with the light of the Yuletide fire, and packed with noisy celebrants awash in holiday cheer. As night drew on, only Rodrigo was sober enough to think about looking in on Mariquita; at about the third verse of a joyous "Un Flambeau, Jeannette, Isabelle," Rodrigo broke away with a plate of food and extra blankets.

The night was cold and clear, which in itself was like an early gift of Christmas in à city where balmy Decembers were too often the norm. Rodrigo looked up at the black dome of the night sky, lavished with stars, and took a deep breath of the bracing air. It was Christmas, he thought, and Mariquita was still with them; even Laron had not anticipated that. As the weeks passed, it became clear that Mariquita was glad for her shelter and, for the time being at least, meant to stay. In all that time she had never uttered so much as a word to either Rodrigo or Laron, though they often sensed that she appreciated what they did for her, and that she liked the attention. And although she frequently left the confines of her shelter to walk about the once-familiar streets of the old quarter, she always found her way back by nightfall.

These thoughts filled Rodrigo's head, and as he approached the shop door he was surprised to hear a strange, unfamiliar sound, something he could not have expected to hear, even though it was the season for miracles: Mariquita was singing. A faltering voice, almost a child's voice, warbled into the still night and found Rodrigo where he lingered just outside the door; he could just make out the words, out of order, disjointed, but a hymn of joy:

"The beautiful Mother
Stood joyously at the crib
In which her child lay;
Through her exultant soul,
Dancing with joy,
Went a song of rejoicing.
O how jubilant and blessed
Was the immaculate
Mother of the Only-begotten!"

Rodrigo could not believe what he was hearing. Surely, no mindless imbecile could know the season, or recall words unsung perhaps since childhood? For the first time since that long-ago spring day, before his thoughts of her were overshadowed by his resentment of Paulo, Rodrigo allowed himself to hope. Even if it were only the sentimentality of the holiday obscuring something about which he should "know better," as Francita frequently admonished, Rodrigo did not care. In this moment, he embraced his quiet joy.

"May your ardour fill me,
May the child be my refuge
In my exile.
Virgin, most exalted among virgins,
Be not bitter towards me,
Let me take the child in my arms."

Slowly, as soundlessly as possible, Rodrigo entered the blacksmith shop and crossed over to the stall. Some weeks past, he and Laron had hung a large blanket across the stall's open gateway to give Mariquita some sense of privacy; he now approached it. If she was aware of him, Mariquita did not give any sign, nor did she cease her singing. Rodrigo bent before the curtain and gingerly laid down the blankets and the plate of food. He backed away slowly and turned around to stoke the bellows of the forge fire.

"When my body dies,
Then let my soul behold

The sight of your first-born."

Mariquita repeated the final verse of the hymn a second, then a third time, but Rodrigo never heard. He had passed out of the shop as quietly as he had entered.

"Mon Dieu! Mon Dieu! Mon Dieu!" Laron was calling on God and running down the Calle de Chartres to the church of St. Louis. It was crowded with worshippers attending the midnight mass, so much so that many found it necessary to stand outside, bathed in the light of a thousand candles and singing responsorials out in the cold night air. Laron approached the press of people with all the politeness of a general approaching a battlefield: he threw himself at it.

"Excusez-moi!" he now repeated as he pushed his way through the joyous assembly. "Excusez-moi! Pardon! Pardon!"

At last Laron made it into the vestibule of the church and poring over the disgruntled faces surrounding him, found two he recognized. "Merci a Dieu!" he said, clasping his hands and looking heavenward. "Rodrigo!" he called now. "Rodrigo!" he repeated louder, over the inevitable scolds and shushes of the crowd.

Rodrigo was standing with Francita on the opposite side of the vestibule, and at last he was aware of Laron, now signaling that he meet him outside. As soon as he and Francita appeared on the church steps, Laron was upon them.

"It's coming!" he panted, grabbing hold of Rodrigo's arm. "The baby! It's coming!"

"Holy Mother!" Francita whispered, and a momentary look of doubt shadowed her face. "And on Christmas! This is not good!" She crossed herself.

"Come on!" Rodrigo cried. "We must hurry!"

They found Mariquita crying out in pain and writhing like a wild thing; she fought both men, and it took their combined strength to control her so that Francita could begin to help.

"Good Lord!" Francita cried. "Shh! Hush now, and let me see." Mariquita began to calm under Francita's gentle encouragement; Francita felt her abdomen. "Ay me! This baby is coming now! I need clean linens, a knife, and two basins; fill one with hot water! Quickly!"

Rodrigo and Laron stood transfixed, not knowing what to do next, but Francita's sharp commands roused them to action; they returned swiftly bearing everything she required.

"Now leave us," she said to them. "But stay close by." At the same moment, a fierce contraction took hold of Mariquita's body. She shrieked, eyes wide with fear. "Holy Mother!" Francita sighed. "I do not think she even knows what is happening to her!"

Rodrigo and Laron took up stations in the stable yard where soon they were joined by Laron's loyal friends, those reliable Frenchmen who knew all about the "guest" in the blacksmith shop's stable. All of the men were subdued, partly in reverence of the event, and partly because they had all imbibed a copious amount of holiday cheer; having shared in the watch, protection, and care of Mariquita over the last several weeks, they all felt a kind of anticipation, and a breathless tension was now palpable in the air. For the better part of an hour, Mariquita's cries were the only sound to punctuate this tension and occasioned the pouring of several more rounds of fortifying drink. When, an hour and a half later, Francita emerged from the blacksmith shop, all these expectant men jumped to their feet.

"My holy mother!" Francita sighed, exhausted and disheveled, looking as if she had just come from taming a wild beast. Then, in answer to all the anxious looks, she said, "She is resting now, and the baby is fine and healthy. It is a boy."

A chorus of cheers erupted from Laron and his friends; bottles rang out in happy toasting, and Laron led the way into the house to procure more. Francita sat down wearily, and Rodrigo settled in beside her and gave her a hug.

"Thank you," he said quietly.

Francita patted his back. "Of course," she said, "of course."

"Do you think the baby will be … safe with her," Rodrigo went on, hesitantly. "I mean – "

"You are right to ask," Francita replied quickly. "And yes, the baby will be safe. When I put him in her arms, her eyes lit up like jewels. She has no will to harm it."

"Good," Rodrigo said, much relieved. "I think there is not a mean bone in all her body."

Francita gave her brother a long, steady look. "Rodrigo," she said at last, "I am your sister, and I feel I can tell you this: there is no hope of a future with that girl." Rodrigo turned away, but Francita pulled him back to face her. "The baby is safe with her, for now. But the best thing would be for it to be sent to an orphanage, or into the holy orders of the church. Her mind is gone, Rodrigo," she held his face and made him look into her eyes, "gone, and she will not recover it; she will never be the same. I know that once you had hopes for this girl, but it would only bring you ruin now. Understand?" Rodrigo did not reply, but nodded to his sister that he understood.

"And there is something else," Francita went on, crossing herself. "You know it is sacrilege for any baby to be born on the day of our Savior's birth."

"Superstition!" Rodrigo scoffed.

"No!" Francita replied. "Sacrilege, I tell you. It is a bad omen, and bad luck for the child; it must be baptized, as well. So that is even more of a reason to make sure this baby – and its mother – are given out of your care as soon as possible!"

Rodrigo opened his mouth to speak, but the glare in his sister's eyes made him reconsider what he was about to say. "Alright," he said, reassuring her, "alright. I understand."

The finer families of New Orleans celebrated Christmas in the traditional European manner, stretched over at least ten days and culminating in the celebrations of the Epiphany on Twelfth Night. But there was no such thing as a long holiday for men like Rodrigo and his fellow workers at the blacksmith shop. Their toil resumed the day after Christmas, and even this was barely soon enough for the rush of carriage and hansom drivers whose horses were worked almost continuously to keep up with the Creole festivities. This left Rodrigo very little time to spend ruminating over Mariquita and her child, which he occasionally heard crying over the din of the shop; he and Laron made certain she had food, but for most of each day she was left on her own. Even when Laron came to tell him, one afternoon close to the end of the year, that Mariquita had once again taken up her habit of going out during the day, and that she was taking her baby with her, Rodrigo only shrugged it off as a sign that her health was improving.

"She's not our prisoner," he said.

Later that night, however, Rodrigo realized that Laron's concern had now become his own, and despite his exhaustion from the work day, he made sure that he was the one to bring Mariquita her supper. As always, he entered the shop as quietly as possible, but even more so now that there was a baby he might disturb; he gingerly stepped over to the blanketed entrance of Mariquita's humble nursery, and put down the plate and cup he had brought. Then, although he felt a great reluctance to do so, he leaned in to steal a peek at the edge of the curtain.

Mariquita lay upon several blankets, facing away from him and cradling her infant in her arms. The baby's face was obscured by her long hair, but Rodrigo could hear the sucking sound as it nursed, and could see its hand moving against her breast. Satisfied that all was well with both mother and child, Rodrigo left them undisturbed, and went off in search of his own bed. He was asleep almost instantly.

It was deep night. Rodrigo shot up in bed. He was sweating and cold, his hair lank and damp across his face, and clutching the bed sheets tightly in his strong fists. A powerful nightmare had disturbed him in which he saw, or dreamt he saw, Mariquita standing at the foot of his bed. She was amorphous, ghost-like, wearing a beautiful white gown and appearing as hale and beautiful as she ever was in the time before her affair with the Spaniard. At first she only smiled at him, with a look of love and kindness upon her face that she had never shown him before. But then it seemed to Rodrigo that she was also speaking to him; he could hear the sounds as a distant whisper, but the words were indecipherable. In another instant, her countenance changed, and her mouth opened wide so that it looked disturbingly like a gaping black hole with eyes; then she screamed, and at first the scream seemed distant, but as Rodrigo strained to hear, it grew stronger and more urgent, buffeting him like the wail of a banshee. The image began to fade, but the scream was still pulsating in his lower consciousness when he sat bolt upright and gasped out loud, "Mariquita!"

He lay back down, but was unable to rest. Shivering, he got out of bed and wrapped himself in his blanket, then went over to the narrow fireplace where a few tiny flames were all that was left of the night's fire; he poked it and fed it with a new log, and immediately it crackled back to life. Then he pulled up a chair and sat, studying the flames and waiting for the drowse of sleep to return. But sleep would not come, and try as he might, he could not get the horrible dream-images out of his mind. So, resigning himself that he would not sleep again that night, he dressed quickly and made his way downstairs.

A ragged antique clock above the cold kitchen hearth loudly ticked out that the time was just after three o'clock. Crossing over to the outside door, Rodrigo opened it slowly until the hinges reached the point of their familiar squeal, then he yanked it in quickly, averting the jarring sound that would surely have roused the entire house. He stepped outside.

The night was cold and clear, and full of a silence that Rodrigo rarely experienced. Everything was frosty and still, and gave him the disconcerting impression that, in the entire world, he was the only living thing awake at that moment. The sound of his own footsteps crunching in the gravel of the work yard made him cringe so much that he tiptoed through the final few steps leading to the shop; he slowly opened the door and passed inside.

Here, too, an unearthly quiet prevailed. The air was warmer, and there was something else, a smell, rancid and slightly noxious. The embers of the forge fire burning low cast a weird play of light and shadows into every nook and cranny, and seemed to transform the familiar workshop into a new and surreal vista. Rodrigo was alarmed to see two feral cats eating from the plate of food he had brought Mariquita the night before. He chased them away but was frustrated because he could not tell if they had actually eaten the meal or were simply stealing from Mariquita's leftovers; the cup of milk was empty.

"Cats!" he thought. "What a stink."

Although a blanket was all that separated him from the stall where Mariquita and her baby lay, Rodrigo stood frozen, staring at the thing as if it were a brightly-patterned brick wall. Perhaps it was the images of his dream preying upon his mind, or maybe it was the otherworldly stillness of the raw winter's night, but a feeling of inexplicable fear suddenly overcame him. For a moment, he did not want to be there anymore, didn't want to have to pull that blanket back, and yet he had no idea why. A few long, tense moments passed before he was able to shake off the feeling and lean forward to look through the inky black gap, the boundary between the blanket and the wall, between the shop and the entirety of Mariquita's world.

It took a few seconds for his eyes to adjust to the spare light of the stall, and several minutes more passed before he thought to consider what the source of the odd, glowing light might be. Mariquita lay in almost exactly the same position as he had observed when last he looked in on her: still, unmoving, her head bent down to her chest so that her thick, black hair obscured her face, he assumed her to be sleeping. Her arm lay across the top of the blankets, pale, the hand turned upward, and looking strangely mottled in the dim light. And that light! It illuminated everything in a sickly glow, but what could it be? In another moment, its source became all too clear.

Rodrigo was suddenly aware of a vaporous, blue mist moving along the cold ground near Mariquita's feet; and in that mist was the opalescent, glowing form of a baby! It pulled itself along with tiny arms and runty, misshapen legs, but a bony, hunched back made movement difficult. The head seemed too big for the diminutive body, and it lolled back and forth as the creature moved; ribbons of drool hung from its messy mouth and about its chin, while its unblinking, opaque eyes remained fixed upon Mariquita. Slowly, with the furtive, lurching movements of the animated dead, the pitiful infant crawled up onto its mother and over her distended belly, finally coming to rest in her stiff, unfeeling arms. It tore at the bodice of its mother's dress with tiny, eager fingers, and with hungry gurgling sounds began to suckle the putrid milk from her corrupted, decomposing breasts.

Secreted in the darkness beyond the blanket-curtain, Rodrigo fought back the nausea that overwhelmed him as he watched the grisly tableau unfold. Horrified, angry, he barely knew what emotion to feel. Mariquita was dead: But when? And how could he not have known? How long had this creature, this ghoul returned to feed upon her corpse? *And where was the body of her baby?*

He closed his eyes and backed away from the horrifying scene; he had seen enough. Warily, and as soundlessly as possible, he moved around the shop. At first he didn't even know what he was looking for, and certainly he had no idea what he was going to do. Then suddenly his eyes fell upon the familiar sight of his own tools, and recognition galvanized his mind. He went over to where several soldering poles were stacked against the forge chimney and cautiously grabbed hold of the longest one, hefting it in his hand to get the feel of its weight. He took a step back toward the monstrous lair when next he saw his long, iron tongs lying across the anvil.

"Now I've got you, you little bastard!" he thought.

Rodrigo was not a man who was easily frightened, but as he approached that loathsome corner he felt a dread the likes of which he had never known before. He hesitated and took a deep breath then, with the metal pole in one hand and the tongs ready in the other he steeled himself to confront – what? What was he confronting? Surely, it was not a baby? He did not allow himself to think about it; in fact, he stopped thinking altogether so that he might act all the more resolutely.

With one sweep of his arm, he threw back the blanket and raced into the stall. The creature, taken unawares, had just enough time to pull away from Mariquita's foul breast and to utter a fearsome, demonic snarl before the tip of the metal rod plunged into its chest. Impaled and struggling, it glared at Rodrigo with fiery red eyes, and uttered such a fantastic howl that for a split-second his resolve almost faded. Then, to

Rodrigo's dismay, the ghoulish little creature began to swell, literally to grow in size; and as it grew it wrapped its little hands around the pole and began to pull itself closer, inch by inch, toward his sweating hand. Alarmed, and of all things not wanting it to get hold of him, Rodrigo reached forward with the tongs and clamped them tightly onto its swelling head. Another fearsome shriek rent the air, and the ghoul let go of the pole; snarling and howling, it grabbed at the tongs, as if the metal itself were causing it pain. It was trying desperately to free itself.

Rodrigo stepped back, and swinging around, thrust the writhing creature into the forge. He primed the bellows furiously, and what had been a smoldering fire was suddenly blasted into a conflagration that roared so loudly it even drowned out the ghoul's devilish shrieks. Rodrigo watched in horror as its flesh was consumed and charred into grisly coal. But the eyes – the nightmarish red eyes – continued to glare at him long after the thing ought to have died and the fire had been rendered a white-hot smelt.

"Die!" Rodrigo cried, pounding the bellows angrily. "DIE!"

Many long, surreal minutes later, the red eyes dimmed, faded, flickered, and – at last – winked out.

Rodrigo collapsed upon the ground, exhausted, as if he had just wrestled with the Devil himself. He stared blankly into the depth of the fire where now nothing was left of the fiendish infant except embers and charcoal; it was as if he could not, or more precisely, perhaps, would not look away. Finally, with a heavy sigh, he got to his feet and made the few painful steps that took him to where he knew he must go: then, he drew back the blanket.

There on the ground lay the once-lovely Spanish beauty, a swollen, putrid corpse upon which here and there flies and maggots had already begun their nefarious work. Thankfully, her face was obscured by the mass of her hair, but Rodrigo could not help but see that the drooping of her head made it seem as if she had no neck; and her arms, which lay exposed, were juxtaposed at such odd angles that the overall impression was of a life-sized rag doll and not a dead woman at all. More sobering, however, and most sickening of all was the sight of her fetid breasts, bulging, oozing a foul, nauseating mixture of bile and clotted milk, and full of deep gashes where tiny claws and razor-sharp teeth had hungrily dug the flesh away!

"Where on earth is the child?" Laron pondered aloud as he stood with Rodrigo beside Mariquita's simple, hastily-constructed casket.

Rodrigo had thought better of telling Laron anything about the horrific events of the early morning hours, but when the sun was fully up had gone to rouse the Frenchman for help getting her body into the casket. Now he only shrugged for, in fact, he had no idea what had happened to Mariquita's baby, and said as much in reply.

Laron shook his head sadly and turned away. He walked out into the work yard where his friends were gathered, downcast and speaking in soft voices. Like Laron, they had all awoken to the shocking news of Mariquita's passing; they had helped with building the casket and tending to her body, and now they waited to accompany Mariquita on her final journey. All that was required now was for the priest to join them, and Francita had been sent to find one. But when she returned alone, the men exchanged knowing looks and pointed her to the blacksmith shop, where Rodrigo waited.

She entered quietly, almost reverently, to the sight of her brother standing alone, gazing down at the body of Mariquita. Francita's heart was breaking because she did not have good news.

"Rodrigo," she said softly, as she came up beside him. "No one would come."

Rodrigo sighed heavily and bit his lip. "None?" he asked, after a moment.

Francita shook her head. "No," she replied sadly. "I'm sorry."

"So, they will let her be damned?" Rodrigo said angrily.

Francita paused, considering what to say. "Rodrigo, to them she has already damned herself, she lived and died in sin – "

Rodrigo threw up his hands and turned away, but Francita continued, "adultery, fornication – Rodrigo you *know* this."

Rodrigo did not reply, and felt, in fact, that there was no good reply in the face of such unrelenting stringency: anyway, Francita had always been religious enough for both of them. He picked up the lid of the casket and after one final look, slid it into place. "Let's go," was all he said.

It was the last day of December and a canopy of heavy, grey clouds hung low over the city. As the mourners carried their sad burden into the Calle de Borbón, a mist of rain began to fall. Abandoned in life, this was not Mariquita's fate in death: Rodrigo led the way, carrying the shovel, and Francita walked at his side; Laron and his friends followed, carefully carrying the simple casket over the precarious patches of frost that had formed during the raw, cold night. Because of the holiday, the streets were nearly empty of merchant traffic, and there were only a few passers-by who had not been compelled by the cold to stay inside their businesses and homes. These few stopped to stare, and to remove their hats in respect for the anonymous dead; some others looked from behind frosted windows and crossed themselves as the makeshift funeral passed by: Rodrigo smirked at the bitter irony.

They were making for the pauper's burying ground on the northern edge of the Carré, where anyone with a shovel and the need could provide a decent burial for their dead – as long as the dead did not mind sharing their eternal rest with criminals, suicides, excommunicates, and the unbaptized. As they approached the entrance of this ragged bit of earth, and were carefully lifting the casket over the narrow gate, Laron lost his footing on a patch of ice and stumbled to the ground. To everyone's dismay, the casket shifted from the hands of its carriers and slipped down, striking the hard, cold ground. The lid was jarred open, and Mariquita's pallid arm unfolded through the gap. Rodrigo rushed back, but was too late to catch the falling casket; from behind, he heard his sister gasp.

"Look!" she cried, crossing herself. "She is pointing!"

The men all looked, and indeed, it appeared that Mariquita's hand was pointing: there, protruding from out of the slimy, wet mud at the base of the nearby gate post was a ragged piece of black lace. Rodrigo felt his heart sink in immediate recognition. He took the shovel and gently dislodged the cloth from the putrid soil. Then, on his knees and with his bare hands, he tugged at the lace, and loosened at last, the earth gave up its tiny secret: the full length of Mariquita's lace mantilla, and the frozen, bloated remains of her dead infant.

"Holy Mother! Oh, my Holy Mother!" Francita whispered, and burst into tears.

"How can this be?" Laron choked, and all the men with him fought back tears.

Rodrigo reached down and gently lifted the tiny corpse from off the icy ground. Now he understood, and the depredations of the ghoulish infant he had consigned to the flames of his forge suddenly made morbid sense: Mariquita, her mind at last unwound, had exposed her child, and had left it to die an awful death out in the biting cold. And it *had* died, but driven by an otherworldly hatred that would not let it rest, it had returned to avenge itself and to take payment in kind from the mother who had so condemned it.

Carefully, respectfully, Rodrigo replaced the little, frozen body in the swath of black lace. He turned to the disheveled casket and gently folded Mariquita's arm back into place; then tenderly, almost lovingly he laid the bundle next to her. "Sueño tranquilo," he whispered. "*Sleep in peace.*"

The lid was replaced, the casket lifted, and the mourners entered the poor burying ground in search of a sheltered place. They found a perfect spot under a spreading cypress tree that in the coming spring would spread its verdant branches protectively over the treasure at its feet – the beautiful, tormented Mariquita and her tiny child of love.

"I've been meaning to tell you something, Rodrigo," Laron said as they left the burying ground, lagging somewhat behind Francita and the other men.

"Oh yes?" Rodrigo chuckled.

"Yes!" Laron replied, and reached up to put his hand on Rodrigo's strong shoulder. "You see my friends there," he nodded toward the Frenchmen walking five abreast in the road ahead.

"Yes," Rodrigo replied warily, not sure where this was going.

"And you know, I mean, well, *we* know they don't just run that shop," Laron whispered, cocking an eyebrow as if he were letting Rodrigo in on a secret he did not already know.

"No!" Rodrigo replied, feigning surprise.

"No!" Laron said now. "And you know that no good, that *salaud* who had his way with poor Mariquita, and then abandoned her?" Rodrigo nodded. "Well," Laron went on, "last I heard there is only one way to get to Havana, and that is by boat; and you might say our friends there," he again nodded toward the Frenchmen, "know something about boats, as that is, you might say, their business."

"Laron . . ." Rodrigo sighed, growing impatient.

"Alright, alright," Laron responded, "I was only going to say that our friends there had something of a fête, you might call it a little going-away party, and that dirty bastard was the guest of honor."

Rodrigo stopped short and stared at Laron. "They did not – "

"Kill him?" Laron said over his shoulder, waiting for Rodrigo to catch up with him. "No," he went on, "but I would say it was close. And I doubt he saw much of the voyage being somewhat – how shall I say it? – indisposed." He held his hands at some distance from his head to illustrate how swollen Paulo's face had been when the French pirates had finished with him.

This struck Rodrigo as extremely funny, and more than a little rewarding. He laughed out loud, and was jarred slightly at hearing the sound of his own laughter again. Francita turned back sharply and tried to scold him into being quiet, but somehow this just made him laugh all the more.

The Zombie

The peoples of Europe from which the earliest settlers of New Orleans came, saw the nature of their wider relationship with the dead demonstrated in the recorded cases of "wandering corpse" activity: when whole communities were victimized by the wandering dead. History and tradition suggest that in almost every case of this kind, those dead who could not rest had led dissolute or impious lives, or had died a "bad death."

It was also common belief that a corpse could exhibit signs of acts committed in life. Often the relics or preserved bodies of saints were used as a measure by which to gauge the profundity of dissoluteness in those dead suspected of being revenants. When exhumed, the bodies of saints were found marvelously intact and smelled faintly sweet, or not at all. But when the corpses of the troubling dead were exhumed or dragged from their resting places, they often showed signs of an unholy condition. The cadavers were grotesque and swollen, with blackened bodies and torpid faces; when struck, they exuded fresh blood that copiously soaked the earth, and even groaned in protest.

But how were dead bodies revived? By evil magic, certainly, and in particular by necromancy, that branch of the dark arts that deals specifically with the reanimation of the dead. Still, did these enlivened corpses have a will of their own? In cases where the use of magic or sorcery was in evidence, probably not; but disturbingly, these conditions were not involved in the majority of cases involving the restless dead. Although people sought answers in theology and Church teachings, popular ideas about the walking dead tended to be much less dogmatic; and in more cases than it might be comfortable to admit, conclusions about the subject were drawn from first-hand experience. When faced with the ravaging corpse of a former neighbor spreading fear and pestilence through the village of its former home, it was natural for common folk to lose sight of the obtuse concepts suggested by Church doctrine. They wanted a real solution to a very real problem.

But ultimately only the proper treatment – and this meant religious treatment – could really put an end to the depredations of the profane dead. In order to fortify those who might be confronted by such a task, the Church provided a broad definition of who could acceptably perform the necessary rites. Therefore, clerics and lay persons alike could absolve the revenants of sins committed in life, could asperge or dab the corpse with holy water, and, significantly, could consign the dead to the flames of a bonfire. This last is a notable departure from the usual proscriptions of the Church against immolation of the dead, and amply demonstrates how seriously the Church perceived the matter to be.

There was little doubt among the people of early New Orleans and the Louisiana colony, coming as they did from the populations of classical Europe that the dead could – and frequently did – return as revenants. They knew these roaming dead were solid and alive, and that no phantom or possessing demon was to blame. But whenever the intervention of magic was suspected, especially if it was the mysterious magic of an enslaved population, the fear – both of the dead, and of becoming one of the dead – was enough to paralyze an entire population. Such was the case when a brigand who first became famous in New Orleans as a hero, fell under the intoxicating powers of primitive magic and, for a time at least, learned how to cheat death and mimic an almighty God.

Bras Coupé, The Zombi King

It was dark night and the late April moon cast fantastic shadows through the moss-hung cypress trees deep in the St. John's Bayou swamps.

Dante ran because his life depended upon it. He splashed along the bayou's edge, following the matted grass of alligator tracks, fearing that creature less than the malice of the more evil thing now pursuing him. Tripping among the cypress knees, scratched and bleeding from the roots of the knotted viperine, panting, weeping, Dante ran on until at last he spied the lights of the Spanish camps glowing faintly through the trees. Hope grew in him. But then, his safety and salvation just within sight, Dante felt the tremendous weight of a powerful hand grabbing at his shoulder.

"Whar're yo' gwon, boy?" said a booming voice that made Dante's blood run cold and paralyzed him in place. "It's feedin' time!"

Dante felt the grip tighten; he was lifted from the ground, kicking and screaming like a porcine about to be slaughtered. At first he had only squeaked, like a tiny mouse caught by a thrice-times-larger hunter; but now Dante screamed fully, wailing pitifully, pleading for his life, though he knew it was useless. "No! No! Oh, Lawd – noooooo!!"

There was a booming sound, like thunder in the distance, the deep laugh of the victorious hell-fiend: carrying his captive over his head with his one good hand, Bras Coupé disappeared into the suffocating darkness of the tangled swamp.

José Planas sat at the long bar of Le Coquet nursing his second glass of red wine, listening to the cacophony of noise from the gambling salon, and watching as the late afternoon shadows lengthened in the Rue Bourbon outside. He had waited the better part of an hour, but still the man he most eagerly wanted to see had not arrived. The bar man came over to him; he gave a meek shrug and said, "He comes every day by this time, Señor. I do not know why today should be different." Planas only nodded.

Suddenly the outside door opened and there, framed in the hot gold of a humid July glow, was the very man for whom Planas had so patiently waited. Tall, made even taller by the height of his top hat, with dark hair and moustache, a wide white smile and a bun-brown complexion, penetrating black eyes that now laughed but could turn in an instant to pools of fulmination, and a voice deep with authority: this was Alphonse Avetante.

Planas watched as Avetante made his way through a flurry of nods and hat-tipping, finally coming to rest on a stool beside him. He perched the top hat over the head of his tall walking stick and set both to rest against the bar. The server fluttered over immediately with a bottle of brandy and a large glass snifter. Avetante watched as the glass was filled to his liking; he took a careful sip and set the glass down again with a deep sigh, then he lifted his piercing gaze to Planas.

"José, my friend!" he said, and cordially extended his hand. "Forgive my tardiness. I was delayed in the Rue Condé."

Planas held up a hand and shook his head. "Do not be concerned with that," he said. "Alphonse," he continued in a low voice, coming closer. Avetante cocked an eyebrow at him over the rim of his brandy glass. "We have found where he hides."

Avetante was silent. He carefully set his glass down and reached for the bottle. Slowly, thoughtfully, he poured out a little more brandy, watching as the rich liquor rolled around the belly of the glass. At last he looked up and with a glint in his eyes, like a flame encased in a smoky, opaque glass, said simply, "Indeed?"

A memory came to Avetante then, recent and painful: a room on the third floor of a beautiful home in the Rue Conti, strangled with the July heat, a table littered with the accoutrements of the sick room, a single bed. On the bed lay a man, once vibrant and strong, now gaunt and wasted, and drawing his last breaths. Doctor Joseph Gottschalk was dying.

Avetante recalled the pain on the face of the man's wife, swollen from crying, and being drawn through the rest of the dying man's family where they clustered in the doorway; a wave of Gottschalk's hand signaled his wish to be alone. With a shaking finger, the ruined hands of a brilliant man, Gottschalk drew Avetante to him and whispered something. Avetante could not make out the words.

"What, old friend?" he said, bending down closer to the quivering lips, the translucent white of the face. "What is it you are saying?"

Gottschalk swallowed hard. With his eyes, he motioned at the glass on the bedside table. Instinctively, Avetante poured some water into the glass; he bent over and helped his friend to drink.

"Alphonse!" Gottschalk gasped, holding tightly to Avetante's hand. "My son . . . yes, as a son you have been to me," he added, and smiled feebly. "You must – must listen to me . . ."

"Of course, Joseph," said Avetante, "only do be restful."

Gottschalk shook his head. "Listen . . . the Fiend will come upon the City now, he will take them all to him. It will be Sainte Domingue, but worse – you must act, and swiftly."

Avetante nodded. He knew what Gottschalk meant. "I know what you would have me do," he said with resignation.

Gottschalk gasped. A cough wracked his body; he held tightly to Avetante's hand. "Alphonse," he said at last, "the City will be overrun." Again he coughed, then, "All will fall under his sway – a dead city . . . I understand now. His body is filled with venom instead of blood, filled with the power of Le Gran Zombi!" The poor man wheezed, struggling to draw breath.

Avetante considered the words. Gottschalk turned and looked at him, his once clear blue gaze clouded with the approach of death. His grip tightened, then he gasped out the words: "Alphonse, remember, he was baptized – *he is a Catholic!*"

The coughing fit returned and Dr. Dumiot, who had waited in an antechamber nearby, came quickly to Gottschalk's aid; the white-clad figures of two ministering nuns rustled by as Avetante took his leave; and the Gottschalk family, now clustered in the hallway, parted again to let him through. Hat in hand, he passed out of that chamber of death.

"Alphonse?" A voice roused Avetante from his dark recollections. "Did you hear me?" It was the voice of José Planas.

Avetante regarded him over the rim of his glass, downing the heady brown liquid in one swift gulp. "Yes, I did," he said at last, his voice rasped with a sting. "Now we come to it. A great work lies ahead of us, José!"

Planas didn't know whether to be excited or afraid. He gazed out the window at the lowering sun and sighed. "Whoever brought that monster here should be cursed!" he said in a low voice.

Avetante's eyes flashed momentarily with the rosy sunset hue. "He is, my friend," he said. "He is."

The myth of the Zombi King had been years in the making, and had grown in the telling and re-telling of his tale. A runaway slave, shot by his master, he went into hiding in the backwaters of the St. John's Bayou swamp. There he had become a brigand and, so the superstitious said, a fearsome conjurer, and thereby he had instantly entered the legends of the Old Carré.

Had he come from San Domingue? This is what many believed; that there, when still just a boy, he had served his master and the French crown loyally against the rebellion of the island's slaves. When the cause was lost, he and his master escaped and ultimately came to New Orleans with thousands of other defeated refugees. In New Orleans he was known as Squire John, or sometimes Big John, the boy who had grown to almost seven feet in height and who, with his Abyssinian black skin and great booming voice, had become the centerpiece of the "bamboulas," the slave celebrations of the Congo Fields. On a time, he had been happy and unknown, and few whites had ever heard of him, or would even have cared if they did.

But something had happened; something dark and sinister had found and overtaken Squire John somewhere in the course of his commonplace life. He was a drunk, everyone knew, and a powerful drunk at that, so that when he was in his cups there were few who could match him in strength. But as his infamy had grown, so had a peculiar cunning, and with that cunning came the admiration of the nefarious and the low until at last the loyal Squire John turned away from good, and never turned back. When, sometime later, he took a bullet while running away and not only walked away from it, but survived, the slaves attributed it to his powerful magic – his *hoodoo*. But there was reason to suspect that this common root-working, familiar to all slaves in one form or another, had met something else in the makeup of Squire John, something preternatural, perhaps otherworldly; and by its power, it seemed he had taken mastery of his own life – even to the defeat of death. Concealed on the outskirts of the city of New Orleans, he was a powerful magnet for the disenfranchised among the free people of color and for other runaway slaves, all of whom he gladly took in. But he was also a source of inspiration for the base and the criminal; these, too, flocked in great numbers to the green savannahs of his lair.

When New Orleans heard rumors of him again, and his fame began to spread in the city, it was by the name he had taken after being shot: Bras Coupé, he of the bloody broken arm, and his powers were said to be nothing short of amazing. Scores of local militia and regular soldiers had gone out into the swamps to capture this hero of the slaves; some did not return, and all who did told stunning tales that only served to increase the brigand's celebrity among his own people. Bras Coupé was impervious to fire, they said, and when set upon with torches had simply laughed as the flames leapt over him then choked themselves out; bullets shot at point-blank range flattened against his bare chest and bounced off; and all spoke with dread of the unearthly strength of his one good hand, saying that for what the Lord had taken away in his withered arm, the Devil had more than compensated in the other.

At the outset of the earliest rumors of who the brigand actually was, the slaves of New Orleans were clucking with delight at the prospect of having so powerful a hero in their midst, and they ignored altogether the fact that Bras Coupé had done nothing on their behalf. Eventually, however, an evil fault-line began to show, a dark, foreboding crack in the mythic façade of their "hero of the savannahs," and things began to change. Where originally any who could readily fled to him, it was not long before runaway slaves were running in the opposite direction of Bras Coupé. Where at first the colored of all castes had trumpeted the heroics and the mythic legend of the indefatigable Bras Coupé, most especially encouraging their youth to defect to him, now they held their young men and women locked in close, or seemed content in their servitude as long as it kept them safe.

Everywhere was the whisper of a terror abiding in the St. John's swamp, one that ate the flesh of the living and practiced every forbidden dark art to enslave the dead to his nefarious ends. Worse, the urgent whispers now said, Bras Coupé, he of the powerful broken arm, was soon intending to unleash upon the citizens of the Old Carré both his physical fury and the supernatural plague of his army of the dead!

"He is making zombies out in that swamp," Avetante said, and he could barely believe the words he was speaking.

Joseph Gottschalk snorted incredulously. "You are not saying this is what the authorities believe?"

"No," Avetante replied, "of course not. They believe him to be nothing more than a common criminal, albeit a dangerous and very elusive one."

"Then why this talk of zombies?" said Gottschalk.

"Joseph, there is not a slave in this city who does not believe that Bras Coupé is conjuring a very bad magic out there," Aventante explained. "Talk to any of them! Why, one of every two either knows someone who has gone missing, or has narrowly escaped being kidnapped themselves."

Gottschalk looked at him for a long moment. "How?" he said at last. "What is he doing – out there?"

"He's a sorcerer," Avetante replied. "He's using black island magic, that's certain. But there is some other element, something . . . I do not know, not so obvious, perhaps? Something that helped him to defy death and that he is using to make necromancy on the dead."

Gottschalk sighed. "I must defer to you in this, Alphonse," he said at last. "I know too little about this 'zombie' magic that you speak of, and I have not your experience with the island practices so prevalent here." He hesitated, then, "*Can* he be stopped?"

Avetante sat in silent thought, gazing dejectedly through a narrow window that frosted over with his every breath. It was the dead middle of a February night and the two men were huddled around a little fireplace in the upper rooms of Gottschalk's surgery in the Rue Conti. A cold rain had fallen just before sunset and now the gables and turrets of the city glistened in deep shadows and cut odd angles, sharp with frost, against the steely night sky. An icy, unrelenting wind blew off the river and swept through the streets, whistling shrilly and prying with icy fingers at the windows and doors.

"You know, the Spaniards along St. John's Bayou live in constant fear of him," Avetante said at last, breaking the oppressive silence that had settled over the little room. "It was the Acolapissa Indians who first helped him, and the Spaniards hold them in low regard for it. They provided all he needed to survive, even gave him weapons. Then they taught him their knowledge of the wild swamp plants . . ." He shook his head.

"And armed him with powerful, more deadly weapons," Gottschalk finished the thought. "Maybe that is what he has paired with this 'island magic,' the *hoodoo* you speak of, maybe this is what makes him so fierce, makes him unassailable with fire and arms . . . ?"

"I have considered that," Avetante said thoughtfully.

"Surely it is a possibility?" Gottschalk mused.

Avetante sighed. "There is something else at play," he added, hesitantly. "At first it seemed that every escaped slave in the city made a run for the swamp to join the renegade. Now, they will not go near the place for love or money. If Squire John was once their hero, this Bras Coupé that he has become is something entirely different in their eyes. They fear him, and they do all they can to protect themselves against him."

Gottschalk shook his head and sighed. "Yet some still flee to him," he said flatly. Avetante looked at him curiously. "Dante," Gottschalk explained, "my cook's son."

"Is he missing?" Avetante replied.

Gottschalk nodded, "For some weeks now," he said. "His mother is driven to distraction, of course, but I am also concerned. All his talk before he went missing was of the exploits of his 'hero with the broken arm' – Bras Coupé, of course. And if what you suspect is true . . ."

Outside the wind wailed bitterly and there was a noise of shingles sliding off the roof, shattering in the empty street below. A thoughtful silence settled over them and the long night wore on.

✦✦✦✦

Dante fell face first onto the cloying wet mud of a newly-dug grave. The taste of the loamy soil mingled with the taste of tears and blood welling in his mouth. Through the throbbing in his brain he could hear laughter – the laughter of Bras Coupé and the other hoodoo men who stood all around. Nearby, just on the edge of sight stood a young black boy, about Dante's age, naked to the waist and holding a machete. There was a thumping sound – something fell beside him in the mud.

"Get on up here!" he heard the voice of Bras Coupé command him. The laughter subsided. "Get on up here, boy!" said the voice, more threatening. Two booted feet stepped up beside the grave. "Or is I gwon't has t'make yo?" The voice was a growl now.

Dante scrambled to his feet as quickly as the muck beneath them would allow. He stood shaking, crying, and staring into the face of Bras Coupé: black, as black as tar, fixed with two yellowed eyes and a broad white smile; and the moon passing in and out of the clouds in the sky above made the huge circumference of that face appear a sickly, grayish blue. The height of the fiend, made monumental by the natty top hat stolen off a mortuary man, the worn black suit with a dangling, knotted sleeve covering the missing forearm . . . Dante was weeping fully by now.

Bras Coupé regarded him, feigning compassion. "Aww," he said, and put his one good hand on Dante's shoulder. "I knows it, I knows it. Such a shame. But it gotta be done, boy." Dante shook with fear. "Yo hear me boy," said the big man, coming closer, almost nose to nose. "It jest gots to be done! Yo see, I gots me some fine seedlings under here – yass, some fine, fine sprouts! But dey ain't gwon't be wurt nothin', no, not a picayune son, if'n dey don't *eat* . . ."

The African giant rose to his full height and pointed to the machete that lay on the ground at Dante's feet. "Pick it up."

Dante could do nothing, frozen to the spot with shock and fear, knowing his fate. He gazed with blurred eyes at the youth across from him who was trying his best to look brave, though the tears in his eyes betrayed his own wild fear. That boy, Dante knew, was going to try to kill him; if the boy did not succeed, then Dante would have to kill him instead.

"Looky here, now" Bras Coupé hissed. Reaching down, he grasped Dante's slippery wet face in his hand. "Pick . . . it . . . up." Dante wept anew, the sobs coming in great gasps now, but he did as he was told – he bent and picked up the machete.

"Nah we gots it!" Bras Coupé shouted and slapped the back of a hoodoo man standing nearby. "Nah we gots us a fight, ya'll!" He spun on the two youths. "Get it goin', boys!"

Dante and his nameless foe approached each other over the mounds of spongy soil. Had they looked more closely, had they been able to see what they were walking through, the boys would have discerned the remnants of human bones and teeth glowing yellow in the mute light of the moon. But each boy was trapped in his own private hell, and each boy had only one thought – to survive.

Suddenly Dante let out a scream, a garbled wail of fear and terror, and with that he charged his young opponent. The clang of the machetes filled the close, humid night, ringing over the laughter of Bras Coupé and his men. As the boys flailed and chopped at the air, the hoodoo men pitched coins and threw the backwash of their bottles at them, the liquor searing the boys' wounds.

Then for Dante, disaster struck. Losing his footing in the muck, he went down to one knee; he felt the sudden impact of his opponent's machete, and cried out in pain. The blade had chopped into his shoulder, and before he could return the blow, another cut into his leg. In agony, Dante threw down his own blade and tried to crawl away. Then came another blow; the other boy had buried his machete in the side of Dante's head.

He stopped crawling then and lay still. He could feel the other boy's foot on his back as he bent to remove the machete from his head; he knew the final blow was coming. His face washed in tears and sweat, Dante could feel his life's blood surging in his mouth and flowing from his body. The laughter of Bras Coupé and his cohorts was growing fainter, and the throbbing in his brain was calming to a gentle drumbeat. Dante was dying.

But just before the death blow fell, with a horror that would abide with his spirit even as it passed the bonds of this world, Dante saw the blood-blackened mud around him begin to crawl as something beneath it pushed its way through. A hand, putrid and scaled, with long yellow nails, burst through the soil; it felt around for a moment then locked upon Dante. And just before his life was spent, as the final blow of the machete separated his head from his body, Dante saw a bloated face rise up from the mud. It turned its popping eyes upon the dying boy and, pulling him face first toward it through the muck, the zombie bit down and began to feed.

"They wanted you to capture Bras Coupé? Alone?" José Planas exclaimed. He was sitting at the reins of a rickety, wooden produce cart with Alphonse Avetante beside him holding onto his hat with one hand and his seat with the other, and feeling that he had never been in more danger of losing his life than at that moment. They were speeding toward St. John's Bayou and the July afternoon was steaming.

"Yes, indeed," Avetante replied, and shrugged at the look José gave him. "What they expected me to do against a supernatural fiend, I cannot imagine."

José smiled at Avetante's feigned modesty. He knew very well why the Creoles and the churchmen of the old Carré had sought Avetante out. An apothecary and surgeon by trade, he was also famous – some said infamous – as a powerful gree-gree man of the Congo Fields, where everyone called him Doctor Cracker because of his white race. "And did you agree to help?"

Avetante nodded deeply. "I did, of course," he replied. "But as you can see I was not very successful. We would not be sitting here otherwise." Then he said quietly, as if to himself, "They offered a reward but it was we who paid the price."

"What do you mean?" José asked. Avetante's comments did not sit well with him.

"I knew I had to counter the magic of a hell-fiend," Avetante explained, "and I doubted; you see, I doubted that I could act alone or even that anything I could do would work against Bras Coupé, for pity's sake! So," he sighed heavily, and held on tighter as the cart shot along over the rut-covered road, "so . . . I went for advice to my dear friend, Joseph Gottschalk."

"Ah, sí! The doctor," said José, recognizing the name. "He died recently, didn't he?"

"Yes, only days ago." Avetante's voice trailed off. Again, Planas did not feel reassured.

At last Avetante opened up and shared the story of his first attempt to find and kill Bras Coupé; how the slave owners of New Orleans, fearing that rebellion was fomenting in the bayou swamps, had appealed to him to find some way to put down the magic of the Zombi King. How he had consulted with Gottschalk, an expert in the occult arts, on how best to accomplish the deed; when Gottschalk offered to help him, his confidence grew tremendously because he would not have to face the task alone. Accompanied by a few brave vodusi men whom they had armed with muskets and knives, he and Gottschalk went off to confront their prey.

"We encountered the giant just outside his encampment near the mouth of St. John's Bayou," he said. "His followers had disappeared ahead of him, leaving only his creatures to defend him." Planas started at these words. Avetante continued.

"He was at his most dangerous then, cornered, having to concentrate so hard to direct his mindless zombies that any mistake could be a fatal one for him. This emboldened us, I suppose. Joseph and I performed a powerful ritual which we had prepared, one that he and I had both performed previously and knew well. Yet it had no effect whatsoever on that monster. Though all our will, all our energy was focused upon the fiend, our failure made us falter. It was as if we were scrambling our brains to find the right key to lock a door holding back a maelstrom. Even a moment's distraction was enough to open us to his power.

"Guided by the fiend's evil will, the creatures began to move in unison toward us. The fire of our muskets had no power to stop them. It was necessary that I do something, somehow, you see, and when I moved my mind to concentrate

upon this, in that instant Bras Coupé was upon Joseph."
Avetante fell silent and the men rode on together for a while,
each lost in his own thoughts.

The little cart sped along, passing in and out of the patches
of sunlight under the oaks of the Bayou Road as if frame-by-
frame through the panes of a stained glass window. A thread-
like glimmer shone in the distance, the waters of St. John's
Bayou sparkling in the afternoon sun.

"He breathed on him," Avetante said at last in a low, angry
voice that could barely be heard above the noise of the cart and
the horse's hooves.

Planas leaned in closer. "Pardon? What was it you said?"

Avetante sat up straight in his seat and coughed to clear his
throat. "He breathed on him," he repeated more clearly. "That
zombie lifted poor Joseph from the ground and cast aside our
holy relics; then he breathed a great sigh into Joseph's face, a
foul breath filled with malevolence and evil."

Staring blankly at the road ahead, Planas considered this,
then said, "His breath killed the doctor?"

Avetante nodded sharply. "Yes," he replied, and looked
Planas squarely in the face. "The breath of the zombie is
miasmic, deadly; it must be avoided at all costs. Bras Coupé
infected Joseph with it, and it rotted him from the inside out."

A palpable silence now fell between them; then Avetante
jumped and seemed to come alive. Animated, excited, he
grabbed José's shoulder. "But Joseph was a Jew!" he said.
"And though my father was a Catholic and raised me in the
Church of Roma, my mother was a Jew!" Planas looked at him
blankly. "We are Jews, don't you see, José? Gottschalk and I:
we are Jews by birth, so we failed!"

José shook his head in confusion.

"The last words Gottschalk said to me were, *'remember – he
is Catholic!'*" Avetante declared with a broad, almost wild
smile. "Bras Coupé was baptized, José! Soon you will see how
important that is! The son-of-a-bitch is a *CATHOLIC!*"

Francisco Garcia, a swarthy, square-shouldered Spaniard, paced the banks of St. John's Bayou impatiently, swinging an iron crow bar which every now and then he hefted from hand to hand.

"What are we waiting on?" he muttered. "We could take care of this problem now, while we still have sunlight! Why must he come along?" he spat, referring to Avetante.

"Because," Raul Planas shrugged, stamping tobacco in his pipe and lighting it, "they want to make sure that this time he dies, and that his legend dies with him! Besides, I'm sure they will pay the reward regardless of if we catch him in the day or the night." A cloud of smoke wreathed around his head, framing his dark silhouette in the glow of the lowering sun.

"Well, your brother had better get him here soon," Garcia replied. "I have no desire to be in that swamp after nightfall. And I'm not splitting the reward with that charlatan Avetante," he added, shaking a scolding finger at no one in particular.

Sitting nearby, Raul's brother Gabriel chuckled. "Do you mean to say you're afraid to go in there, Cisco?" He cocked his head toward the dark canopy of the nearby swamp.

"I didn't say any such thing," Garcia replied, but Gabriel and Raul just laughed. "You know how easy it can be to get lost in there," Garcia sputtered on.

"Oh, of course!" Raul chortled sarcastically.

"Ah! Of course!" Gabriel echoed, nodding deeply.

Garcia glowered at the brothers. "You will not be laughing soon!" he grumbled.

"And," Gabriel replied, "*that* is exactly why we are waiting on Avetante!"

The men fell silent, listening to the sounds of late afternoon stealing over the bayou, watching the dragonflies swaying on the tall grasses and the cranes picking their way along the water's edge. Now and then a fish jumped up and fell back into the water with a "slap." A warm breeze wafted the smell of cut grass down from the Carrollton fields.

"You know what that thing does in there," Garcia said in a low voice, referring to Bras Coupé. He stared at the deep-shaded cypress trees looming not far away.

"I know what they *say* he does," Raul replied.

"Oh, he does it," Garcia said, once again feeling the weight of the crow bar in his hand.

Raul and Gabriel sat thoughtfully. They each remembered a summer night the year before when they, and all their family, had been startled from sleep by screams and otherworldly moans coming across the water from the pitch black of the swamps. The screams and garbled voices had gone on for many minutes when suddenly a loud, booming voice sounded out. No one could make out any words, but the pitiful screaming ended and the booming voice laughed; then silence again settled over the bayou. The event had so frightened Gabriel's wife that she took her infant son and all the youngest children of the family, and went to stay at her mother's home in the city for some days.

"You remember that old slave come out of there this past spring?" Garcia said, and the brothers nodded. "Remember he was all eaten up with mosquitoes and leeches and who knows what else? Remember the way he walked and the look in his eyes, and how he walked right into the water there?"

"I remember," said Raul. "He would have drowned if we hadn't pulled him out."

"But it took a banana gaff to get him, remember?" Garcia whispered hoarsely, leaning in close to the others. "And when we hooked him, he didn't even flinch. Any man would have screamed, would have fought us or something."

"Yes," Raul said, puffing thoughtfully on his pipe, "yes, I remember, and you're right. And remember that doctor who came and took the man away, what was his name?"

"Truxille," Gabriel said. "Doctor Truxille."

"Who knows what happened to him after that . . ." said Garcia.

The men were suddenly distracted by a cloud of dust approaching from the Bayou Road; in the midst of it were a galloping horse and the familiar sight of José Planas's cart.

"Get in!" he called to his brothers and Garcia, as he drove the cart directly up to them, straining the horse to a halt. The men jumped into the back of the cart which was littered with machetes, some rope, a pick-axe, a roll of canvas, and a large net.

José snapped the reins. The cart lurched on, leaving the portage docks behind and heading north along the bayou's edge. The path narrowed; trees and tall grasses soon closed in, swiping the men on either side. They were riding through the overgrowth of a small, fingerlike peninsula of land that protruded slightly into the bayou. Near these thickets were the ruins of old Spanish soldiers' cottages; at the water's edge was an old dock, still sometimes used by the Planas brothers, who kept a small piloting skiff moored there. "Whoa!" José cried, and drew to a halt.

"Get the boat ready!" said Avetante, jumping quickly down from the cart. The others also jumped down and busily set about readying the skiff.

A golden gloaming, peaceful and eerily quiet, was stealing over the marshy banks, reflecting on the mirrored face of the still bayou waters. The men abruptly stopped, listening anxiously, and gazing at the tree line on the far shore. Their hearts all fell in unison as the tall bushes there suddenly began to rustle . . .

⚜⚜⚜⚜

José Planas and his wife, Pauline, sat gazing in silence at the two-hundred and fifty American dollars that lay on the table between them. The flickering of a single oil lamp was all the light illuminating the tiny galley; the remainder of their houseboat lay silent under a canopy of darkness. Pauline lifted her eyes. She didn't have to say a word; José could feel her inquisitive gaze upon him. Then, hesitantly, he went on with his story.

As the men were preparing to cross the bayou, a figure approached, rustling through the marsh grass on the far side. It was a holy Abbe, a brother of the Church, wearing the long cassock of a mendicant friar; his face was obscured under his heavy hood. He held a large book and a slim metal box under one arm; from his other hand a small brass censer hung suspended on a long chain and was already smoking with the heavy scent of holy incense.

Avetante jumped from the little skiff as soon as it came aground and rushed over to the Abbe. They exchanged a few words and nods then Avetante returned to where Francisco Garcia and the Planas brothers were waiting.

"Take this!" he said, and tossed the net to José, then, "You, take this!" He tossed the rope and canvas into Gabriel's hands. Next he lifted the pick axe and swung it over his shoulder. "All of you, arm yourselves," he told them, looking into each of their faces in turn and motioning to the machetes remaining in the bottom of the skiff.

"I am armed!" Garcia declared. Avetante looked over Garcia and his crowbar with an arched eyebrow and a slightly bemused expression.

"Good," he said at last. "You can lead the way!"

Garcia seemed to lose his bluster for a moment. "Very well," he coughed, and stepped toward the front of the group. He hesitated. The others exchanged knowing glances.

Avetante stepped over to him. "It was you who found him, wasn't it?" he asked, to which Garcia nodded. "And you do know the way, don't you?" Again, Garcia nodded. Avetante held out an arm toward the mossy, lowering darkness of the swamp. "Après vou!"

Garcia steeled himself and stepped forward. Avetante and the Abbe followed, with José and Gabriel just behind; a resolute Raul brought up the rear.

The little group wound their way in silence through the suffocating pathways of the swamp; darkness had overtaken them, and a night of no moon. On Avetante's orders, Garcia was provided with only a small, partially-concealed lantern to light his way. Any brighter light, Avetante said, might alert the Zombi King to their presence long before they could see him. At first the night noises of the marshland were overwhelming; the whelping of frogs, the buzzing of insects, and fish and tiny animals plopping here and there among the gnarled cypress knees were oddly magnified amid the claustrophobia of the trees. But as the men continued to advance, a brooding silence began to settle over everything, and the trees and brush seemed to bend in closer on either side; the swamp was watchful, almost as if it were a thing alive and aware of their intrusion.

They had walked some little distance when slowly, insidiously, a powerful stench overcame them, a heavy miasma of swamp rot, decay, and the unmistakable smell of death. They advanced slowly into an area where the trees and undergrowth were thin and soon found themselves exposed, standing on the sloping edge of a patch of boggy, wet earth. Avetante held up a hand and the men came to a halt in a bunch behind him. Together with the Abbe, he stepped forward tentatively, pacing up and down along the edge of the bog; though the ground looked firm enough, they were hesitant to cross over it. The two men exchanged a few, hushed words, and nodded, apparently coming to an agreement.

The Abbe stepped forward carefully and made the Sign of the Cross saying, "In nomine Patris, et Filii, et Spiritus sancti. Amen." Avetante and the others followed suit. "Adjutorium nostrum in nomine Domine qui fecit cælum et terram, Amen," the Abbe went on. "Our help is in the name of the Lord who hath made heaven and earth. Amen." And the men all said, "Amen."

The Abbe blew the smoking censer into life and extended it over the clearing, and pacing back and forth, prayed quietly under his breath. If he crossed himself, the men standing nearby did the same; if he said "Amen," they echoed him. Then the Abbe nodded at Avetante; he turned to the men. "Pray with him now," he said, and they all prayed: "May the almighty and merciful Lord grant us pardon, absolution, and remission of our sins. Thou shalt turn again, O God, and quicken us, and Thy people shall rejoice in Thee."

Suddenly, Garcia, who stood closest to the rank, spongy earth, screamed and cried out in a shrill voice, "Madre de Dios!" He fell to the ground; the lantern snuffed out. "Help me!" he cried. "Help!"

The Planas brothers rushed to his aid but quickly recoiled in horror. A putrid arm, grey and swollen, a hand with blackened flesh flaking under long, yellowed fingernails, had Garcia's leg in a powerful grip and was pulling him into the earth. In abject terror, Garcia beat frantically at the arm with his iron crowbar.

"Sistrenatus!" Avetante called out to the Abbe, as another yellowed arm broke from the ground.

Sistrenatus rushed over and cried in a commanding voice, "Show us Thy mercy, O Lord, and grant us Thy salvation!" He waved the censer furiously over the moving earth. "O Lord, hear my prayer, and let my cry come unto Thee! Amen!"

"Zombies!" Avetante cried through gritted teeth as he at last pulled Garcia free. He rolled out of the reach of the monstrous arms and crawled to the feet of the Planas brothers who sat transfixed, gaping wide-mouthed at the sight unfolding before them. The mucky, black earth was *moving* . . . The mud itself was crawling, as if a hundred snakes lay beneath it, struggling toward the surface. A vile, squalid smell filled all the air around them – the smell of putrefaction and death made their stomachs churn.

"Take away from us our iniquities, we beseech Thee, O Lord," Abbe Sistrenatus prayed, "that we may be worthy to enter with pure minds into the Holy of Holies!"

Avetante, realizing he must retain control and keep the men calm, motioned for them to join the prayer. "This we beseech Thee, O Lord, by the merits of all Thy saints," Sistrenatus went on, and here the men joined in vigorously, "that Thou wouldst vouchsafe to forgive us our sins, Amen."

The ground was roiling now, alive with furtive movements, and the smell was nearly unbearable. The Abbe, unmoved, continued praying and calmly incensed the earth, though it writhed before him like a hellish quicksand. Garcia and the Planas brothers drew back toward the trees.

"May this incense which Thou hast blessed, O Lord, ascend to Thee, and may Thy mercy descend upon us," the Abbe prayed. Then from out of the metal box he removed a bottle, opened it, and with wide, sweeping motions cast its contents about upon the ground saying, "I saw water flowing from the right side of the Temple, Alleluia!" And all the men said, "Alleluia!"

"And all unto whom that water came were saved, and they shall say, Alleluia! Alleluia!" Sistrenatus cried, and the holy water hissed as it fell upon the fouled earth. "O, praise the Lord, for He is good, His mercy endureth forever. Amen!" And all the men said, "Amen!" The writhing mass recoiled at the touch of the holy water, and from beneath the puckering earth came a groaning sound, like the doors of tombs being forced open against ancient, rusted hinges.

Now the Abbe took out a consecrated Eucharist, the Body of Christ. He broke it and cast it upon the ground, where, to the frightful amazement of the others, the putrid heads and faces of decomposing corpses could now be clearly seen. The Abbe said: "I will take the bread of heaven and will call upon the Lord. May the Body of our Lord Jesus Christ save these souls and preserve them to life everlasting. Take the bread of the Lord, call upon the Lord and be saved. Amen!" The men all crossed themselves and said, "Amen!"

Very soon a fright even greater than before came over them, and even Avetante, who had stood staunchly by all this time, assisting the Abbe, stepped back cautiously. The random boiling of the earth had stopped, but the entire clearing now appeared to rise up and then go down, up and down; it belched forth a foul mist that hung heavy in the air, as if the ground itself was breathing!

"Move back!" Avetante cried, and pulled out his handkerchief. "Cover your faces! Do not breathe the air!" The men all did as he ordered, their kerchiefs flapping out surreally like little white sails in the smothering darkness.

Sistrenatus knew he must act quickly. He cast his hood back and, swinging the smoking censer in wide arcs with one hand, he held up his other hand over the swollen earth and cried: "If Thou, O Lord, should keep account of sins, who could stand before Thee? Those that have been humbled shall rejoice in the Lord, Amen! A hymn, O God, becometh Thee in Sion, and a vow shall be paid to Thee in Jerusalem: O Lord, hear my prayer: All flesh shall come to Thee! Amen!"

The Abbe reached into a leather bag that hung upon the cincture about his waist and pulled forth several shiny objects that looked like silver coins. These he cast widely upon the earth and said: "Almighty Lord, their debt is paid! Eternal rest grant unto them, O Lord, and let perpetual light shine upon them! O God, through whose mercy the souls of the faithful find rest, be pleased to bless this grave. Send Thy holy angels and loose from the bonds of sin the souls of those whose bodies here lie buried, that they may ever rejoice in Thee with Thy saints and angels, through Christ, Our Lord, Amen!"

Avetante and the other men stepped back into the line of trees, so foul had the air become, and so loud the sound of breathing; it seemed the ground was about to explode. Then there came from the moldy earth a hiss, as of a long sigh of breath extended after great effort. The ground shook slightly and then was still, and the air, that only moments before had hung so heavily with the foul reek of death, now suddenly cleared. The festering zombies that Bras Coupé had created and confined to the earth in that spot to be his wards, his watchmen, his soldiers, had all been exorcised and their souls released by the ritual which the holy Abbe had performed.

Sistrenatus solemnly replaced his hood, but not before José Planas caught a glimpse of him: a Spaniard, with the brown skin of his race, a rugged, handsome face framed with a mass of black hair except where a shock of white was brushed back from the forehead. There, it appeared to José, Sistrenatus had been clawed by something, and still bore the mark; four deep gashes marred his face from the hairline into his cheek. His right eye was black as ink, but his left eye, where the scars had crossed his heavy brow, gleamed like an icy blue marble in the rekindled lantern's light. Sistrenatus motioned silently for them all to move on.

Garcia no longer wished to be in the lead and so José moved forward to take his place, with him giving directions from behind. The men stepped gingerly along the edge of what was now a sanctified grave, and as he walked along, José peered at the back of the Abbe's rough cassock hood.

"He is a brave man," he whispered to Avetante.

"That was nothing," Avetante replied. José felt a knot rise in his throat and swallowed hard.

They walked on. No one spoke; each man was listening intently. The silence that had previously plagued them had returned, more oppressive than before. Nothing stirred. It seemed the entire swamp was pensive, listening, watchful and alive.

There was more than the supernatural to fear under the dark, vaulted canopy of the cypress trees. Living things, too, posed a danger to them, as here and there they came upon a poisonous viper or heard the demon-like hissing of alligators, unseen, but lurking too close for comfort in the shadows. With only the spare lantern light and the stuttering directions of a frightened Garcia to guide them, the going was slow. At last they reached a patch of swamp so thickly overgrown that it seemed they could go no further. Yet here, Garcia said, was the very edge of the hiding place of the Zombi King.

Avetante went forward and looked about, examining the thick brush and hanging vines closely. The men watched as he reached out toward a tree whose branches hung low with small green fruit; he withdrew his hand quickly and with an audible gasp. "Mancenillier!" he hissed, looking above and all around. The trees were thick overhead, nearly blocking out the sky; the sickly green fruit hung over them and littered the ground under their feet. "Get back!" Avetante barked. "Move away!"

"What is it?" José asked.

"Mancenillier!" Avetante replied, rubbing his hand on his chest, even though he had not touched a thing. "Deadly poisonous! The sap can kill within minutes." He snapped his fingers to illustrate the point. "Even a drop of rain that has passed the leaf of the mancenillier can sicken a strong man if it touches his skin! We cannot go this way."

Gabriel poked Garcia in his back. "You have gotten us lost!" he whispered angrily. Raul, standing close beside his brother, sighed wearily.

Garcia was about to reply when a sudden crack, like the sound of a twig snapping underfoot, came from the area behind them. Avetante blew out the lantern. Instinctively, the men drew close together, forming a circle, weapons ready. There came a creaking, followed by a snap, then another crack and the sound of brush underfoot. Footfalls. Something was walking out in the inky-blackness of the swamp.

"Something is out there," José whispered.

"Some swamp animal," Gabriel choked hopefully, but even he didn't believe it.

"Hush!" said Avetante. He took a single step forward, peering at the wall of darkness around them, as if his very gaze could pierce trees, shadow, and night. Soon he could discern many shining points of light moving through the darkness, in and out of the twisted shafts of the trees, coming closer. Aware of the looming danger of the mancenillier grove behind them, he knew they would have to make a stand against whatever approached. "They are coming," he said.

José felt his heart leap into his mouth; beside him, Francisco Garcia swayed as if he might faint. José held him firm. Gabriel and Raul raised their machetes, though they could see nothing approaching, neither friend nor foe. Suddenly, however, the men caught sight of what Avetante's sharp eyes had already seen.

"Holy God," José whispered.

"Zombies!" Garcia choked.

Abbe Sistrenatus drew out his holy water and anointed the men and himself, and then asperged a circle around them. He blew the smoking censer into renewed life and completed another circle, encasing them all in heady fragrance. Then in a whisper, he began to pray.

The sound of the approaching zombies filled the swamp around them, furtive steps and a rustling sound, drawing an ever-tightening noose about the little group. Eyes, like shining dots of silver, flickered among the trees; the men could now perceive the shadowy forms moving through the brush, from tree to tree, coming closer and closer. The air around the men was filled with the sound of labored breathing and hollow groanings that made every hair on their bodies stand on end. Fear grew with every excruciating moment.

José Planas stood frozen, grasping tightly to the handle of his machete, and propping up a quaking Garcia with his back. He was aware of what was happening, of the very real danger in which he now found himself, and yet the whole thing seemed surreal, like a vision from a dark nightmare. At any moment, he thought, Pauline would shake him awake and laugh at his fit, and the bright light of a summer morning would be flooding through the windows of their little houseboat. He was in his bed, he thought, safe and sound.

Sistrenatus drew back his hood and, holding up the golden crucifix that hung about his neck, said in a loud voice: "Help me, O Lord, my God, because Thy servant has exercised himself in Thy commands!"

Then Avetante joined him saying, "Blessed are the undefiled in the way, who walk in the law of the Lord! Help us, O Lord, my God: save us for Thy mercy's sake!"

The rustling and groaning in the woods grew louder: the first of the zombies were now breaking through the tangle of the trees. The men could just see their twisted features; their bulbous eyes transfixed and staring, their broken, yellowed teeth snapping in mouths full of rotting flesh; their emaciated forms draped with the ragged, filthy remains of clothing. They passed surreally in and out of sight, moving through the shadows of the trees; they glowed a deathly grey as they here and there crossed open spaces, and the faint moonlight illuminated their skin. Their awful groans turned to growls as all at once they caught sight of the living men, and the momentum of their movements quickened as they advanced upon their prey. The air was choked with the unbearable stench of death.

"Ready, men!" Avetante cried. "They are upon us!" At once, a tall, gangly zombie moved toward Avetante, growling and grinding its awful teeth. José and the others watched in amazement as Avetante swung out with his pick axe and buried it in the zombie's head. But they could not watch for long, as soon they were also fighting off other zombies. Machete blades swung, and blood flew everywhere, and the black maw of the swamp belched forth more and more of the hellish creatures.

Undeterred, Sistrenatus continued to pray, crying out in a loud voice to be heard over the din of the dead: "Bless the Lord, all ye his Angels!" he cried. "You that are mighty in strength and execute His word, hearken to the voice of His orders! Bless the Lord, O my soul; and let all that is within me bless His holy name!" He drew out holy water and sprinkled it over the group, and as drops of the blessed water flicked onto the zombies, they hissed and growled.

"Alleluia! Alleluia! Saint Michael Archangel," Sistrenatus prayed, "defend us in the day of battle, that we may not perish in the dreadful judgment! Alleluia! All ye angels of the Lord, bless the Lord: sing a hymn, and exalt Him above all forever!

Out of the depths we cry to Thee, O Lord! Lord, hear our prayer!"

The noise of the approaching zombies was now at a fever pitch and as they reached for the men with mottled, rotting arms, it was all the group could do to fend off the attacks; in front of Avetante a little mound of zombie bodies had piled up. There was barely time to think, but the Planas brothers exchanged knowing looks, silently acknowledging their bonds of memory and love, each believing he was entering the last moments of his life on this earth. Then, suddenly, the zombies stopped their attack; indeed, they stopped moving altogether and stood absolutely still. The sickly glow of their eyes winked out, the groaning ceased – all was stench and absolute silence. Yet there was a feeling . . . It permeated the very air: Something was coming, something *else*.

Sistrenatus had not ceased praying; though he only whispered now, in the ominous vacuum that had suddenly formed around them the men heard his every word. "Thou shalt not be afraid for the terror by night; nor for the arrow that flieth by day," he whispered. "Nor for the pestilence that walketh in darkness . . ."

Suddenly, as if in answer to those very words, the mossy, vine-strangled cypress trees facing them were torn away in one tangled mass, as if a cannon ball had struck and blown them down. In place of the trees stood an enormous shadowy mass, man-shaped and panting like an angry bull. It towered over them, a black hole against the black night sky.

⚜⚜⚜⚜

José leaned forward wearily and rubbed his face. Pauline, who had until now sat silent and transfixed, reached out and took her husband's hands in hers.

"You don't need to go on," she said, soothing him in her soft Irish voice.

José shook his head. "No," he said. "No, you should hear this. Ah! Pauline, I have never been so frightened in my life. But you should have seen it! Power against power, force against force!"

Pauline looked puzzled. "What do you mean?"

"I mean the Abbe, and Avetante!" José replied, almost laughing. "*They* had no fear, I can tell you! No, indeed!"

"Well, tell me!" Pauline cried, anxious now to hear the rest of the story. "Go on!"

José looked at her and sighed. "Well . . ."

※※※※

"This is it, men!" Avetante cried, hoisting the pick-axe into his hands. "Have no fear of this shadow man! Shadow and smoke are all he is!"

The shadowy mass stood to its full, incredible height and seemed to draw a breath meant to deprive the very night of air. "So I'm nothin' to fear, am I?" said a deep voice from inside the blackness, a fearsome growl from the bottom of a pit. "We'll see 'bout dat! Yass! We gwon't see 'bout dat!"

Avetante laughed, an unexpected sound in that tense darkness. "Yes, *we is*!" he said, mockingly, goading the thing to anger. "Bras Coupé, your time has come!" he went on. "Time to answer for the souls you have stolen, the men and women you have killed!"

The huge shadow swayed back and forth; far above them, where it seemed the face of the monster must have been, two points of red fire glowed. Avetante's eyes were fixed on these points as all the while he was reaching deep inside his coat pocket. In another instant, he drew out a small bottle – something strange was inside, the contents flashed as he swept it into the air. "Get back, shadow man!" he cried, and with that threw the bottle to the ground.

There was a small explosion and a tremendous flash of blinding white light that sparked like blue-white stars and lit up the fetid darkness. It was as if the liquid from the bottle had a mind of its own and the men, who had up to now been cowering behind Avetante, watched in amazement as a fiery, white ring spread out, encircling the shadowy shape of the monstrous Bras Coupé.

Now they could clearly see his human form, a tall black man with skin like onyx, waving with his one good arm as the

flames leapt up around him. But his face was not like any
man's: bloodied, red lips stretched wide in a howling scream
and revealed a mouth full of broken, yellowed, fang-like teeth;
his eyes were not like human eyes at all, but instead were two
solid orbs like flaming rubies filled with a supernatural glow;
even his ears were Devil-like, long and pointed, and standing
up almost like horns astride the obsidian-black dome of his
bare head; but strangest of all were the markings, like letters of
a weird, fantastic alphabet, shining red as a hot poker all across
the throbbing surface of his skin. He was hideous to behold, a
thing ruined and possessed, now only barely human.

Avetante laughed again, his face brightened by the slowly-
fading flare of his potion. Lifting the pick-axe above his head,
he swung it and let it fall, striking Bras Coupé in the ribs under
his ruined arm. The Zombi King let out a fearsome, demonic
howl – he seemed surprised that the blow had injured him!
This was the signal for the others and they now moved forward
in unison, hacking and cutting with the machetes, Francisco
Garcia pounding blindly with his crow bar. Bras Coupé yowled
and twisted under the blows like a demon in the abyss of Hell.
Avetante's ruse and the fierceness of the attack that followed
had indeed taken the creature off his guard, shaking him and
preventing him from rallying a response. But the attack on his
body had not dulled his mind; as they continued to hack and
beat, the men were once again aware of movements around
them and in the woods nearby: Bras Coupé was calling upon
his zombies. But Avetante was thinking swiftly, too.

"Get the net!" he cried. Quickly, José and Gabriel moved to
unfurl the net. "Sistrenatus!" Avetante called, and the Abbe
stepped forward as if on cue.

He again asperged a circle around the men, now grappling
hand-to-hand with the struggling fiend; then he threw out the
contents of the censer, and the incense combined with the
remnants of the strange fire Avetante had thrown, reigniting it
in a rainbow flare of smoke, scent, and color. The Abbe drew
out his holy book once more and, holding up his golden
crucifix, began to intone: "To Thee, O Lord, have I lifted up
my soul. In Thee, my God, I put my trust: let me not be

ashamed. Neither let my enemies laugh at me, for none of them that wait on Thee shall be confounded."

The men felt Bras Coupé falter under their grasp as Sistrenatus spoke these words; then, just as quickly, he was fighting with renewed vigor.

"Bind him!" Avetante ordered. The men wrapped the yards of netting around the body of the great Zombi King; Avetante turned his attention to the other zombies approaching from the swamps, but this time he used a simple approach: fire. He broke the lantern and poured its oil over the smoldering remnants of his potion and the incense. A circle of flames roared into life around them; it kept the advancing zombies at bay and cast a hellish light on what was quickly becoming the demise of their maker.

"Remember not, Lord, our offenses," Sistrenatus cried, "nor the offenses of our forefathers, neither take Thou vengeance upon our sins. Our Father," he began, and the men prayed along as they worked. At the moment of "Amen," Avetante again buried his pick-axe deep into the back of the Zombi King. The beast cried out, fighting violently, and blood spewed from his wound.

"Save thy servant, O my God" Sistrenatus cried loudly.

"That putteth his trust in Thee," Avetante responded, breathing hard.

"Be unto him, O Lord, a fortified tower," said Sistrenatus.

"From the face of his enemy," Avetante responded, wrapping canvas about the head of the creature, lest he breathe on them all.

"Let the enemy have no advantage of him," said Sistrenatus.

"Nor the son of wickedness approach to hurt him," Avetante replied, as nearby Raul and Garcia were unwinding the rope with which to bind the beast.

"Send him help, O Lord, from Thy sanctuary," Sistrenatus cried.

"And strengthen him out of Sion," Avetante made response.

"Lord, hear my prayer," Sistrenatus prayed.

"And let my cry come unto Thee!" Avetante replied through gritted teeth as Bras Coupé fought anew, crying now with a man's voice, muffled under the canvas.

"The Lord, be with you," said Sistrenatus.

"And also with you," all the men replied, as much out of old habit as of fear.

"Hold him!" Avetante ordered as he stepped away to rekindle the flaming ring of naphtha that protected them. José and the others held fast. Bras Coupé fought in violent spasms and then would relax. At first he had growled like a wild, trapped beast, but now he cried out audibly, like a man, and under the canvas his shoulders shook, as if he were crying.

"Leave me alone," he sobbed, "go away! I ain't hurt nobody! Ain't gwon't hurt nobody! Where mah drank? I jes' wants to live free! I jes wants to has mah drank!"

"Don't listen to him," Avetante said, his eyes flashing. "Pay him no heed! Bind him!" he pointed at the rope in Raul's hand.

Nearby, Sistrenatus continued to pray. "O God, Whose property is ever to have mercy and to forgive: receive our supplications and prayers, that of Thy mercy and loving-kindness Thou wilt set free this Thy servant who is fast bound by the chain of his sins!"

At this Bras Coupé roared and fought anew, kicking and ripping at the canvas covering. "No! Damn yo, priest! Damn yo to Hell! I ain't gwon nowhere," he added, with an evil laugh.

Sistrenatus sprinkled the holy water; again Bras Coupé roared. The Abbe continued: "O holy Lord, Father Almighty, Eternal God, the Father of our Lord Jesus Christ: Who hast assigned that tyrant and apostate to the fires of hell; and hast sent Thine Only Begotten Son into the world, that He might bruise him as he roars after his prey: make haste, tarry not, to deliver this man, created in Thine Own image and likeness, from ruin, and from the noon-day devil!"

It was at this moment that José, and perhaps the other men, too, realized that while they bound the body of Bras Coupé, Sistrenatus and Avetante were exorcising him, and binding his spirit to free his soul. Bras Coupé was fighting violently now; clearly he realized this, too. At one point he nearly ripped through the canvas, at another he kicked so fiercely that Gabriel was tossed back, nearly into the deadly hands of the growling zombies. Avetante stood over them, covered in blood and panting fiercely.

"Is he secure?" he cried.

"I think so, yes!" José replied.

"Good," Avetante said, and taking Garcia's heavy crow bar he swung high and came down upon the head of Bras Coupé where it strained under the canvas. The blow made a horrible rending sound, a "pop" like a ripe melon when it is dropped on hard ground. The men stood in shocked silence, staring at the gruesome red stain spreading on the canvas. Avetante threw the crowbar aside. "Drag him," he panted, and stepped over the dying circle of flames.

"But the others – !" José cried, coming back to his wits.

"Are dead," Avetante said flatly.

Dawn was just blushing in the eastern sky when the men, dragging their heavy captive, came once again to the shore of St. John's Bayou. Avetante had spoken the truth. The zombie slaves of Bras Coupé had all perished when his power was broken. As he came upon their bodies, in various stages of putrefaction and decomposition, Sistrenatus rendered blessings, and watching this, José came to understand the purpose. The zombies had once been human, and out of compassion the priest was giving them the sacrament of forgiveness so that their souls might enter heaven. Sistrenatus continued, too, in the exorcism of Bras Coupé, who was not dead, but lapsed in and out of consciousness in his canvas snare. Now and then he cursed the priest and struggled, but most of the time he simply wept and moaned, begging to be let out, begging for a drink.

With great effort they loaded the body of Bras Coupé onto the little skiff. José was given the oars. Avetante and Sistrenatus accompanied him and stayed with the body on the far shore as the others came across. It took all their efforts to lift the huge man into José's cart, but it was accomplished. The men piled in, shocked, exhausted, and bloodstained; with Garcia at the reins, they struck out toward the Bayou Road and the Old Carré.

"You can imagine the sight," José told his attentive wife, "five men, full of blood, a monk, and a cargo waking up and screaming out at random moments. We did not get very far before we were overtaken by the militia. Avetante did all the talking; at least one of the men appeared to recognize him. Of course, they did not believe him when he said that we had the body of Bras Coupé in the bottom of the cart. They climbed up and made us pull back the canvas . . ." His voice trailed off. Pauline waited patiently.

"He woke up again," José continued, "Bras Coupé – he was awake, well, only barely. His face was all bloody, and his brains, they were," he lifted his hand to his head to demonstrate, "coming out between the cracks in his skull . . . Anyway, the militiamen offered to escort us, but really they were taking things over. Two of them jumped up onto the cart. They were French, and they kept kicking the body, saying things that I didn't understand. I didn't want to. And they pulled at the canvas, wanting to see more of him. They only stopped because Avetante made them.

"'A lot of hard work went into that,' he told them. 'I do not want it undone.' He gave them a long look and they sat very still. But I had to fix the canvas, wrap it back tightly and secure the rope – Gabriel and Raul wanted nothing more to do with it – and it was the strangest thing, maybe the very strangest thing out of the whole experience . . ."

Again, José's voice trailed off and he fell silent. Pauline waited. After a few tense minutes she said, "What?" José looked at her. "What was strange?" she cried.

He sighed. "I can't explain it," he replied and shook his head. "Bras Coupé was still alive. He was moving and making sounds – he looked right at me, right into my eyes, but . . ."

"But what?" Pauline asked, now anxious to know.

"In the daylight he was pale, almost grey," José said, "and not from loss of blood. His skin looked . . . dead. There is no other way to describe it. His eyes were clouded like those of a corpse that has been dead many days, but he moved and spoke. And the smell! Pah!" He lifted his hands to his nose. "The smell that came up from him," he said, shaking his head, "it was awful, unbearable. He smelled like an open grave! And when I was tightening the canvas around his shoulders," here José shuddered, *"his skin moved under my hand!* It was putrid, decomposing, the flesh of a dead man!"

There was a long silence. At last Pauline spoke. "Then it was all true," she said quietly, "what they said about him, that he was undead, a corpse kept alive, a . . ."

"A zombie," José finished her sentence. "A zombie," he repeated, and nodded. "Yes. Somehow, I don't know how, he kept himself alive out there," here he turned to look at the pitch black tree line of the distant swamp. "He should have died – maybe he did die – when his master shot him. But that was *three years ago!"*

"He might have survived the gunshot," Pauline mused.

"But everyone said he could not be killed," José replied, and shook his head. "Is it because *he was already dead?"*

José went on to tell his wife how a crowd of the idle and the curious had quickly congregated around the little cart and followed it where it crossed the Rue des Ramparts into the Esplanade. Word of their approach preceded them and as Garcia turned the cart into Cathedral Alley, they found it jammed with people: they lined balconies and spilled over into the Rue Condé and the Rue Royale, and were filling the Place d'Armes. Jose and the others could see the doors of the calaboose standing open, but they could not drive through the throngs of people to get to it.

Finally, the militiamen jumped down from the cart and began to push the people back; Garcia got out and inched the horse forward, with Avetante now standing up at the reins. It was all the Planas brothers could do to keep back the hands of the curious, who reached into the cart and tugged at the canvas and ropes, eager to get a glimpse of the body of the Zombi King. This was the moment José noticed that Sistrenatus was no longer with them: wanting nothing to do with the mayhem, and there being nothing more he could do, the Abbe had quietly slipped away.

At last the cart and the body of Bras Coupé came before the gates of the calaboose. Several official-looking men came out to inspect the body; they seemed delighted to hear that the brigand was still alive, if only barely. But as they leaned in for a better view, they all recoiled from the smell, and hid their faces behind their kerchiefs and cravats. A great commotion ensued; people came and went, running here and there. Avetante was called inside the calaboose and motioned for the men to follow him, but José and his brothers refused.

"But the reward . . ." Avetante said.

José held up a hand and pointed to Garcia, "Go get it," he said, and wearily slid down the whitewashed calaboose wall.

More militiamen poured out of the calaboose doors and took up positions around the wooden cart. Not long afterward, Avetante and Garcia emerged, the latter holding an important-looking document. They came over to where José, Gabriel, and Raul sat.

"Sign this," Garcia said, waving the document and a pen before their faces.

José looked up wearily. "What is it?"

"A statement of the capture," Avetante told him.

"You all have to sign, if you want the money," Garcia said.

José shook his head. "You sign," he said, waving Garcia away. "You can have the credit."

"Don't you want your portion of the reward?" Garcia said incredulously.

José looked at him and sighed. "We trust you," he said, at which Gabriel and Raul both nodded. "Avetante is our witness."

Garcia seemed exasperated. "Very well," he said, and stomped back toward the calaboose gate. Avetante bent down and put a hand on José's shoulder.

"Are you alright, my friend?" he asked.

"Yes," José said, managing a wan smile. "I am very tired."

Avetante nodded. "I understand. Well, it is nearly over."

The mayor dispersed the militia to all corners of the Carré to announce the capture of Bras Coupé, and to compel every slave and person of color in the old city to assemble immediately in the Place d'Armes.

"Why are they doing that?" José asked distractedly as he was counting through his portion of the reward money. Avetante had refused to accept any portion, so Garcia and each of the Planas brothers received the handsome sum of two-hundred and fifty American dollars for their efforts.

"They want them all to witness the hanging," Garcia said, matter-of-factly.

José stared at Garcia. "Hanging?"

"Yes," Garcia shrugged. "They want to make an example of him, to show those scoundrels that if they forget their place, or want to start another rebellion, the same fate will befall them."

José was speechless. He stuffed the cash into his pocket and walked wearily over to his cart where Bras Coupé lay under guard. Explaining that he was its owner, he unbridled his horse, and with a long look to his brothers, slowly turned and walked away. Gabriel and Raul fell in step behind and Avetante, with a last nod to Garcia, hurried to catch them up.

As they walked on, from everywhere, from every corner of the city, in long lines and clustered in frightened groups, a steady stream of people flowed past them. Men, women, children - all came, slave and free black, passing like estuaries of a vast, murmuring river, all heeding the call to be witnesses to the death of their fallen hero.

※※※※

José fell silent and for several minutes Pauline did not move or speak. Her gaze was fixed upon the money where it lay on the tabletop. Then, she looked up at her husband and, without saying a word, pushed the money away.

The next morning, José rose early and made the long trek back into the city along the Bayou Road. Not in a hurry, he wound his way through the familiar streets until he found himself at the steps of the Cathedral. He could not keep from looking across the expanse of the Place d'Armes to where the gallows stood, empty now because the corpse of the Zombi King had so offended with its horrible odor that after only two hours it was taken down and secretly buried. The tinkling of a bell called José out of his thoughts.

There, on the corner of St. Anthony's Alley, stood the now-familiar figure of Abbe Sistrenatus. He rang a small bell and held a metal money box in his hand, which he extended to passers-by as he called out in a monotone voice, "Animabus in purgatorio! Animabus in purgatorio! Animabus in purgatorio!"

José went over to Sistrenatus. A few coins littered the bottom of the metal box, and José recalled how Sistrenatus spread coins upon the zombie grave. Not certain if he believed in a heaven or a purgatory, but certain that he had been shown a glimpse of hell, José thought of all the unhallowed graves that might yet be littering the St. John's swamp. He reached into his pocket and, pulling out his reward money, placed it in the box. The Abbe nodded a silent acknowledgement and went on with his work.

As he walked away, José sent up a supplication, a little prayer for those lonely graves and the victims sleeping fitfully in them. "Requiescant in pace!" he said. "Requiescant in pace!"

"Strange rumors were in circulation of this subject. Sometimes it was a detachment of troops that had ventured to the haunt of this brigand, who disappeared without any trace . . . Sometimes it was the hunter whose ball was flattened against the breast of the brigand, whose skin was rendered invulnerable by certain herbs with which he rubbed it. The Negroes asserted that his look fascinated, and that he fed on human flesh . . . He was finally captured and sentenced to be hung in the Square opposite the Spanish church . . . and the infecting odors exhaled by his corpse but two hours after his execution made them bury him, contrary to the law that condemned him to remain suspended on the gallows for two days."

L. Moreau Gottschalk, **Notes of a Pianist**

PART THREE: LORE

The Ghost

True to their spectral natures, ghosts defy neat categorization. Fortunately, folklore provides an abundance of evidence describing various types of ghosts, and since the bulk of this folklore originates in the European countries that helped populate New Orleans, we can most easily refer to this for a better understanding of the types of ghosts early New Orleanians would have known.

They would certainly recognize the transiting spirit of someone recently deceased, and there is barely an old family in New Orleans that cannot offer a tale of seeing the apparition of a family member at the time of his or her passing. Sometimes it is the voice of the loved one heard when no apparition is seen, or evidence of some old habit – the smell of coffee in an empty kitchen, a favorite perfume – that serves to reassure those family members left behind that the spirit of the departed lives on, if invisible to the physical world.

Ghosts with an innocuous purpose could easily have populated the supernatural atmosphere of old New Orleans, especially when the transience of life in those early years is taken into consideration. Disease, pestilence, attack, and traditions such as dueling – all these factors and more played into the background of daily life in the city. Yellow fever, cholera, malaria, and the other unforgiving plagues of the wild environment plucked more than their "fair share" from the very bloom of life; many times a vibrant breakfast partner could be suddenly sickened and lie dead in the family home that night.

Often the spirits of these dead, forced into such untimely departures, would linger near family and friends to fulfill a certain purpose. Many New Orleans families have stories to tell of how the ghosts of dead loved ones assisted them in discovering lost treasure and documents; others can relate how the persistent apparition of a loved one helped to solve crimes or reconcile feuding families. Like purposeful ghosts the world over, once these spirits have accomplished their goal, they are able to move on through death and are usually never seen again. Not so the haunting entity or vengeful ghost. These are the most frightening of all ghostly encounters because there is a definite sense that an actual personality is present – and that it has an agenda all its own.

Entities will haunt a particular place for an extended period of time usually without any apparent purpose beyond frightening the living. A wide range of phenomena accompanies the entity haunting and most of it can be extremely unnerving. Pale images, mists, or shadows are often seen, sounds are heard deep in the night, ghostly touches are felt; the atmosphere will feel oppressive, unwholesome, and often cold and, perhaps most disturbing, it quickly becomes evident that the spirit behind these activities is cognizant and capable of thought. Such spirits are often the result of tragic circumstances that have occurred in a particular place: violent death, insanity, abuse, neglect – these are tragedies that can keep a spirit bound to a place long after everyone else involved has passed on. In modern times, occultists and paranormal investigators have learned ways of dealing with such negative entities that might not have been considered or even known to previous generations; in many cases, a person or family can often be freed from oppression by such entities.

A spirit set on vengeance, however, is far more dangerous to the living and far less likely to respond to efforts to drive it away. Vengeful ghosts are very often the result of some horrible wrong committed against them in life, and they will resist entirely any effort to dissuade them from their goal which is, quite simply, to avenge themselves on the person or persons responsible for their awful situation. The vengeful ghost will not rest until its victims meet an unpleasant fate and more often than not death is the final outcome of this spirit's depredations. A question long-pondered by occultists is whether or not such insatiable vengeance, once enacted in the physical world, persists against the spirits of the victims of this type of ghost once they, too, join it in the realm of the unseen.

The Vampire

The occult tradition that lies behind the legend and lore of the vampire is one that is aimed at achieving personal immortality by deliberately evading death, usually through magical means. Before the onset of the Scientific Revolution – and later in spite of it – occult practitioners, very wise scholars, and even Church fathers were taught to understand that death was a process. Not simply the immediate cessation of life, the process of dying is a gradual detachment of the spirit from the physical world. It is when a spirit does not complete the entire process that it remains within reach of our world and is able to trouble the living.

Ghosts can become accidentally trapped in this condition, but in the case of the vampire there is usually a resistance to the normal death process. The spirit of the would-be vampire might be particularly strong and able to remain conscious in the dreamy, after-death twilight, or it may be frightened enough to be aware of its condition and therefore able to work to avoid its final transition into the realm of the dead.

Perhaps the spirit's attachment to the material world, with all its physical pleasures and addictions, is enough to galvanize it into quickly learning how to stabilize itself in the etheric realm before the disintegration of the death process becomes too advanced. As long as this stabilization can be maintained, the spirit body will remain intact. Therefore the goal of the vampire become's keeping its spirit body strong enough to continue to resist natural disintegration; this can only be achieved successfully when two other conditions are met.

The first of these is the preservation of the vampire's physical body in a state that will allow the spirit to continue to take refuge in it; this is why destruction of the corpse is such an important step in destroying a vampire. As long as a physical remnant of the vampire's body remains, its spirit is assured stability. This condition does much to explain why the vampire is so prevalent in the lore of New Orleans, a city well-known for its necropolises of above-ground tombs and mausoleums. Many of the oldest tombs and wall vaults have received burials almost continuously since the founding of the city; there are certainly plenty of physical remains that might hold the anchor of a vampire's existence.

The second condition necessary for the vampire's survival is a continuous source of fresh energy on which to feed. The sources used by living people to sustain our physical life are shut out to the vampire, and so it must rely on predations of the living to replenish what it loses in the course of its nefarious existence. Since the time it was founded New Orleans has bustled with the energy of the living, gathering here in throngs, even today; certainly, there is food enough for any vampire here.

Only once in living memory has there been a time when the undead apparently went hungry: In the dark days following Hurricane Katrina, when New Orleans was empty of its residents and its tourists, a palpable shadow hung over the old city and moved through the streets. For weeks following the storm, returning New Orleanians reported feeling a heavy sense of oppression in every corner of the city, and news of bizarre incidents – including a horrific, cannibalistic murder – floated on the heavy air. These were the days when the dead went hungry.

The Monster

The Plaquemines Parish of the nineteenth century was a swampy marshland bordering the Mississippi River and extending down to the shores of the Gulf of Mexico. Even in modern times some areas of Plaquemines are still inaccessible except by boat, and although Plaquemines' development parallels the growth of New Orleans, its remoteness and isolation have certainly helped to shape its unique historic landscape.

In New Orleans, Voodoo is a form of religion mixed with magic and is very personal to its practitioners. Its rituals can vary from devotee to devotee, but generally a priest or priestess is recognized as the main conduit through which the world of spirit connects with that of the living, granting petitions and favors, and helping devotees. A slave religion, Voodoo was preserved throughout the African Diaspora via a wise effort on the part of its practitioners to "syncretize" it with the prevailing faith of their white masters. Thus, by aligning its most powerful spirits with the images of saints and religious figures familiar to their host culture, voodoo practitioners were able to continue practicing their faith while giving all the appearance of adhering to the faith of their masters. This type of syncretized belief system is readily evident in New Orleans. However, the voodoo practiced by the slave populations of Plaquemines Parish differed greatly from its counterpart upriver.

The slaves of Plaquemines came to Louisiana with the Isleños, Spanish settlers from the Canary Islands. These Isleños brought a particular type of slave, one that was at variance with the prevailing ethnicity and culture of the majority of other slaves in the Louisiana colony. While most Louisiana slaves could trace their origins to the West Indies and ultimately to places like the Congo and Dahomey on the western coast of Africa, the slaves of the Isleños called eastern Africa home, and one country in particular: Ethiopia.

While the West African slaves developed a form of voodoo that is immediately familiar to anyone with even a passing knowledge of the magical practices of New Orleans, in Plaquemines an entirely different form of voodoo prevailed. The saints, candles, mojos and dolls that so distinguish New Orleans voodoo were nowhere to be found in the rites of the Plaquemines Parish slaves. Instead, the Ethiopians practiced a fetish-based religion centered in the creation and worship of material idols. The Ethiops developed practices through which, they believed, these idols were brought to life and could see, hear, understand, and most importantly act on behalf of their worshippers. These crude figures were constructed from river clay and other materials found in the swamp environment, and ranged in size from small ritual fetishes to substantial, life-sized statues. Locals often called the larger, imposing figures "mud men" and avoided altogether the open clearings hacked out of the swamp by the Ethiops to accommodate the strange rituals associated with their creations.

Locals of European extraction recognized an old craft at work, one that mirrored the practices of medieval Jews who were known to have created and brought to life mud figures called "golems" to serve them as powerful protectors and fearsome avengers. According to some accounts from Plaquemines, the mud men of the Ethiops, quickened by voodoo rituals, walked far abroad from their ritual circles, intent on serving the will of their dark masters and devotees. Not surprisingly, locals fell into the familiar habit of identifying these frightening creatures as "golems of the swamp." This is interesting, too, in light of the fact that the Ethiopians of Africa have long nursed the belief that they are one of the "lost tribes" of ancient Israel.

It is said that hoodoo doctors and rootworkers in Plaquemines continue the tradition of creating and worshipping the swamp golems. What is more alarming are stories that suggest these "mud men" are still being used today to strike fear in the hearts of non-believers and those who pry too deeply into the ways of the dark Louisiana swamps.

The Ghoul

The vengeful infant that returned to maim its mother was well-known in the folklore of Europe and Scandinavia where it even had a name – "utburd," Old Norse for "child [put] outside." The practice of exposing infants was unfortunately common in times of famine, or in instances involving sick or deformed babies, or the progeny of unwed mothers. These unwanted children would be carried outside immediately after birth and placed in a shallow hole in a lonely place, there to die from exposure or the depredations of wild animals; many times mud or snow was stuffed into the infant's mouth to hasten the death process. Though the act may have seemed justified in the moment, the ghosts that were created from these tiny corpses burned with hatred and thirsted for revenge, especially against their mothers. It was widely believed that, in compensation for the infants' helplessness during its few painful days or hours of life, the ghosts of these children were gifted with enormous strength, making them one of the most formidable ghosts anyone could have the misfortune to encounter.

In some instances the rage of these abandoned infants endured long after the mother was dead and gone, and these ghosts often continued to haunt the places connected to their birth and death. Sometimes the mournful crying of the ghosts would be heard near the little grave in which the infant died; and occasionally a traveler might even see, under the nearby brush or in the gnarled roots of an old tree, the phantom of the murdered infant. Most travelers knew better than to approach the spot, or to look too inquisitively into the source of the plaintive cries. To do so might only embolden the creature to leave its grave and take on its supernatural form – that of a powerful, angry, invisible entity burning with hatred for all humankind. If disturbed, it might pursue and attack the wayfarer, leaving only a ravaged body out in the lonely wastes to be found days or weeks later, or in some cases never found at all.

In the pre-modern European mindset, which certainly directly influenced the cultural references of the settlers of New Orleans, ghosts like the "utburd" were part of a broader type of supernatural being that also included the ghoul. Ghouls or ghoulish entities like the "utburd," were distinguished by their propensity to bother, ravage, and even devour the corpses of dead human beings; children killed by their mothers, or those who died before being baptized, were thought to return as ghouls. Inhabiting the waste places surrounding burial grounds, these ghoul-children could be seen in various stages of manifestation, rocking in tree branches and moaning, or sitting in the road, weeping piteously. Some begged to be released by baptism; some begged for passersby to give them a name, and thus release their spirits; others, full of rage, lured the unwary to dangerous places, like cliffs or still ponds, where death was swift to follow, forever entangling the wayfarer's spirit with the wretched infants' ghosts.

Since at least the 1720's there has been a house at the corner of Bourbon and St. Phillip streets. In the days of the Spanish domination the site was also the location of a busy blacksmith shop, and its chief smiths served as designated farriers for the Spanish colonial troops. While the soldiers were garrisoned in the barracks of the "Calle del Arsenal" nearby, their horses were housed in stables adjacent to the smithy. The grassy square between Bourbon and Dauphine streets was where the horses grazed, and was known as the Spanish meadow.

It is generally accepted that the pirate Jean Lafitte used the house and shop as a front for his smuggling operations when the location was owned by Rene Beluche, a known privateer and friend of Lafitte's, and the captain of an infamous pirate vessel, the "Spy." While his brother Pierre ran the smithy, Jean was busy distinguishing himself as a privateer, a spy, and ultimately as a hero in the Battle of New Orleans where he assisted General Andrew Jackson in the defeat of the British.

In modern times the building, the second-oldest in New Orleans, houses the popular Lafitte's Blacksmith Shop bar. The ghosts of pirates, blacksmiths, and the occasional long-standing patron are said to haunt the bar, and sometimes a pair of frightening red eyes are seen to glow in the pitch dark opening of the old fireplace. But the building's most mysterious specter is that of a beautiful, dark-haired woman who appears dressed in black with a black veil covering her face. She is said to manifest in the bar area late at night, keeping to the shadows, and is occasionally seen wandering upstairs or as a mist crossing the bar's exterior courtyard. Although some have suggested that this might be the ghost of a pirate's mistress, the obscure story – related above – of a beautiful Spanish woman who died in that spot may at last reveal the identity of this more-infamous ghost.

The Zombie

"Sometimes Sally interrupted my grandmother to exorcise a 'zombie' of which, she said, she felt the breath on her face. We narrowed our circle, shivering with fright, around my grandmother, who, after crossing herself and scolding Sally, took up her story where she had left off."

Louis Moreau Gottschalk, **Notes of a Pianist**

In the passage above, nineteenth-century New Orleans composer Louis Moreau Gottschalk is recalling a scene from his childhood in which his nurse – the beloved slave Sally – is reacting to the presence of a zombie that she believes is haunting her in spirit form. Meanwhile, Gottschalk's maternal grandmother is telling fireside tales about the fall of her homeland, the French island of Ste. Domingue, and the slave rebellions that ultimately transformed it into that most pivotal source of zombie lore – Haiti.

Throughout his life Gottschalk would often return in his mind to that shadowy place, a source of very real horror and fear for him because so many of his maternal relatives had suffered "unspeakable outrages" at the hands of the rebels and had died there. Passing within sight of the island one night years later during a trip to South America, Gottschalk watched the dark hulk of it rise on the horizon, the rolling backbone of its mountains arching black against the evening sky, and heard its palm-shrouded coast whispering from the impenetrable darkness of its shore. He shivered to recall his grandmother's tales, and yet there was something oddly compelling, almost magical about the place; despite being emblematic of the great suffering of his French ancestors, for Gottschalk the bitter memories mingled with the sweet of that dark island to inspire many of the most brilliant compositions of his long career.

The lore of the zombie was well-known in New Orleans and south Louisiana. Tales of the reanimated dead told among the earliest African slaves were enhanced with the folklore of free people of color and a large island slave population brought there by Ste. Domingue's French refugees. It is obvious from his writings that Gottschalk was familiar with the zombie and probably with the other supernatural beings of that fallen island. In his childhood fantasies, the zombie did not walk alone.

In Haiti the word "zombie" is most frequently used to describe a corpse that has been reanimated through some form of necromancy practiced by the "bokor," voodoo's evil conjurer. The conjurer accomplishes the reanimation with the aid of evil spirits who lurk in cemeteries, waiting among the dead for the opportunity to possess a body and thereby have physical influence on the material world. By providing these spirits with a mortal vessel in which to abide the bokor gains control of the corpse, and thereby the spirit; both become thralls to the conjurer's will. But the evil bokor does not control every aspect of the corpse's new existence; for all his tremendous power he cannot forestall indefinitely the natural decay of the once-human shell. After time, the process of decomposition sets in and even the most indebted spirit will ultimately be able to escape the power of the bokor's spell once the putrefying body becomes uninhabitable.

To avoid this circumstance, evil-minded bokors will often choose to zombify the body of a still-living human being. The shrewd conjurer will often choose the most impressionable and superstitious man or woman he can find from among his followers or neighbors. Once chosen, the zombie "candidate" will unwittingly be subjected to a near-constant regimen of manipulation by the bokor, who will play on both the person's superstitious nature (by amplifying his or her greatest fears) and the prevailing cultural mores concerning the living and the dead. Through the use of ritual and the introduction of just the right amounts of toxic herbs and other substances, the bokor will ultimately achieve a state of suspended animation in the individual that is nearly indistinguishable from actual death. The proper "zombie ingredients" can cause paralysis, loss of reflexes, cessation of pulse, and apparent absence of breathing which the individual's family and friends will easily mistake as the results of natural death.

Owing directly to Haitian fear of zombies, the "dead" person will be hastily buried. Paradoxically, inside the mind of the person now presumed dead, the same superstition and fear that is dictating the actions of family and friends is also at work. "Awaking" in a death state when exhumed by the bokor, the victim is fully convinced not only of having, in fact, died, but also of the obvious fate of having been made into a zombie. What the bokor really exhumes from the grave is a ready-made servant that he will continue to ply with drugs in order to maintain its zombified state. Enthralled by the conjurer, the zombie can easily be manipulated to cause no end of havoc on its master's behalf. Zombies have been used to terrorize and kill their surviving family members and friends; to destroy livestock and cattle; to rob and steal; and even to abduct children and animals for use in magical rituals. But ultimately a zombie's main purpose is to protect its maker, and to serve his or her deadly, nefarious will. Unlike the reanimated corpse, the living zombie will not rapidly decompose, but once created will continue to exist in a normal, if magically-amplified, physical state. Some zombies have been known to outlive their masters and have even been bequeathed by bokors to their descendants whom the zombie will continue to serve as a supernatural slave until the natural span of its own life has been spent.

The bodiless spirit zombie feared by Gottschalk's nurse Sally is also familiar in New Orleans zombie lore. These "astral" zombies are usually the spirit personalities of dead human beings who subsist in a state similar to that of the psychic vampire, though they have been known to attach to and even possess the living. Spirit zombies can be captured – usually inside a bottle – and depending upon the will of the captor can be made to do everything from predicting the future, to healing or harming the living, or even attracting a lover. These captive zombies, very like the proverbial "genie in a bottle," are often passed down through generations in a family that it has sworn to serve by solemn oath. Some believe that it is morally right to free such a captive spirit after a long period of such servitude; others will hold onto them for years upon years.

Because zombies are the products of strong and complicated magic, destroying them is not an easy task. Decapitation is one traditional method of dispatching a zombie, and a good way to be certain it will not reanimate; but this requires gaining close proximity to the creature, something nearly anyone would want to avoid. Salt, the great banisher and cleanser of the magical realm, is also useful against zombies; salt spread around a house, on the windowsills, and all over the path to your door is sure to keep a zombie away. According to folklore, if a zombie ingests salt its spirit is immediately set free to return to God.

In deeply-Catholic south Louisiana the zombie is looked upon as a creature of God brought low and possessed by an invading spirit. Even though the zombie is outwardly a ruined, monstrous being, to the faithful there is still a spark of life within him or her that is worthy of salvation because it was put there by God. In the supernatural world of old New Orleans, where the dark, mysterious island practices that give us the living dead share space with the uplifting faith of our ancestral founders, it is the Catholic funeral rites that are most often used to drive away and destroy a zombie, while at the same time redeeming its immortal soul.

THE END

ALYNE PUSTANIO:
AUTHOR, OCCULTIST, PARANORMALIST

Alyne Pustanio is recognized as one of the foremost authorities in the field of paranormal research, the supernatural, and the occult, and is considered an expert in the folklore and haunted history of her hometown, New Orleans.

Alyne's work in the paranormal field is the natural result of a lifetime of exposure to the supernatural and unexplained. A survivor of supernatural attacks and demonic hauntings, Alyne is especially focused on raising awareness in the paranormal community of the many supernatural dangers inherent in the field of paranormal exploration.

Alyne is a sixth-generation New Orleanian, a descendant of the family of American classical composer Louis Moreau Gottschalk, and many of her ancestors were present for some of the most famous events in New Orleans' haunted history. From the capture of Bras Coupe, the notorious "Zombie King" to the opening of the attic doors amid the flames of the infamous Lalaurie House, many of these firsthand accounts have been passed down through generations and inform every one of Alyne's "Haunting Tales of Old New Orleans."

As an expert in the paranormal field, Alyne has appeared on the popular "Ghost Hunters" television series, and on the History Channel series "Haunted History," and has been sought out as a consultant for numerous other productions airing on the SyFy Channel, the Travel Channel, the Discovery Channel, the Destination America Channel, BIO, H2, and NatGeo. She is a popular and frequent guest on radio talk shows exploring the occult, the supernatural, and paranormal exploration.

Alyne is the author of <u>Purloined Stories and Early Tales of Old New Orleans</u> (Copyright © 2013, Creole Moon Publications), and a contributing author of <u>The Hoodoo Almanac</u> and <u>Hoodoo and Conjure New Orleans</u> magazine. Her work has also been featured in numerous publications by paranormal expert Brad Steiger including, <u>Real Zombies</u>, <u>Real Monsters</u>, and <u>The Werewolf Book: Second Edition</u>.

Learn more about Alyne Pustanio by visiting her website www.alynepustanio.net

Made in the USA
Columbia, SC
25 June 2025

59844838R00122